# SACRED HEARTS

# SACRED HEARTS

## A Mystery Introducing Sister Agnes

Alison Joseph

St. Martin's Press ⋈ New York

ISBN 0-312-14405-9

First published in Great Britain by Headline Book
Publishing

First U.S. Edition: May 1996

10  9  8  7  6  5  4  3  2  1

# ACKNOWLEDGMENTS

I would like to thank Gilda O'Neill and all the Material Girls, Tanja Howarth and Charlotte Oldfield, and Anne Williams at Headline. Also, ex-Detective Sergeant Bob Hinde, and Sarah Dobson IBVM; Huw Edwards and Paul Durrant for their computing know-how, the Hermitage for the wine notes, Jane Cain for her outstanding talents in looking after my children, and Tim Boon for everything.

# Prologue

He knew she was dead. It was only the eyes, the way they stared out above the mask, that made it difficult to believe. He found himself talking to her.

'Philippa – you stupid bitch—' and her eyes followed him with unblinking gaze as he paced his huge lounge, the knife still in his hands. 'Pip – what the hell did you think you were doing?' And his voice cracked in the heavy silence of the room. He looked down at the kitchen knife in his hands, at the sticky red trails on his cream linen suit, and then looked at her again. She was seated where he'd placed her, in an armchair, her arms and legs awkwardly akimbo, despite their manacles, despite the leather straps that crossed her torso, the neck collar with heavy silver studs, the half-mask above which her eyes still stared at him with that same empty green accusing gaze. He felt only disgust.

'Well, you stupid whore,' Hugo said to her. '*C'est fini*. At last.' He put down the kitchen knife and glanced again at his wife's body. Even in death she seemed to provoke him; the accusing look in her eyes had given way to a blank, ghastly triumph. He felt his anger, which had abated, rise into his throat again, and roughly he bent and closed her eyelids, his fingers leaving smears across her bruised and swollen face. How he hated her. Well, that was that.

'No more,' he heard himself murmur, as he began to pace the room. 'No more.'

It occurred to him that he couldn't just leave her there for ever – some action was required of him. Bury her in the

1

garden? He'd be bound to be seen, by the gardener if not by a passing neighbour. 'Just digging a grave for the wife,' he'd have to say, and the thought made him laugh, a strange rasping sound in the hushed room. He was still laughing when he got through on the phone to the local police station.

'Yes, you can help me. It's about my wife. The stupid bitch has just got herself murdered.'

# Chapter One

There was a weariness about the room, as if the grinding distant rumble of the traffic had worn away any style it might once have had. A woman sat on the shabby single bed wearing only her underwear. She sat perfectly still. Her body was large-boned and trim and not young, flattered by the confection of silk and lace that now, barely, covered it. She had short, thick hair, dark brown mixed with grey. Over her knees a long garment was draped in heavy folds, which now as she stood up took on the shape of a nun's habit. She was surprisingly tall. She bent down and gently laid the habit out on the bed, pausing to pay her last respects, briefly touching with her fingertips the crisp white collar. There was a battered old leather suitcase on the bed, and she began to rummage through it with impatience, picking out dresses, skirts and blouses, flinging them aside. Something caught her eye; she lifted out a worn Hermès silk scarf and allowed it to float across her fingers, frowning at it as though it might explain how she came to be here.

The phone rang, and she jumped.

'Hello?'

'Hello, Agnes, it's Sister Katherine,' said the voice at the other end. 'I was thinking of you. We all are.'

Agnes grimaced. 'I can imagine. Not you, Katy, I mean the others.'

'How's the new life?' Katherine asked.

Agnes smiled. 'Oh, not so bad. Except, I haven't got a thing to wear.'

'But – even without a habit – you're still one of us, aren't you?' Katy's voice was tentative, uncertain.

'I'm as much a nun as I ever was.'

'And you still believe?'

'Katy, what a question. Of course I do – it's like the lettering on a stick of rock, my faith is etched right through me.'

But after their conversation, as she replaced the receiver, Agnes felt her confidence drain from her. She might still be a nun, but it had been an awkward compromise. Looking around her shabby rented room, she wondered whether it had really been God's will. At the time it had felt like an inevitable outcome, a relief after all the anguish, the battles with her superiors that had resulted in her final ejection. Now it felt more like a defeat, and a great sense of loss swept over her as she remembered the smooth, worn flagstones of the convent, the tiny chapel, the ancient pillars of the cloisters which had always seemed to her to hold up not just the building, but the rock-solid certainties of the Faith itself.

How she had struggled with those certainties. For more than fifteen years she had been locked in a battle where the forces of doubt and reason had raged against the quiet mysteries of the convent. How she had longed to give in, to allow the gentle words of her fellow sisters and the love of God to lead her softly into a resolution. But, no, it was not possible; and now, looking back, all she could see was her own devilment. She had heard the voice of God Himself calling to her, and she had deliberately covered her ears. How often had she prayed, 'Thy will be done,' and yet she had turned away from His will with a selfish, bloody-minded, destructive will of her own.

She went over to the window. Staring through the grimy glass at the London rooftops she tried to remember the elation she'd felt on emerging from her last meeting with the Mother Superior. She had walked tall, while Reverend Mother had thrown up her hands in the face of Agnes's cool intellect and blatant disobedience. Agnes tried now to recall the relief as she had walked out through the heavy iron gates for the last time, the joy on looking back and realizing that she was now on the outside; but the memory was weak, muffled by the grey fog which nestled outside her window, snagged on the cobwebs which hung from the musty frames.

She recalled her discussions with Father Julius about the struggle between Faith and Doubt, and how Julius would tease her about her 'brilliant analytical mind' – and when things got tough he'd just say, 'Well, no one said it would be easy.' Now she stood by her window, trying to glimpse the River Thames beyond the drab towers, and wondered why she always destroyed that which she loved the most; and the demon within her whispered softly cruel words, words that said, over and over again, 'Everything you do turns bad.' She stared around the room encrusted with generations of dirt; it seemed as if all its misery would engulf her, as if the sticky floor itself were rising up and inviting her to join it. Suddenly, she was on her knees, attacking it furiously with the silk scarf, spitting and scrubbing as if possessed, until one tiny corner revealed shiny floorboards – and the scarf was in rags. She sat on the floor, still in her underwear, still gripping the torn silk. In utter weariness she leaned her head on her knees.

She was startled by a knock at the door. 'Who is it?' she cried out, hoarsely.

'Julius. Who d'you think?'

'Oh, *mon Dieu.*' She stumbled to her feet, rummaged amongst the garments on the bed until she found a suitably decent dressing gown, and unlocked the door. Julius walked in, calm and smiling, surveying the room as if it were a luxury hotel suite. He was slightly taller than Agnes, with soft white hair and a lined face. He wore a black cassock, and over it an old rust-coloured cardigan. Under one arm he carried a take-away pizza which brought into the room with it a delicious warm smell. His eyes, when they turned to her, were piercing blue. 'It'll do, won't it, Agnes?' he said, pronouncing her name the French way, *An-yes*. 'Supper?'

They sat opposite each other, Agnes on her bed, Julius on the one intact chair. Julius said grace over the pizza and they munched on slices of peperoni. Agnes looked down and realized there was a smear of tomato sauce on the silk of her robe, and laughed. 'It's from my old life; all this stuff is,' and as she waved an arm to gesture at the pile of clothes next to her, she was aware that a flash of cream lace revealed itself between the loose folds of the gown. This, to a man who had got used to her appearance only in full habit. Julius said, in his calm, low voice, 'It's all different now.' Their eyes met and she wondered what he meant.

'I'm still a nun,' she said, dabbing at the stain with a red paper napkin.

'A nun at large,' he laughed.

'No,' she protested. 'I made vows of poverty, obedience and chastity. Nothing's changed.'

'Well,' he said, still smiling, 'I'll remind you about the poverty when you complain about your wages. And I'm not sure you can be obedient without an Order to be obedient to.'

'Technically speaking, as you well know, I'm still part of the Order. It's just that, rather than put up with me living there and being a bad influence, they've gratefully accepted your job offer. And who can blame them after the way I've behaved? And anyway,' Agnes went on, 'my vows of obedience were made to the Lord.'

She got up and filled the kettle, and searched around for a socket to plug it in.

'And chastity?' said Julius, and his eyes seemed to dance.

She smiled, suddenly conscious of her *déshabillé*, and said again, 'Nothing's changed. Except, I really could do with some new clothes.'

The room was dark. Agnes ignored the bulb in the middle of the ceiling and lit candles instead. They sat in the warm, flickering light and drank tea, and discussed the job that

Julius had created for her as a member of his team on a project for teenage runaways.

As he left, much later, he hesitated at her door.

'It'll be all right. Really, it will.' His lips brushed her cheek, and he was gone.

She shut the door behind him; and wished fervently that he might be right.

That night, Agnes heard in her dreams the swish of dark habits against flagstone floors like waves lapping against rocks, gnawing, eroding, wearing away. She awoke to a grey morning and the tolling of the church bell, as Julius called the faithful to eight o'clock mass. She stumbled into the clothes by her bed and ran down the stairs of the block, almost colliding at the bottom with a woman who was coming in. In the hurried mutual apologies Agnes just had time to notice her neighbour's youthful bearing and the elegance of her clothes, even though, Agnes reckoned in the few seconds it took, they must have been about the same age. As she hurried down the street she was aware of her own dowdiness, and arrived breathless at church, thinking only how awkward and shabby she must have appeared. As Julius chanted the opening phrases of the mass for the few stragglers that made up his congregation on a weekday morning, she tried hard to confess her vanity as a sin; and even harder to mean it.

Afterwards, as Julius shook hands at the door with his parishioners, she lingered in the church, waiting for him. Wordlessly they went past the vestry to Julius's little office.

It was a comfortable room, with deep old chairs and crimson cushions, and little leaded windows, through which the sun now scattered lines of light across the worn carpet. Julius put on the kettle and produced dark roast Arabica coffee and a cafetière.

'What am I doing today then?' she asked, but in answer he showed her the morning's paper.

'I thought you'd better see this,' he said.

The headline said, 'HUSBAND HELD OVER WIFE'S STABBING', and underneath she read:

The husband of Philippa Bourdillon, the woman found stabbed to death at their Gloucestershire home on Sunday, was yesterday held for questioning by police regarding the murder. He was named as Hugo Bourdillon.

'I thought you ought to know,' said Julius quietly. He poured two mugs of coffee, handed her one, then settled down at his desk with some papers. She stood in the middle of the room, reading the paragraph over and over again. Eventually she said, 'Stabbed.'

Julius looked up. 'Sorry?'

'Oh, nothing.'

She put the paper down and came over to Julius's desk where she peered over his shoulder at his papers.

'So the Council thinks it might have a building we could use?' she said, reading a letter on his desk.

'Yes, they've got one or two suggestions. I wondered if you could pop in and have a chat with the woman from the planning department, over at Borough. See what they've got. Nothing too small. We'll need at least three storeys.'

She prepared to leave the room, then paused on the threshold. 'I just meant, stabbing – it's not something he'd do.'

She put her hand to her neck, thoughtfully. Then she shrugged. 'Still, who am I to know? Maybe he's changed his style.'

She returned to the office at lunchtime, and they discussed the options for premises over smoked salmon bagels and more strong coffee. Agnes spent the afternoon on the phone, making contacts with the local police and social services. She turned down Julius's invitation for supper, determined to spend the evening making her room habitable. On the way home she bought a large selection of cleaning fluids, cloths and brushes; and an evening paper. It was only after some hours spent cleaning that she picked up the paper, holding it in one hand while she stirred a saucepan of tinned asparagus soup with the other. Finally, she sat at her table and, after saying grace over the little bowl, she began to eat and to read the latest report of the murder.

The evening paper said that Hugo had been released without being charged, and added that the victim was his second wife. It did not say that the police were widening their murder inquiry, however, which she thought must mean that Hugo was still their prime suspect. She sat over her empty bowl, frowning. Then she got up and rummaged once again through her luggage, picking out an old shoebox of photographs. As she pulled it from the case, the frail cardboard gave way, and several dozen photos cascaded on to the floor. She sat amongst these fragments of her past like the pieces of a shattered mirror – and remembered.

There she was, a seventeen-year-old débutante, the adored daughter of an English father and a French mother. Throughout her coming-out season, her mother had fended off all English suitors with steely determination in her insistence that only a Frenchman would truly understand her daughter.

Agnes remembered being eighteen, holding out against these conspiracies, bewildered by the whispered hints about marriage from her mother's elegant friends, the giggling conferences with the girls, the obscure but well-meaning utterances from her father, and through it all her mother with her iron will and sparkling eyes, whirling her through the season's ballrooms in an array of beautiful gowns, pausing from time to time in front of several fine examples of Parisian manhood.

And then, at last, it happened. As Agnes was introduced to him, a hush seemed to fall on the glittering ballroom and his brooding gaze burned through her.

9

She hardly dared now to look down at the photos, knowing she would see those eyes again, but there they were, staring up at her from a photograph taken on her wedding day. It had been taken by one of their photographer friends in a deliberately *paparazzi* style on the Champs Elysées outside the Hotel George V. It showed the swinging Paris of 1963, her friends in shiny white boots, large houndstooth-check dresses; the men with loud ties and hair which dared to touch their ears. And there he was, his broad shoulders managing to carry those wide lapels with some style, his dark curls obeying no rules of fashion, his square jaw, those eyes. Oh, how she remembered his looks; his body. There was a confidence about his bearing that told of his background, his wealth, his privileged education, his studies at the Ecole Polytechnique; his estates in the Loire valley, his skill at shooting and on horseback; his easy way with friends, his generosity at the gaming tables, his sportsmanship whether winning or losing.

Nothing could have prepared her for the reality. It amazed her to think of it, that they really did have a white wedding, and that her husband had 'behaved himself' until the wedding night. And then she had found out that this beautiful man she had freely chosen as her mate was not what he'd seemed. Or perhaps, was everything he'd seemed. The memory of that wedding night would never be clear to her, yet it was etched through her very being. It was impossible to disentangle the pain, the cruelty – the astonishment that such a beautiful man could possess such an ugly soul. It had all invaded her so profoundly that she could recall only snatches of the night. She remembered clearly the expression on his face as she had undressed, and how she had basked in his appreciation; not yet understanding that he was admiring her the way he might admire the grace of a deer seen through the sights of his gun. Then there was his touch, gentle, thrilling, his hands, his lips, her own gasps of pleasure and surprise. And then his face changed into a mask of cruelty;

he was huge and powerful, towering over her as if he could do anything he wanted. And after that a blur, in which she heard only his laughter and her cries, and there was such pain, and fear; but there was such pleasure too.

Sister Agnes sat on the floor of her room, and held the wedding photo in her trembling hand. I didn't stand a chance, she thought. She shuddered, and looked at the young people in the photo, and read all their names; and underneath the young bridegroom it said 'Hugo Bourdillon'. She wondered if she really had shared all those years of her life with a murderer; and then wondered why, given what she knew of Hugo, the idea should surprise her.

# Chapter Two

Borough High Street was grey and gritty and chilly that February morning. Agnes wore her old Burberry raincoat, the collar pulled around her face against the cold. Julius was wearing his cassock, his old cardigan, and a bright stripy scarf that looked as if it had been knitted by a committee. They were deep in conversation. As Julius took her arm to cross the road, Agnes said, 'But why should we all wear bloody crowns of thorns?'

People turned to stare, as the beeping of the pedestrian lights drowned out Julius's answer.

'It's unhealthy, making people want to be like that,' she continued.

Julius said, 'It's only symbolic.'

'What do you mean, only? Don't you remember that yearning when you were a child, wanting to be completely and utterly good, and feeling that you had to suffer for it? Or perhaps you were never a child,' she said, taking his arm again and laughing. 'Perhaps you've always been an old old man with beautiful eyes and baby-soft curls.' She ruffled his hair and people stared again and she laughed.

'It's about the Pearl within,' Julius said. 'Purity. Prising open the oyster to get at the Pearl. In our sinful worldly state we fall short of what God intends us to be.'

'Woolly mysticism,' scoffed Agnes.

'Oh well,' smiled Julius, 'it's obviously too much even for your brilliant analytical mind. Here we are.'

They'd stopped in front of a large Victorian house, which

was once, in its heyday, a family home. Agnes imagined children and their nannies issuing forth from its heavy front door and tradesmen calling at the side gate. Now it was shabby and neglected, with broken windows and gaping holes in the roof, a home only for pigeons. They picked their way up the front steps and went inside.

'There's lots of space,' said Agnes, as they trod gingerly through the large rooms. 'You could sleep hundreds. Sling them in hammocks from the ceiling two feet apart.'

Julius looked at her thoughtfully. 'I think, Agnes, if you're going to be in charge of this project, you'd better do a crash course in "Joining the Caring Professions".'

That afternoon, on the way back to the convent from a committee meeting, Sister Katherine dropped in to visit her friend.

'I'm sure the Bishop thinks we should be converting the heathen children like in the old days. Still, everyone else showed some common sense, in the end.' Katherine yawned. 'Got any biscuits?'

While Agnes went and fetched some from her tiny kitchen, Katy looked around her room. She was fascinated by the sudden blossoming of Agnes's personality as she'd begun to make her mark upon the room. It had started as dull as her convent cell, once she'd cleaned it and painted it white; then, in a matter of days, touches of ornament had appeared; a few cushions on the sofa bed, covered in beautiful antique embroidery. 'French, from before,' was all Agnes had said. A painting now hung on the wall; a modern still-life of fruit, chaotic brushstrokes of thick paint in deep brown and dark grey and purple. 'From my marriage.' She would say no more.

Katherine looked across at her friend, who was also munching biscuits now. Agnes never failed to surprise her. Like that time at the convent, some months ago, when she had opened the old leather trunk in her room and revealed a collection of beautiful gowns. And she had begun to dance and sing, and hold them up against her, the soft velvet and silk floating against the coarse fabric of her habit. Katherine had been terrified when they were discovered by the Mother Superior, but Agnes had shown only a cool composure, had even smiled as she had lovingly packed away the dresses under Reverend Mother's steely gaze. Katherine had blamed herself for the ensuing disputes and anguish and the Order's final compromise with Agnes, though in time had come to realize that it had just been a detail in a much more protracted battle, the truth about which Agnes refused to discuss, just as she refused to reveal anything about the gowns, or the former life which involved a husband, or these exquisite objects that had appeared over the last fortnight in her room. And now it was all resolved, apparently, now that Father Julius had managed to persuade the Archdiocese to employ her, even though theirs was an Order which preferred to keep its sisters firmly within its own four walls. An unusual arrangement, thought Katy; but then, Agnes had never been an ordinary nun.

Katherine's musings were interrupted by Agnes.

'What are you smiling at, Katy?'

Katy grinned at her friend. 'I was just wondering if there was such a thing as an ordinary nun.'

Agnes smiled. 'Whatever it is, I'm not. Is that what you meant?'

'You must admit your particular path has been – unusual.'

'Yes,' sighed Agnes. 'And many's the time I've wished it wasn't.' She looked at her watch, and said, a little wistfully, 'It's vespers in half an hour – you'd better get a move on.'

'Surely you can still join us for worship?'

'Once the dust has settled, I'm sure I shall.'

Katy stood up and stretched. 'I gather . . .' she began. 'I mean, I've heard that your – er – husband, your ex-husband . . .'

'Still the same old convent, eh? You'd think the girls would have found someone else to talk about by now.'

'Oh no,' said Katy earnestly. 'No one could be as interesting as you.'

'Well,' said Agnes, 'yes, my dear ex-husband is about to be charged with murdering his second wife.'

Katy's eyes were wide. 'And did he?'

'I'm absolutely certain he didn't. The thing about Hugo is, he'll kill anything. The fish of the sea, the fowl of the air, anything that moves. But not human beings. You see, he enjoys torturing them when they're alive far too much to want them dead.'

Katy stared, committing her words to memory, ready for the questions of the sisters on her return to the convent.

After she'd gone, Agnes began to sort through the later photographs, carefully posed images of husband and wife artfully arranged in beautiful drawing rooms. How the camera lied, she thought.

After a year or two his delight in those most private and terrible moments had waned, and she assumed he'd found other women with whom to share such things. She settled into an isolated life, dividing her seemingly endless days between the Château Savigny in the Loire and the Paris apartment, relieved by Hugo's distance and by the absence of children, and yet fiercely and agonizingly jealous of the shadowy female figures that seemed to haunt their married life. But there was worse than loneliness; and on the occasions when Hugo did come back to her, it was with such viciousness that she began to fear for her life.

She held up one of the beautiful images, a photograph of 'M. et Mme Bourdillon', and saw in her mind her twenty-year-old self kneeling in a corner of a huge bedroom, clutching a garish postcard of the Virgin and praying, over and over again, for the strength to bear her fate. Her faith had been fierce and devout, yet it had never occurred to her to ask for deliverance from her misery. Now she shuddered to think how, when Hugo would rant and rave, she had believed his words; and when he would tell her she was worthless, that she deserved what he was going to do, and even wanted it – somewhere deep in her being she believed him.

About three years after her marriage, the parish of Savigny had acquired a young Irish curate called Julius. He noticed, amongst his congregation, the beautiful and pious young wife from the Château. He noticed how her eyes would fill with tears during prayers. He heard her halting, whispered confessions which betrayed a life in crisis. Gradually he came to see that under her well-bred poise this pale young woman was living on the edge of an abyss into which she might fall at any moment. One day he accompanied her back to the Château along the brook that ran past her husband's vineyards; and after that their Sunday stroll became a regular event. Thus it was that without any details, sometimes with barely a word spoken, the truth of her life became clear to him. He was appalled by the cruelty with which she was forced to live; but also, he was appalled at her meek acceptance, at the way her faith enchained her.

One afternoon in early September they had paused to admire a meadow which had been left fallow and which now bloomed with a last burst of summer, as patches of red and blue and gold came alive in the warm light and honey bees snatched a last late harvest before the winter. Agnes was tense and drawn, anticipating Hugo's arrival that evening. The young curate looked at her nervous face, half hidden beneath her thick, dark hair, and found himself saying. 'You deserve to be happier than this.'

She turned to him in anguish. 'But what can I do?'

He stared at his feet, aware that there were boundaries that must be observed, and mumbled something about the examples of the saints.

'Exactly,' she exclaimed, and her voice was full of despair. 'The Blessed Virgin herself accepted all that the Lord asked of her. What else can I do?'

Her eyes burned with an anguish so profound that Julius

17

took her by the shoulders, and said, 'No, no, you mustn't think that. Mary said yes because she was free to say yes.'

Agnes shook her head, and her hair seemed to throw off sparks in the golden light. 'Well then, she was luckier than me.' Their eyes met. Julius took his hands from her shoulders, and they continued their walk in silence, while the sun sank lower in the sky and their shadows grew longer.

And then came the day when she really was in fear for her life, and there was simply nowhere else to go; and it was Julius who had found the half-dead, terrified young woman on the steps of the church, hid her in the vestry, arranged for her to flee. In a matter of days he had found her a place in a convent in London, fixed tickets and money and smoothed over all objections on the grounds of her dubious marital status, appealing, in the end, to the Holy Father himself. She always said afterwards that Julius had saved her life.

Two years after her flight, he joined her in Southwark as the local parish priest at St Simeon's. So peaceful were those middle years at the convent that when she heard that Hugo had remarried, an Englishwoman, and had fled from Paris in some sordid trouble to do with gaming debts, it had barely caused a ripple in her equilibrium. He'd settled in the Cotswolds – Chidscombe, she was pretty sure that was the village.

Now there was the tragedy of his poor second wife. The thought occurred to her that perhaps Hugo had carried through his murderous intent with Philippa beyond the limits he had, for whatever reason, respected in his first marriage.

Late that night Julius and Agnes bumped through London in a van packed with four cheerful volunteers, fifty catering packs of cheap white sliced bread and a large urn of soup. Wherever they stopped, people in straggling groups would appear out of the night and cluster around the van, taking their steaming plastic cups in hostile silence, or with a grunt of thanks, or even a few words of gossip. In the darkest part

18

of the night they arrived at the edge of Smithfield market, by a patch of waste ground where a fire blazed. The flames illumined faces in the shadows: a vulnerable girl with large eyes made larger by hunger and smears of eye make-up; an older man, whose face seemed lined with the dirt of years of London streets but whose teeth grinned brightly in the firelight. The plastic cups were dotted around the fire, held tightly for warmth, as people ate in private. Eventually the volunteers got a lift home, and Julius drained the last of the soup into two cups and looked round for Agnes.

He saw her beyond the fire, sitting on a rusty oil drum. Her hair was dishevelled; her face, softly framed by a cashmere scarf, reflected the smoky warmth of the fire as she stared into the flames. Her eyes seemed dark and haunted, as if she could see something in the embers that frightened her. In that moment Julius feared for her. He saw, suddenly, that he'd done what he could; but maybe that wasn't enough.

She came over to him and they drank their soup in companionable silence. As the night turned from black to grey, they packed up the van and drove off through the city, and a cold dawn crept over the river.

'I'll walk the last bit,' Agnes said suddenly, and she got out of the van on London Bridge. As Julius drove off, he looked in his mirror and saw her standing there, the early stirrings of the river breeze ruffling her hair. He knew she would make a decision; and he feared that, once again, it would be the wrong one.

Agnes looked out at the murky waters of the Thames. An idea that had formed in the smoky darkness of Smithfield was now becoming bright and clear in her mind, like the shiny glass of the redeveloped quay across the river; like the sparse rays of the sunrise on the water. She remembered Julius's face as he'd watched her by the fire; but the image was as fleeting as the sunlight, and her resolution was as harsh and as chilling as the day had now become.

\* \* \*

'You don't look much like a nun,' the young man at the desk said cheerfully.

Agnes looked at the name tag on the striped shirt, which said: 'Kwik Cars. Alan. Happy to Help,' and said, 'Don't I?'

Alan typed her date of birth on to his keyboard and said, 'I thought they all wore them things, you know.'

Agnes smiled. 'At least it's easy to spell.'

Alan typed three letters, and without looking up said, 'It was the Jag you wanted, wasn't it?'

An hour and a half later, Agnes turned off the A40 at Hillingdon and stopped at a garage. She emerged clutching a cassette tape. As she pulled away from the forecourt, the opening strains of Bach's *St Matthew Passion* filled the car at full volume, and Agnes put her foot down hard and screeched away from the other cars.

Leaving London behind, and approaching the rolling hills of Berkshire and then Oxfordshire, she was reminded of her arrival in England all those years ago. The gentle green landscape had given her a feeling of peace and safety after the nightmare of her life with Hugo. Even now, driving towards him again, the reassuring curves of the countryside with their nestling villages made her feel that nothing could harm her after all these years.

Back in London, Julius would be reading the note she'd left. 'Have gone to Gloucestershire for the day. See you tomorrow. A.' Agnes turned off towards Burford and admitted to herself that it had been cowardice not to tell him face to face.

It began to drizzle as she drove into the town of Chidding Ford. It was a little market town, built squarely in Cotswold stone, and it seemed to have taken upon itself to represent all that is solid, traditional and genteel, with its tea rooms and little shops and its two hotels, each of which had their loyal following among the locals.

She passed waxed jackets and green wellingtons, farmers walking dogs, dogs walking ladies, and a group of young people loitering by the war memorial, their brightly dyed hair a startling splash of colour against the subtle stone.

Leaving the town she headed for the village of Chidscombe, driving slowly as she looked out for the house. When she reached the tall iron fence with its intricate wrought-iron gate, and the long drive lined with rhododendrons, she knew she'd arrived. She parked the car out of sight of the house and walked up the drive, wondering what it would be like to live here; to live here with him; or rather to die here, as poor Philippa had done. She wondered what she'd say to him; what he'd look like now. She saw someone working in the garden, stooped and middle-aged, and was about to ask him where she might find Hugo; but he straightened up as she approached him, and she realized that this dishevelled, staring figure was the gloriously handsome man she'd married in Paris all those years ago.

He gazed upon her as she approached him, and the nearer she got the more grizzled and panic-stricken he appeared, as if he were about to flee from some phantom of his past. 'You – you . . .' he was saying in a voice harsh with late nights and cigarettes. Agnes looked at him, and all she could feel was that for some unknown reason she was very glad she'd come, very glad indeed. But the pleasure was shortlived. He drew himself up to stand broad and straight in front of her, and his mouth twisted into a sneer.

'Come to gloat, have you? Heard about the mad axeman of Chidscombe? I'm their prime suspect, you know – they think I'm dangerous. And now here you are, turned up like the proverbial, eh? Sniffing around this dung heap that I call my life. Drawn by the stink, were you? *Ça pue, n'est-ce pas?* Well, have a good look, go on, breathe it in – you love it don't you?'

He paused, panting, his arms outstretched in a clumsy, unnatural posture. Agnes turned slightly to inspect a winter jasmine, bending to take in its sweet fragrance. Quietly, she said, 'Why did you do it, Hugo?'

His bravado drained from him, and his voice when he spoke sounded lost.

'I didn't, Agnes. I know I didn't . . . they're telling me I did, and sometimes I believe them . . . but that knife . . . that blood . . .'

'Well,' said Agnes briskly, 'that's what I've come about.'

It was only afterwards that it struck her as macabre. At the time it seemed perfectly normal that he should lead her into his huge sitting room and gesture vaguely towards the bloodstained curtains, the splashes across the walls, and say, 'Sorry – I've kind of got used to it.'

He stumbled over to the drinks cabinet, poured two large whiskies, passed one to her then threw himself into an armchair. So they sat in the room which bore the scars of the crime and sipped their drinks, and the afternoon sun sent pink streaks across the ceiling as the rain cleared.

Much later he lifted the whisky bottle again, and found it was empty. He grinned at her across the room. 'S'probably time you were off.' She smiled back and drained her glass.

Outside it was dark. He leaned unsteadily against the door and said, 'If anyone had told me that of all the people – all the people to come to me now – it would be you – that it would be you who believed me . . .'

He shook his head blearily, then with one huge clumsy gesture he enfolded her in his arms and kissed her with extraordinary tenderness. She walked away from him, down the long drive, and her hands trembled as she unlocked the door of her car. All the way back to London, through the smooth purr of the engine and the zipping headlights of passing cars, she felt his kiss like a shudder through her body.

'But what did you talk about?' Julius's cassock flapped against the altar steps as he replaced a candle.

'Oh, this and that,' said Agnes quietly, leafing through a

prayer book in a front pew. 'And the funny thing is, we spoke in English – mostly, anyway.'

'I can't believe it,' flustered Julius, tending the wick of the other candle. 'Him of all people. Just when you could get your life together – but that man, you go to that man and spend hours drinking his whisky, in that very room—'

'I wish we said "quick" in our creed, like the Anglicans used to.'

Julius looked across to her in exasperation. She continued, 'Look – it says, "and He shall come again in glory to judge both the quick and the dead," instead of "the living and the dead." I'd like to say quick. It's a bigger word. Like hearts beating, or blood pumping. Like life itself.'

She stood up. 'Oh well. Better get on.' But as she walked out of the church, she felt once again that shudder through her body; and Julius felt it too.

What had she and Hugo talked about? She tried to remember through the whisky haze. He'd seemed surprised about her leaving the Order, but she hadn't explained because he'd never understand. And anyway, he wasn't really interested. He had begun to talk about Philippa, about how she was spoilt, selfish, and only interested in money. The marriage had been a terrible mistake. Yes, thought Agnes, there are two sides to that story, I expect. At least, there were.

As Hugo had poured himself another whisky, he'd told her that Philippa had had loads of lovers – 'most of them I didn't know about, but then I didn't care either. Whoring bitch. She had it coming to her.' Agnes began to think she'd been a fool to come.

'Still,' he'd gone on, 'that's that, eh? All over. No more lovers. No more bloody anything.'

He'd begun to laugh, and the horrible drunken sound had made Agnes gather her woollen jacket around her and take another sip of whisky.

His rant had continued for hours. She could see him now,

standing in front of the french windows as the sunlight faded. He was an unhappy man – all his words betrayed that simple fact. No amount of boasting now, no reeling off lists of his business turnover for the last two years, of the houses in France he'd bought and then sold for five times the price, of all the racehorses he had shares in, could change that about him. The room grew dark and he seemed to become larger and larger within it, and his misery too seemed to become almost separate from him, until as the moon rose it threw shards of pure icy light across the room, and Agnes saw Hugo's misery etched across his face like a scar.

At last, all talked out, he slumped into his chair and refilled his glass. The smoke from his cigar hung in uneven shapes in the air, and silence settled on the room, until Agnes said at last, 'Hugo – did you do it?'

In answer he had stretched out both arms and looked her straight in the eyes across the darkness and said, 'Agnes – you know me for what I am. Am I a murderer?'

Thinking about it now, as she closed the church door quietly behind her, she realized that the shudder had begun then as a tiny tremor deep within her body. But she had said, quietly, 'Well – who do you think did it?'

Suddenly, unpredictably, he was on his feet. 'Who do I think? I was always the last to know. Find some crone to talk to her on the Other Side. Then you'll get an answer.'

He quietened and paced the room, then said, in a voice of steely calm, 'There'll be enough who wanted her dead. Once you'd had Philippa . . .'

His words tailed off. He stood in the middle of the room and the red dot of his cigar glowed brightly.

'God knows, I wanted her dead too. That very day, I'd gone for her. They'll tell you all about that, *les flics*. They love it. She was seen that evening with bruises on her neck. Beauties they were. Caused by me. With provocation, I can tell you, more than enough . . . Yeah, I went for her. But you know, it bored me, to have that fucking treacherous lily-white neck between my hands like this–' in silhouette, Agnes saw him grip his hands together – 'and anyway, I liked seeing her walking about with the bruises.'

Again he laughed his brittle laugh, and in the darkness, there in his room, Agnes had put a hand to her own neck. No, she'd thought, he hadn't changed at all. After all these years, he was still the man she'd married.

Leaving Julius to tend to his church, Agnes strode off towards the Thames embankment. As she paced the streets by the river's edge, she felt enmeshed in a sense of lurking doom, which seemed to feed on the dull greyness of the day and the muddy swirls of the water.

That night she crept back to the church, letting herself in with her key. Her steps echoed as she went to the little Lady Chapel and settled down to pray. The church was dark, and she felt strangely comforted by the shadows that seemed to enfold her, as she allowed herself to breathe once more the mysteries of her faith, feeling the love of that God, expressed over the centuries, express itself again anew in her own quiet dialogue.

Much later she left the church, setting off home through the deserted blackness of the streets and the sparse traffic rumble. Once again, she thought, I am unworthy. What I am about to do is self-willed, vain and egocentric; and utterly inevitable. She felt suddenly, terribly, alone.

# Chapter Three

'How long are you going to be away?' Julius looked up from his desk to face her.

'I don't know. As long as it takes, I suppose.' The morning sun flecked the old worn carpet as Agnes stood there, defiant and determined. 'The point is,' she went on, 'he didn't do it, and I intend to find out who did.'

Julius looked at Agnes's weary expression, at the dark shadows under her eyes. He guessed she'd hardly slept the night before. His hand went to the crucifix at his neck the way it always did when he was upset, but his blue eyes were clear and calm. 'Why?'

She looked at the carpet, tracing with her shoe the breaks in the pattern where the threads showed through. Eventually she said, sitting down wearily, 'I don't know.'

They sat in silence for a few moments, and then she said, 'Perhaps it's just the pursuit of truth.' She tried to laugh, and then added, 'You see, all the evidence points to Hugo – but not quite.'

Julius's eyes were still upon her. 'You mean, God's Truth must out?'

She looked up at him gratefully. 'Yes, that's it.'

Julius jumped to his feet. 'My God, Agnes, that man nearly killed you once – and now he's gone and done it for real. So the police get their man – but you have to rush in talking your nonsense for some reason best known to yourself . . .'

He began to pace the room, his face white. 'You remember in France, how you used to starve yourself, drink yourself silly, jump the most dangerous fences – well, nothing's changed, has it? Fifteen years of convent life and you still want to do yourself in. Only now it's not the danger and the booze. Now you just have to go and sniff around the putrescence of that man's life, like a rat in a rubbish tip.'

The anguish on his face made her want to take him in her arms. But instead she heard herself say, through a false smile, 'That's funny. That's just what he said.'

In his fury, Julius grabbed her by both arms and shouted into her face, 'I will not be compared to him—' But the look of triumph in her eyes stopped him in his tracks. He let go and stood by her chair, clasping and unclasping his fists, until he could trust himself to speak again.

'No, Agnes. I'm not Hugo. Thank God.' He sat exhausted in his chair, leaning his head on one hand.

Agnes came over and stood before him and her eyes filled with tears. She seemed to be about to speak, but no words came. Then she bent and kissed his forehead, and in a swish of Burberry raincoat was gone.

Julius sat still. He touched his forehead where she'd wet it with her tears, then took his hand away and stared blankly at his fingers. He stayed like that, motionless, long after the echoes of her footsteps had faded away.

The Cotswold Crest was a modern and anonymous hotel near to Chidscombe. That evening Agnes sat wearily over a whisky in the synthetic plush of the lounge, where the Muzak seemed to trickle from the very wallpaper, and wished that she might merge completely with her surroundings and become soft and pink and inoffensive like the room itself.

That night she forced open her bedroom window, which had probably been painted shut all its life, and leaned out. The night air was raw, and something large and winged like a bat or a huge moth brushed past her face. She lay down, leaving the window open, and eventually drifted off to sleep. But in the dead of night she felt a webbed wing brush her face, and woke in terror. With trembling hands she reached for the light, expecting to see the ceiling black with flying creatures, and was amazed to find that everything was clean and bright and normal. In the morning when she awoke after an uneasy night the light was still on.

Two hours later, Agnes stood at the counter of the local police station and wondered how to explain. She was just rehearsing her words – you see, I'm the wife of the accused, no, not the dead one, the first wife – when she heard the duty officer say, 'Can I help you, madam?'

'Yes, I mean, I think so. It's about Hugo Bourdillon. I've come to help.'

As soon as she had stuttered out the words she regretted it, as the young man seemed to exchange a glance with someone hidden behind the frosted-glass panel.

'Perhaps if you would invite me in, I can explain what I mean,' she said more firmly.

'Sure, I'll let you in,' said the sergeant. 'Only I have to remind you, madam, that wasting police time is an offence.'

Agnes's mug of instant coffee stood untasted on the desk as she finished her explanation of why she'd come. Opposite her in the windowless interview room sat Detective Inspector Lowry, and Sergeant Driscoll.

'So you married Mr Bourdillon and lived to tell the tale,' said Lowry. His voice had a trace of Yorkshire accent. 'Would you say these outbursts of violence were a new thing, then?'

Agnes shook her head. 'No.'

'I thought not,' said Lowry. 'These men never change. Until one day, they go too far.'

'But stabbing,' said Agnes forcefully. 'He's never even tried before.'

'Well, maybe he never wanted to before. I mean, from what we know, he and the missus have a row, he tries to strangle her, leaves the house, some time later comes back, and tries again to kill her, this time with the knife – and this time he succeeds.'

'I just don't believe he wanted her dead,' said Agnes.

'He never tried to kill you, then?' asked Lowry bluntly.

Agnes tried to force down a mouthful of undrinkable coffee. Lowry got up suddenly and picked a large box file off a shelf.

'Evidence you see – fingerprints – the knife had only his prints on it – alibis, statements from the servants, people who knew them – blood groups, saliva samples . . . You can protest his innocence if you like, but you'll be on your own. They all think he did it – oh, except for that Greek woman, what was her name—'

Driscoll checked the file. 'Mrs – here we are, Mrs Paneotou, Athena Paneotou. Striking looking bird.'

'Yes, and she was no help either,' said Lowry drily. 'The man's found with a dripping knife, a fresh corpse and a history of violence.'

Driscoll said, after a respectful pause, 'There's one thing on his side; which is that he phoned us. Told us she was dead. I took the call. But then, to hear him, laughing and that—'

'And no one can give him an alibi,' added Lowry. 'He says he went for a walk to calm down after the row. No one saw him. To be honest with you, Mrs er . . .'

'Sister Agnes. I'm a nun—'

Lowry blinked and continued, 'To be honest, if it was up to me I'd have had him charged days ago. But these days you have to be careful. I'm just sitting it out waiting for the rest of the stuff from the labs, or until I find someone who can tell me what time he went back to the house. And there will be someone. In this life we can't do 'owt without there being someone who knows about it.'

He got up to show her out. At the door, he said, 'If you do find anything, you'll let us know, won't you.'

The only Gaggia machine in Chidding Ford, the nearest

town, belonged to a sandwich bar called Di Maggio's. It took
Agnes approximately seven minutes to sniff it out. She sat
over a cappuccino, feeling foolish about playing lady detective
when the police had so much information at their fingertips.
She wondered whether to give up and go straight back to
London, particularly as the rates at the Cotswold Crest were
way beyond her means. But she'd arranged to have
lunch with Hugo; although even that seemed like a bad idea
now.

She arrived at South Grove House deliberately early, as
Hugo had said he wouldn't be home all morning. There was
no reply, so she walked round the back of the house. Through
the cracked glass of a shabby door she saw a man sitting at a
kitchen table. She knocked, and he jumped, then nervously
opened the door. He was in his thirties, plump with pale
brown hair and a shabby checked shirt. He said shortly, 'Mr
Bourdillon's not at home. I suggest you—'

Agnes said firmly, 'It's not Mr Bourdillon I want to see.'

'Then who—'

'My name's Sister Agnes,' she said gently, offering him her
hand, which he shook hesitantly. 'And you are—'

'Fielding. Colin Fielding. I'm Mr Bourdillon's man – at
least I were, until . . .'

'The murder? Terrible thing. I'm an old friend of the family,'
she said, walking into the kitchen. He gestured to her warily
to sit down. She sat at the table.

'Doesn't Mr Bourdillon need a handyman any more?'

'Well, it's not that so much as—'

Agnes smiled gently at him, and he went on, with some
feeling, 'It's whether I can stand it any more. Which I can't.
I'm off just as soon as I can find another job. The others,
they've already gone.'

'Do you mind me asking – did he do it, then?'

Colin's face clouded.

'To be honest, ma'am, I don't know. Marie-Pierre, she's the
housekeeper, she's sure he did. Always said it was only a

matter of time. But you see, there's more to it than that, I
think.'

'Go on.'

But his manner became suddenly evasive. 'Course, the
police are sure it was 'im. And I s'pose they know a thing or
two.'

'Were you in the house when it happened?'

'No, none of us. Sunday afternoon, our day off. In fact, Mr
Bourdillon insisted that we stay away till the Monday
morning. Jane was at her mother's, Marie-Pierre was with a
friend, and I went to Bristol and drove back early on the
Monday.'

Agnes registered all this. 'So – so why aren't you sure it
was him?'

'Oh, it's not that,' he said hesitantly.

Agnes was suddenly aware of Colin as a man with a
burden, perhaps some secret knowledge that was too much
for him. She said gently, 'I'm not the police, you know. This'll
go no further. You see,' she took a tiny risk, 'I'm Hugo's first
wife. I just need to know.'

Colin blinked. 'Oh. Well, well. I'd heard rumours, I mean,
with respect . . .' He checked himself, and she smiled.

'So you see, it's not as if I'm official or anything. In fact, I'd
rather he didn't know we'd had this conversation.'

'No, no indeed,' Colin agreed vigorously. Agnes waited,
and after a brief pause he said, 'It was Philippa. She was
blackmailing people. Men, you know.' He bit his lip.

'How do you know?'

He sighed and said, 'It's my brother Jimmie. I promised
not to tell, but . . . You see, he's well off. Runs a business over
in Cirencester. Been married ten years or so. She met him,
didn't know it was my brother, got to know him, if you see
what I mean, then threatened to spill the beans. So he paid
her. Over some months. It was only by chance that he told
me. And we're pretty sure he wasn't the only one.' He sat in
silence, chewing his lip.

'Dangerous game,' said Agnes thoughtfully.

Colin looked up. 'If you knew Philippa—' he began, then stopped.

'Could I talk to your brother, do you think?'

Colin looked panic-stricken. 'I promised 'im I wouldn't tell. Stupid bastard, he's got the sweetest wife in the whole world and he has to go for that cheap bit of—' He sighed again.

Agnes wrote her hotel phone number down on a scrap of paper. 'Have a chat with your brother. If he feels like talking to anyone, I'd be happy to listen.'

Colin put the paper in his pocket. 'Can't promise, mind,' he said. Then a thought occurred to him. 'You mustn't think he did it – I mean – what I'm saying is, he wasn't the only one. I reckon there were lots of 'em who wanted her out of the way.' He gestured to the door. 'He'll be back in a moment. You'd better get yourself round to the front so's you can arrive normal like.'

Hugo walked into the Feathers Hotel with his head held high and Agnes on his arm. 'Bourdillon,' he boomed, as the head waiter checked his table reservation. They waited by the glass-panelled doors of the restaurant, and Agnes gazed at the elegant interior with its low oak beams, white linen tablecloths and clinking crystal glassware. People sat at discreet distances from each other, agonizing in low voices over the Châteaubriand or the Escalope, and how did they do the lobster, whilst eyeing the other diners surreptitiously. Only one table was impervious to such etiquette. It was occupied by three men in shiny grey suits who were eating with laddish merriment and with no concern for their fellow guests. Salesmen, thought Agnes. Definitely not locals. Beyond them were two elderly ladies, sitting opposite each other and giving off such a comfortable sense of belonging that Agnes concluded they probably ate here most days. One wore thick tweeds and was keeping the conversation going single-handed;

her companion was in a well-preserved beige suit and seemed happy to listen.

Then the waiter reappeared and they were ushered to their table, 'By the window,' Hugo had insisted; and as they walked through the restaurant every head was raised from the menus, and the voices fell completely silent. Gone were the polite and secret glances, replaced by blatant, un-English curiosity. Agnes allowed Hugo to take her arm again as they ran this gauntlet, and she smiled inwardly, flushed with a strange pride. As they took their seats at the table she saw the heads all lower once more, and heard the whispering begin. Only the three salesmen had resumed their conversation, unaware of the drama that had just unfolded before them. The tweedy lady was heard to say loudly to her companion, 'But I don't believe he did it, you know.' Hugo and Agnes exchanged glances of nervous amusement.

They ordered whitebait, with Dover sole to follow, his with black butter and capers, hers plain grilled; and a bottle of 1986 Meursault.

Then Agnes said to him, 'Right. So who was at your house on the day of the murder?'

Hugo grimaced and said, 'Can't we talk about something else?'

'No, we can't; now tell me.'

He gave an exaggerated sigh, then said, 'Well, we'd had a lunch that day. An old friend called Arnie – Anthony Littlejohn – came. There was me and Philippa; and – the vicar, I'm afraid.'

'Afraid?'

'Well, it was one of Philippa's little whims – she'd got religion recently, and went to church every Sunday; it was an excuse to wear a hat, Athena said—'

'Who's Athena?'

Hugo appeared to check himself before replying. 'Oh, a friend. She was at the lunch too.'

34

Agnes took all this in, then said, 'And what about that morning?'

'Marie-Pierre, my housekeeper – housekeeper that was – had been there all morning preparing the food. And Jane, the maid. And Colin – he still lives there, though he's talking of going. And bloody David Mellersh had the cheek to pop by while we were at church that morning – don't laugh,' he said, seeing the corners of Agnes's mouth twitch as she imagined him at his devotions. 'I only went the once, promise. Anyway, the police know all this. I made sure they knew particularly about the bastard Mellersh. He must have known we'd be out.'

'Why did he come round then? Who is he?'

'Supposed business partner of Philippa's. God knows what he wanted.'

'Did she ever find out?'

'You're like the old cops, you are. We'll never know,' he said with an exaggerated smile.

They paused while the waiter removed their empty plates.

'What about later on?'

'In the evening?'

'Yes.'

Hugo raised his eyes heavenwards. 'I've done all this already.'

'Did Philippa go out?'

'Don't think so.'

'Did you go out?'

'Only after the row. I went out then, for a walk, and didn't get back until about ten, and that's when I found the body.'

Agnes watched as the Dover sole was placed before them, and remembered how Hugo would blink rapidly when he was telling a lie, which in their long association had been very often; and she wondered why he was lying now. She changed tack.

'Did you know Philippa was blackmailing people?'

Hugo sliced through the delicate flesh of his sole, and

35

deftly removed a stray bone which he gazed at with interest.

'Wouldn't surprise me,' he said calmly. 'Any other questions?'

'Yes. Is there anyone in your lives who might have been upset at Philippa's death? Because that's what seems to be lacking in this business. Any woman friends? Athena?'

The ruse worked. Hugo hissed, 'Oh yes, they were friends. Stupid bitches. But I showed her.' He spoke in a whisper, as if talking to himself.

Agnes committed these words to memory, then said, 'Anyone else?'

'Anyone else what?'

'Who might miss Philippa?'

'Oh, er . . . well, no, not really. Arnie was quite sad, but that's because he's a decent bloke. I've tried telling him his fine feelings would be lost on Philippa.' Hugo's face was a sneer.

'Was it the same knife?'

'What?'

'The murder weapon. Was it the carving knife from lunch?'

'Must you play detectives? It's so tiresome.'

'Just wondered. Whose prints did they find on it?'

'Just mine. Anyway, *les flics* have kept it. I've had to buy a new one.'

'What was Philippa's business?'

'Oh, something to keep her happy. Not that it worked. Some kind of handicrafts thing. She was supposed to knit tea cosies or something and sell them to the tourist shops. But I'll tell you one thing' – Hugo leaned heavily across the table and grinned – 'there's no way Mellersh wanted her for her needlework skills.'

Agnes smiled politely and sipped her wine, aware of Hugo's eyes upon her. They finished their fish in silence, and the waiters cleared their plates. Agnes heard the elderly lady say to her polite companion, 'Sick with in-breeding, that's the problem, Grace. Father–daughter incest, the lot. You never know who they'll mate with next. That's why I won't allow Mitzi out any more, not since that dreadful incident with the tom from number thirty-four—'

The dessert trolley appeared and Agnes ordered a slice of French apple tart. She took a mouthful and made a face.

'Why can't these English ever get it right? You'd think after all these years of the Common Market they'd have learnt how to make a decent *tarte aux pommes*. I should know better than to order it, but I live in hope.'

Hugo was smiling opposite her. She continued, 'So where did you go that Sunday afternoon after lunch – before the row?'

She was unprepared for the sudden change in Hugo. His amiable manner vanished and the relaxed cheerfulness of his face was replaced by a scowl of fury. She felt herself cowering, in spite of herself, as she remembered with a sudden shock what was to come. He fired words at her like gunshot.

'You haven't changed one bit, have you?' His voice became louder. 'You just can't leave me alone. Coming back all trusting, pretending you think I didn't do it . . .'

Agnes tried to keep her voice level. 'Hugo, you were lying. I need to know—'

'You need?' he sneered, bounding to his feet, his chair tumbling loudly to the floor. 'You need? What about me, eh? I need to be believed, that's what I need. You're just like all the rest – no, you're worse. I know you; I knew you when I married you and I know you now. To think I was taken in . . .'

His face was twisted and ugly. Agnes sat still in her chair, but fear gripped her stomach – an old, old fear. She saw him reach for the empty wine bottle.

'Hugo, no—' she tried to say, but he was shouting.

'You disgust me – do you know that? And you always did.' He spat out the last words.

She saw him lift up the bottle and she cowered in her chair, her arm across her face, as the bottle hit her elbow

sharply, then smashed uselessly and messily on the parquet
floor. Hugo stood and stared at it, and Agnes caught the look
of defeat in his eyes, a look that reminded her of scenes of
such horror in her past that she began to shake. He saw her
shaking, and smiled, and then walked out of the restaurant,
out of the hotel, his head held high, his fists clenched at his
side.

Agnes sat in her chair, ashen-faced, rubbing her elbow,
waiting for the trembling to stop. The silence around her
rustled with whispered thoughts: Well, if people will have
lunch with murderers, what can they expect . . . She got to
her feet, hoping her legs would be strong enough to carry her
out with what was left of her dignity. As she left she heard
once again that tweedy English voice.

'I'm not often wrong, Grace, as you know, but I'm the first
to admit it when I am – and when I said he didn't do it . . .'

Agnes drove shakily back to the Cotswold Crest Hotel, lay
down on her bed, and fell into a fitful sleep which seemed to
echo with dreams: of a man's voice shouting, shouting; of the
roar of waves in a storm; the tolling of a funeral bell.

She was woken by the phone. She sat up, and shivered, and
wondered why she felt so awful; then she remembered. The
phone was still ringing. Wearily she put out a hand to pick it
up, with a flicker of hope that it might be Julius. But instead
she heard a woman's voice, warm and well-spoken.

'Sister Agnes? Do excuse me for bothering you like this,
but I'd heard you were here. I thought we might have a little
talk. Oh, forgive me, of course, my name's Paneotou – Athena
Paneotou. It's just, I'd heard you were asking questions
about this beastly business with Hugo and Philippa and,
well, you know, if there's anything I can do . . .'

Agnes tried to shake off her weariness. 'Ah, yes. Athena.
Well, why don't we meet?'

'That would be delightful. Shall I come to your hotel this
evening?'

'Er, no, not here. The bar is all chipboard and plastic horse brasses, and we'd be bothered by middle-aged men all evening—'

'Sounds like heaven, darling.' Athena's laughter pealed loudly down the phone. 'Still, as you like – there's a charming wine bar down by the canal at Chalford. We can meet there, at, say – nine o'clock?'

Her hand still on the receiver, Agnes gathered the quilt around her. She felt cold and her head ached. It was ten past five. She ordered a pot of tea from room service, and as she drank it she went over the events of the afternoon. What had really surprised her was the public display of Hugo's violence. In her day, he'd specialized in private cruelty; like the way he'd take her arm in public, the gesture of an affectionate and protective husband; when only she could feel the viciousness of his grip, only she would know the bruises that were forming under his fingers, that he would admire later on in the privacy of their bedroom.

She sighed, and wondered, again, whether a man who could smash wine bottles at the Feathers might not be a murderer, even if the man she'd married wasn't. At all events, she concluded wearily, preparing to go down for an early supper, she was in too deep now. And maybe Athena, for all her charming manners and girlish giggles, might have something to say.

# Chapter Four

Athena, Agnes realized, as she arrived deliberately a few minutes late, was the sort of person you recognize at once. Sitting in a prominent corner of the wine bar was a woman dressed in red, with waves of shiny black hair cascading over her shoulders. The crimson plush of the seats and the antique mirrors behind her seemed to add to her glamour. She had broad shoulders and a large nose. As Agnes approached, she realized two things. One was that Athena was about the same age as she was. The other was that everything about this first impression had been carefully staged. Athena raised her expertly made-up eyes from a copy of the *Tatler*, and smiled in greeting.

'You must be Agnes. Can I get you a drink?'

'Thank you. Whatever you're having.'

Agnes regretted this when Athena appeared with two tall glasses of bright pink fizzy liquid. She giggled, then beamed at Agnes.

'Well! Here we are. And how was your lunch with Hugo? Charming place, the Feathers. I'm often to be found there at teatime. One of the few civilized English traditions, don't you think?'

'Oh, er . . .'

'I gather he got a teensy-weensy bit cross.'

Agnes stared at her, then collected herself and said, 'So you'll know about the smashed wine bottle then?'

'That too? He is a naughty boy. Still, I imagine you got used to all that in the old days.'

41

Agnes took a sip of drink, aware of Athena's large dark eyes upon her, and wondered why this brash and tiresome woman had made it her business to find out so much about her.

'I'm sorry,' said Athena suddenly, then jumped up, poured the contents of Agnes's glass into her own, which was already half empty, and strode to the bar, returning some minutes later with a glass of white wine. 'I should have known, you being French and all that. The Campari, I mean. So vulgar, darling, but I'm too old to care.'

Agnes warmed to her a little, but kept her voice cool. 'Thank you. So, how do you know Hugo?'

'Oh, just around and about. Philippa was a friend of mine. I used to do her hair.'

'You're a hairdresser then?'

'Just for my friends these days. It's so tedious. Anything is if you do it all the time. Except sex.' She giggled again. 'Though you being a nun—'

Agnes broke in swiftly. 'Especially sex. Wouldn't you say?' She allowed herself to smile warmly at Athena. Really, a tiresome woman, she thought to herself. Then said, 'So – why were you so keen to meet me?'

'Oh, you know, curiosity. Hugo's wife a nun.'

'Ex-wife.'

'Ex-nun, I hear.'

'You haven't answered my question.'

'Which was—'

'Why do you want to talk to me?'

Athena smiled a smile of sunshine and olive groves. She placed on Agnes's hand, which was pale, delicate and chilled, her own, which was warm, brown and effusive.

'Because, my dear, you and I alone on this earth believe that Hugo is innocent. Another drink?'

Why is it, thought Agnes sleepily, why is it that no one around here is bothered about telling the truth? She took a sip of wine from the glass that Athena had replaced yet again and leaned awkwardly against the wine-bar bench, her head resting uncomfortably on a fake mahogany picture frame. Athena was sitting the other side of the table, though it seemed a long way off, with a man on each side of her. The men seemed grey and similar, in fact, the more Agnes stared at them the more they seemed to merge into each other, becoming a two-headed mass of polyester suit with Athena a bright splash of red in the middle. Athena was laughing, and they were finding her very amusing indeed.

Athena is lying. Hugo is lying. Why do they bother? It must be sex, concluded Agnes, thinking herself very wise, as Athena leaned forward and allowed the polyester suit on her right to admire her cleavage.

Lust, thought Agnes. It forges unholy alliances, it makes people loyal to falsehood and traitors to truth.

She was rather pleased with this, and when she found that Athena was leaning across the table – surely there was a button missing from that blouse – and saying, 'What did you just say darling?' Agnes was happy to reply.

'I said, Loyal to Falsehood and Traitors to Truth.'

'What does your friend do, then?' one of the men was saying. Athena's eyes danced.

'You'd better ask her yourself.'

'I said, what do you do? Your mate here is a spy for the Greek government – so what about you?'

'I'm a nun.'

The men roared with laughter. 'Nah, you've blown it now.'

'She is.' Athena was enjoying herself. 'And in fact, I'm considering signing up as one too.'

They considered this even funnier.

'Not you, darling. You'd miss it, know what I mean?'

'Miss what, Dave?' said Athena coolly.

'Tell her, Frank.'

'Come on,' said Frank. 'Let's go on somewhere. I've got the BMW outside.'

'You mean the K reg. seven-series in the car park?' asked Agnes suddenly.

Frank and Dave stared. 'Yeah.'

'Three-way catalytic converter, sixteen-valver, nought to sixty in eight point five—'

They stared some more. 'Yeah . . .'

'Just wondered. Mind you, I gather they're discontinuing the seven-series in favour of a common platform five- and seven-series range with a revised four-cylinder engine.' She turned sweetly to Dave. 'So the C reg. Ford Escort parked next to it must be yours?'

Dave nodded, suddenly sullen.

'What a shame,' Agnes continued. 'At the convent we had a fleet of Jags, until we replaced them with Peugeots.'

'At the convent?' echoed Dave. Agnes caught sight of Athena trying to keep a straight face. 'Well, yes, it was difficult,' she continued, 'because Reverend Mother wanted us to have convertibles. She said nothing could beat a good burn-up on the A13 with the wind in your hair.'

Frank drained his glass. 'I thought we were going on somewhere,' he said, sharply. Athena yawned.

'Oh, I dunno. It's late, isn't it?'

Dave turned to Agnes. 'Anyway, aren't your type supposed to live in poverty?'

'Oh, we did,' smiled Agnes. 'Company cars are tax deductible in the eyes of the Lord.'

Dave suddenly put his arm round Athena and turned cold grey eyes on Agnes. 'Well, if you're a nun, you won't be after a shag, will you?'

His tone was distinctly unfriendly. Athena brushed off his arm. Agnes faltered, 'Sorry?'

Dave stood up, towering over Agnes where she sat.

'I said, you won't be wanting a shag then.' Agnes allowed her gaze to pass from his sweaty forehead to his groin, where it lingered, and then back up to his face. Looking at him levelly, she said, 'With you? Good heavens, no.'

44

Athena burst into giggles, then jumped up and grabbed Agnes's arm, and said, 'Come on, let's go,' and they both stumbled round the table, dragging coats and bags with them, and out into the cold night. Still giggling, they ran along the canal towpath, until at last they stopped for breath.

Agnes stared into the inky reeds and realized she was really very drunk.

'I like you,' Athena said.

'Are you a spy?'

'Do I look like one?'

'Yes.' They thought this very funny.

'You know Hugo?' Agnes mumbled at last.

'Yes?'

'Well, you're sleeping with him, aren't you.'

'Don't complain, you had your turn. Was he good in bed when you knew him?'

Agnes giggled. 'No, he was very very naughty,' she slurred. They both laughed some more.

'No, but really, you are, aren't you,' she persisted.

'It's a long story. Listen, you need some decent clothes. Get Hugo to write a fat cheque, I'll call for you on Saturday morning and we'll go shopping in Cheltenham. We can have a girlie lunch. It'll be fun. I like you,' she added, taking Agnes's arm as they walked back to the car park. 'And I'll tell you everything there is to tell.'

I doubt it, thought Agnes woozily. I doubt you'll tell me anything at all.

Agnes rose late the next morning, and went out and bought a notebook at the corner shop. Then she sat in the deserted hotel bar with a tray of black coffee and orange juice. She opened the book and wrote:

Hugo – Philippa.

Then she wrote:

45

Athena

She paused and remembered Hugo's hissing response to her name; and felt less sure of her drunken certainty of the night before that she and Hugo were lovers. Then she wrote:

Anthony/Arnie
Jimmie

She stared at the words for some time. Then wrote:

*Le silence eternel de ces espaces infinis*
*m'effraie*

and closed the book. She picked up the nearest newspaper and idly flicked through its garish pages, until her eye was caught by a headline:

'LOVER IN CLIFF TOP HORROR KILLING'.

A jealous husband in Southampton had broken into his wife's love nest, shot her dead, forced her lover at gunpoint to help him put the body in the boot of the wife's car, and then made him drive to the coast, where he tied the man up in the car and pushed it over a cliff.

Agnes closed the newspaper. Her mind fell to wondering how the police had pieced that story together – had the man's body been washed up first? Had the car been found with its grim cargo, floating in the harbour? Had the forensic team followed a grisly trail of bloodstains and tyre marks? She opened her notebook again and, turning to a blank page, wrote:

EVIDENCE

Under it she wrote:

Hugo, Sunday – a.m. Church 1 p.m. Lunch. Afternoon: Out somewhere. Returns home, has a row, goes out again(?) returns to find body.

After a while, she wrote:

### Bruises

She sat and stared at the words for a long time. She thought about Inspector Lowry and his fat file, and realized that only she knew that Hugo was lying about that afternoon. Perhaps, she thought, she should try and trade information with the police – although why she should still persist in helping Hugo clear his name after his appalling behaviour, the Lord alone knew. Just as the Lord knows all my other failings, she thought. It occurred to her that if she were to tell that nice police inspector everything she knew about Hugo, he'd probably be behind bars within the week; the idea was immensely appealing. Except, she thought, except for the fact that he didn't do it. I know he didn't do it.

As she passed the hotel reception on her way back to her room, she was greeted by one of the young managers smiling a professional smile, as if at a private joke. He handed her two notes in neat envelopes. She nodded, and went to the lift. Unlocking the door of her room, she was amazed. Every surface of her room was covered in flowers – vases here, jugs there – of carnations, roses and lilies, in hugh chaotic displays. She didn't need to read the note to know who they were from. It said,

> I'm saying it with flowers. Enjoy them. H.
> PS I've paid your hotel bill for the next month.
> PPS Please find enclosed cheque.

A piece of paper fluttered to the floor; Agnes caught sight of the amount written on it: one thousand pounds.

The second note said:

Last night was a hoot. We need each other. See you
Saturday.

It was signed 'Athena' in an elaborate script.

Agnes lay on her bed and clasped her hands behind her
head. So, here she was, a nun, installed in a hotel room by
her ex-husband, surrounded by flowers sent by him, and
about to have her dress sense reawakened by a woman who
was possibly his mistress. She smiled, then chuckled, and
then stopped, arrested by a sudden acute loneliness. Who
was there to share the joke with? No one. Kate wouldn't
understand. Julius was her best friend, but even he . . . No,
absolutely not.

We need each other, Athena had said. Agnes suddenly
found she was looking forward to Saturday very much.
She got up from the bed, and for the next twenty
minutes was lost in prayer, in preparation for the day,
absorbed in contemplation of the holy mysteries that wove
like a silken thread through her very being. Emerging once
again into more worldly things, she decided to visit the
police.

As she approached the police station, she saw a tall, stooping
figure emerge. He seemed intent on carrying on his way, but
she caught up with him.

'Hugo – thanks for the flowers.'

'What? Oh, yeah. Them.'

Her heart sank. 'What are you doing here?'

'Another grilling. Another fucking grilling. All the same
bloody questions. Who came to the house? Did Philippa have
friends I didn't know? Might she have invited someone else to
the house? Who came to the house? Who was there that day?
Try and remember, Mr Bourdillon, we only want to help you.
Bastards.'

They walked in silence. Then he burst out, 'And her underwear.'

'What about her underwear?'

'Did I know anyone who might have had access to her private things, like her underwear? I mean, what the fuck does that mean? I said, with that whore, your guess is as good as mine.'

Agnes paced silently next to him. 'Presumably they've found evidence—'

'Of someone fiddling in her drawers? Well, so fucking what?'

They walked in silence, through the village, past his house.

'Aren't you going home now?' said Agnes.

'Should I? Should I tell you if I was?' Hugo was shouting now. 'You and who else? Every bloody busybodying person in this fucking village wants to know where I am and what I'm doing. Well, you can all fuck off.'

He stormed off towards a bridleway that led through the fields.

So much for the flowers, thought Agnes. She turned back towards the police station; then a new idea strengthened her step.

Colin was in exactly the same place she'd first seen him, in the large kitchen at the back of the house. He let her in with a nod, and put the kettle on.

'You've missed him. He had to go to the nick again.'

'I know. I've just seen him.'

'Still at large then?'

Agnes looked thoughtful. 'Yes. You wouldn't know of any visitor to this house who was – intimate – with Philippa?'

Colin's expression clouded, and he shook his head. He stirred instant coffee into two mugs, and then said, his voice flat, 'Jimmie not phone you then?'

'I'm afraid not. I wish he would. I'm sure I could help.'

'I'm sure you could,' said Colin with some warmth. 'It's doing him no good at all. Amy's getting suspicious now, just when it's all over. Stupid really.'

'What's he doing then?'

'He's just, you know. Brooding, like. Acting like a guilty man. Only, he isn't.'

'Has he said anything to you? Anything more?'

'Nope.'

They sipped their coffee. With a sudden resolution, Colin grabbed a piece of paper and wrote down a phone number.

'Try him. Like as not he'll hang up on you. But try.'

'Thanks. I will.' She got up. 'I'm going to er – investigate – upstairs. Can you warn me if you-know-who appears on the horizon?'

As she went quietly up the stairs, Agnes wondered how much longer Colin would stay. Allowing a complete stranger to explore one's master's house was hardly the action of a loyal employee. But then, Hugo in his present state was incapable of inspiring loyalty in anyone; apart from her own misplaced, self-destructive loyalty.

She headed for the large front room, which, as she'd guessed, was the master bedroom. A huge double bed dominated the room, a heavy wooden bedstead draped in an exotic quilt of dark red Indian fabric embroidered with green and gold. She found herself suddenly fearful; it was so Hugo, so dark and large and strong; and as she looked around the room she found it difficult to imagine a woman had ever shared it. There was a dressing table with some face creams and perfumes on it, and a hairbrush, from which she picked out some long, auburn hairs. There was a wardrobe full of dresses and suits and skirts, and in which were stacked a large number of shoes. Agnes felt strange as she searched through the wardrobe and chests of drawers, as if she were going through the costumes for a play.

She sat on the bed, and watched her pale hands trace the patterns of bright thread. It was as if Hugo had adorned his room with all the signs of female life, without ever truly allowing a woman to live there. That was exactly how her life had been with him; and no doubt Philippa's; and even now there was probably someone else waiting in the wings to come on and play the part of Hugo's wife all over again. And would she survive? Agnes thought of Athena again, so bold, so self-assured. Not someone who could be sucked into this dark, empty stage set. Or were his mistresses different from his wives?

She got up and left the room, suddenly feeling cold. All she knew so far was that Philippa had long wavy red hair, wore size 10 clothes and shoe size 5. That she liked perfume by Guerlain (but then, so did Hugo), linen suits with elegant pleated skirts, stockings rather than tights, and that her underwear was rather ordinary: chainstore cotton knickers and plain white bras. The mysterious underwear rifler must have had rather odd taste, she thought. If he existed and wasn't just something invented by Hugo.

She explored the bathroom: large, in black, white and chrome, with jade marble touches; a spare bedroom, empty and dusty. The square, imposing study, which she knew to be Hugo's as soon as she set foot in it, and which was so frighteningly similar to the one he had had in France that she felt the same young girl's trepidation as she approached the large mahogany desk, glancing up at the collections of rare books carefully arranged around the walls, almost as if she expected Hugo to be sitting there, ready to bark out, with heavy sarcasm, 'And to what do I owe this unexpected pleasure?' and to fly into a rage at her having dared to interrupt him, yet pleased at her transgression because it had provided him with an excuse to punish her. Again.

Not that he had ever needed an excuse. Trembling, she left the room and sat in the window seat of the wide elegant landing. She looked out at the view, at the front lawns which slipped away from the house, at the trees which obscured all view of the road, and wondered whether Philippa had sat here, like a prisoner looking out through invisible bars. On the wall opposite there was an oil painting which seemed to show a garden party, with a large house in the background; glamorous people painted in such detail they looked like photographs; a large table of food, around which hovered beautiful people, the men in dinner jackets, the women in stark, bright shift dresses and high heels. And everyone looked suspicious and preoccupied.

There was one door left, tucked away at the end of the landing. Agnes went through it and found herself in what she took to be a little girl's room. Through white lace curtains and pink chintz she could see the gardens at the back of the house. There was a schoolroom desk, and a divan bed in one corner, draped in a white quilt of the English country style and scattered with pink and white cushions. But the room was disordered, with cupboard doors and drawers thrown open; and its innocence was destroyed by what they revealed.

Agnes could see black leather leggings, carefully ripped jeans, tiny black basque tops studded with fake diamonds. A leather peaked cap; a hand-printed black T-shirt with the words 'One Aim, One Destiny' splashed anarchically across it. Leather trousers punched with studs, zips and chains, size 8. An evening dress made of a scrap of scarlet chiffon, also size 8. The underwear was black, exotic and, Agnes supposed, very sexy. She sat on the one chair in the room next to the desk, and stared around her, then idly lifted the lid. Stacked inside were three notebooks with twee Edwardian pictures of children playing on the covers. They appeared to be diaries, although hardly anything was recorded in them. Next to them was a leather file-type engagement diary, again hardly marked. Agnes began to search through the desk for the pages from previous years.

A noise behind her made her jump. A doll had fallen from the windowsill on to a pile of clothes on the floor. It was old and shabby, with a pale china face and matted brown hair. One eye was half shut, the other stared out from ragged eyelashes. The yellowing lace of its clothes stood out against the jagged denim and black fishnet, and as Agnes went to replace it she had to disentangle the tiny dress from the teeth of a zip which cut across a black leather jacket.

Ten minutes later, she was back in the kitchen, reassured by its warmth and sunlight.

'Did the police take much away?' she asked Colin.

'Not as far as I know. They fingerprinted everywhere. Took the kitchen knife, and some bloodstained clothes.'

'That room of Philippa's?'

'At the end? We never went in. She said we weren't to.'

'Did the police take much from there?'

'Don't think so. They taped it shut, and took all them swabs and things, you know, bits in plastic bags. But now it's much as she left it.'

Except for Philippa's diaries, which were now carefully distributed between Agnes's large dowdy cardigan pockets and shoplifter's sleeves.

When at last she settled down to read them that evening in her room, she was disappointed. The journals were hardly kept at all. Whole weeks were blank; occasionally she'd find the odd note in blue biro in small, schoolgirlish handwriting, mostly, it seemed, inspired by odd bursts of dieting:

January 23rd – Have only lost two pounds.
April 8th – One pound. No good.
June 14th – My birthday. H. took me out to dinner and was nice.

To Agnes, this entry had great poignancy.

Halfway through the second journal, Agnes read:

She thinks she's about to go, but she won't. She'll stay right where she is. For ever.

After that the book was mostly blank. The few remaining entries were in the same form, comments on weight loss interspersed with anguished little outbursts.

Agnes opened her own notebook and wrote down the T-shirt slogan, 'One Aim, One Destiny' – it probably meant nothing, she thought, but the phrase appealed to her. She closed the books and stared out of the window into the night. Then she picked up the phone and dialled Jimmie's number. A woman answered.

'Hello, I'm from Centraglaze. Your husband approached us regarding some work he wanted doing on your home . . .'

Agnes heard the receiver being thumped down hard, and then the woman in the background. 'Jim, have you been talking to those bloody windows people?'

There was a pause, then a gruff man's voice came on the line. 'Hello?'

'Listen to me. I'm not selling double glazing at all. I think I can help you. Your brother said—'

The man's voice was a harsh whisper. 'You can't help me. She's dead. Dead and gone. Like the clothes. I burnt them, OK?'

The line went dead.

Agnes knew enough about guilt to recognize it in its naked form. This was a man on the edge. He'd talk; it was only a matter of time.

# Chapter Five

Inspector Lowry was adamant.

'I'm sorry, Sister, our files are classified information. We can't show them to any passing bod who asks to see them.'

'But we're covering the same ground—'

'If you want to go talking to the Bourdillon set, that's up to you.'

Agnes was about to mention her hunch, but something changed her mind.

'Of course, Inspector. And if I do find anything—'

'We're always here, madam.'

She put down the phone and then in her mind ran through the guests at Hugo and Philippa's lunch party. A call to directory enquiries found her the first number she needed.

'All Saints Vicarage.'

'Is that Father, I mean, Reverend Robert Evans?'

'Speaking.'

'My name is Sister Agnes. I believe you knew my friend Philippa Bourdillon.'

'Ah. Yes.'

'I'm sorry to trouble you. I imagine the police have already talked to you.'

'Yes they have.'

'It's just, there're a few things I need to know about her. I'm sure you understand how it is. I wondered whether you'd be kind enough to see me, maybe later on today, if you're free at all.'

'Her friend, you say? Well, um, yes, I suppose so. Um, I

have some time from three o'clock – drop by then. We'll have tea.'

Tea with the vicar, thought Agnes, after thanking him warmly and ringing off. How Protestant. How English. It made her smile.

She ordered coffee from room service and then arranged Philippa's diaries in front of her, the three journals in one pile, the leather file with its extra pages next to them. She leafed carefully through the second journal, until she came to an entry on 19 April (nearly a year ago, she thought):

She hates him. She hates him so much it will kill her.

On 15 May it said:

She locks herself away. No one will know.
May 17th – I lost two pounds in two days.

There followed several blank weeks. On 23 August it said:

Jesus is her only friend.
September 1st – To the bunker.
September 14th – The thin one looks on. They all hate her.
September 28th – Look at them, eating eating eating.
October 4th – I lost three pounds.
December 6th – She is more powerful than they are.
January 3rd – She must turn and face them.
January 15th – She is in danger now.
January 29th – They only pretend to care.
February 3rd – She must get away before it's too late.
February 9th – I'm frightened of him. I think he wants to kill me.

That was the last entry, two days before her murder. Agnes was reminded of something, and tried to think what. Of course. Sister Olivia, who had left the convent some years ago. Sister Olivia who had only talked of herself as 'she', and who, at the time of being sent away because of her eating disorders, had weighed less than six stone.

Agnes thought about this 'she' – an object, someone outside oneself. That also explained the clothes at the house: size 10 for Hugo, for her respectable self, her neat linen suits, her effort to appear normal. Size 8 for her true, thin self in the secrecy of her own room.

She turned to the file diary, leafing through the loose pages for the previous year. They offered even less than the journals: a few haphazard dates, lunches with Athena, a horse ride or two, occasional dinner parties. The letter P was marked at irregular intervals. Agnes counted them: at least thirty-two days apart, sometimes more, sometimes no period at all. Which would support the anorexia idea, unless it was a hormone imbalance – or drug abuse. She'd ask Athena.

There was next to nothing marked for the two months before her death. Agnes turned to the notes pages in the back. No addresses or phone numbers. But then Agnes found, on some finely lined sheets, lists and lists of numbers, all in columns. At the end of a page it said '£4021.69'. It must be accounts, she thought, for Philippa's business with that man Hugo mentioned, Mellersh. Here we are: 'Shop: £350 up to end of year'.

There followed a sum, extracting £350 from £5948.61, and leaving a total underlined twice. Next to this she'd written 'DM 50% = £2799.30. December'. And then, on a scrap of paper clipped to the accounts pages, she found the words, 'NB Athena money Friday (No.2)'.

The image of Athena at her stitching, making pretty things for tourists, made Agnes want to laugh out loud. There was something very odd about this. She got up and wandered over to the window, and the phrases from the journals about people eating slipped back into her mind. It all reminded her of something else, something she'd seen recently; something on the edges of her mind. But it was time for tea.

She dressed carefully, hesitating as she saw her habit hanging, neglected, in the wardrobe. It would be nice to be wearing it, she thought, when one was holding a dainty bone china tea cup in one hand and a delicate cucumber sandwich in the other. But then, you never knew with Protestants.

Agnes sat down opposite Revd Evans and looked hopefully at the tea tray, but all she could see were two mugs of thick brown tea and two ragged slices of shop sponge cake, one of which Revd Evans passed affably to her.

'Cake – um – Sister?'

'Thank you.'

'I'm glad you're not in uniform – if you don't mind my saying so . . .'

'Do you mean habit, Vicar?'

'The name's Bob. It's just, those of us out and about doing our bit for the Lord aren't used to the formalities. Sugar?'

'No thank you,' said Agnes. She was thinking with regret of the entrance she might have made, swishing across his drafty hallway in her heavy grey robe, white wimple flashing, rosary beads jangling loudly at her waist . . . Then she remembered to smile.

'It's very kind of you to see me.'

'Oh, not at all, if I can be of help. It's been a disturbing time for them all.'

'How well did you know them?'

'Well. Mrs Bourdillon was a recent acquaintance, but, I may say, one of my successes.'

While Agnes was struggling to work out how a murder victim could be described as a success, he continued, 'It's the old one about the prodigal son, isn't it, um, Sister—'

'Agnes—'

'Agnes. Those sheep that stray the furthest, the Good Shepherd is the most pleased to see return to the fold.'

'And how far had Philippa strayed?'

'Well, you knew her of course,' Revd Evans replied.

'Mmm,' said Agnes.

'But then,' the vicar said suddenly, 'Jesus never lets us take the direct route to find Him, does He?'

'You mean, her – unusual leisure activities?' asked Agnes, fishing hard.

'Oh, not just that; the whole story. Such a troubled life. The broken home, dropping out of school. Drugs.' He said the word the way a schoolboy might say 'bosoms', and Agnes suddenly saw him as he must have been twenty-five years ago, awkwardly brushing a thick lock of sandy hair from his forehead as he was doing now, blinking at her with pale blue eyes behind gingery eyelashes, looking vaguely furtive and yet making an effort to be jolly. She imagined he must have this eager and cheery manner with all his parishioners, and was glad she wasn't one of them. She was aware he was saying, '. . . and of course, she kicked the drugs habit altogether then.'

'Er – with your help?'

'Oh, no, that was long before me.'

'And was she really a Christian?' Even from the little Agnes knew of her, this seemed unlikely.

'She told me only a few days before the – er – event, that she had taken Jesus into her heart. I only wish she'd been able to share the good news with the others, but she was – taken from us so soon afterwards. At least we know she's with Him now.'

Agnes replaced her mug on the tray and arranged the cushions behind her.

'It must be difficult to preach the – er – Good News in a traditional village like this.'

'Oh, you'd be surprised. I mean, at first I had to wake them up a bit – they'd got used to their little ways. You know, incense, bells, all that stuff. But you see, when you allow Him to, Jesus will speak directly to His people, as I'm sure you know, Agnes.'

'Um, yes.'

'I've been here two years, and so far thirty-four people have welcomed Him into their lives.'

'And what about the others?' Agnes said through tight lips.

'What others?' Revd Evans beamed placidly, oblivious of the acid tone of her voice.

'The other believing and faithful people who come to your church without "taking Jesus into their lives"?'

'Oh, give them time, Agnes. Jesus can move the hardest of hearts.'

A silence hung in the room; and Bob Evans failed to realize how uncomfortable it was. After a moment he continued, 'I mean, take our Philippa. She'd never set foot in church before she came to our group. And even then she had to be dragged along by a friend – that often happens amongst young people.'

'Who was the friend?'

'Gosh, um, now you're asking. Not one of my successes, never came back.'

'What was she like?'

Revd Evans scratched his head. 'Funny-looking girl, if I remember rightly. Quite young. Not very – um – clean, to be honest.'

'And you never saw her again?'

'Young people round here are always moving on, moving away. But Pippa stayed.'

'And you met Hugo.'

The gingery eyelashes flickered nervously. 'Yes. Very, um, hospitable to me, considering he was an unbeliever. I had thought that his, um, unfortunate experience might lead him to Christ, but so far there's little hope on that horizon. I did visit after the, um, death, and left some booklets, but I think I chose my time rather badly.'

Agnes took a large mouthful of powdery cake at the thought of Hugo chasing this gingery man down his driveway, harsh words and little booklets flying. After a moment she said, 'Do you have any thoughts as to who might have wanted to kill Philippa?'

The pale eyes widened in the freckled face. 'I really couldn't say. Ours is not to point the finger. There is someone out there, and he knows who he is, who is even now suffering for the terrible thing he's done. All we can do is wait and hope and pray that at some time he'll allow Jesus to be his friend.'

Agnes struggled to swallow another mouthful of cake.

'Did you make a statement to the police?'

'Oh yes, we all had to.'

'And what did you say in that?'

'Well, that I'd known Philippa for some months, though only well in the last few weeks; and that I had lunch there on the day of the, um, event; and what time I'd left, that sort of thing.'

'How long ago did she come to your group?'

'It must have been about two or three months ago.'

'Did she ever seem frightened?'

The vicar paused. 'She was a person in crisis, wasn't she. Spiritually speaking. I know she managed to hide it from you all, especially Hugo. But she was longing for Jesus's love.' Agnes bit the inside of her lip. 'That's why I was so glad she came to me.'

'Hmmm. One more thing. Would you have the name and address of the girl who brought her?'

'Oh no, it's very informal, our group. It's important that young people feel comfortable and I find that pinning them down frightens them away. More tea?'

Agnes smiled. 'I really mustn't take up any more of your time, Bob. You've been a great help.'

At the door, Revd Evans shook her by the hand. 'Of course, we all miss Philippa a great deal. But knowing that she is at last with Christ is a source of great joy to us all.'

As Agnes closed the wobbly old vicarage gate behind her, she thought of the lunch party – the cynical Hugo, the nervous and vulnerable Philippa, the vivacious and worldly Athena – and wondered how on earth they'd all put up with him.

'Hello, Athena, it's Sister Agnes here.'

'Darling, where are you? Not enjoying the nightlife of Chidding Ford?'

'No, a quiet night in for once. Listen, I've been thinking about Philippa and I wanted to ask you a couple of things.'

'Sure.'

'Was she an orderly person?'

Athena laughed. 'About as orderly as a whirlwind.'

'Did she make lists?'

'Darling, she was hopeless. About once a month she'd decide to be the efficient housewife, drag you off to Tesco's and emerge two hours later with one tin of chestnut purée and some Brillo pads. Without Marie-Pierre they'd have all starved to death.'

'There's something else. When you visited her, which room would she use?'

'You've found the inner temple then? What will Hugo say?'

Agnes blinked. 'Would she take her friends in there?'

'Only me, I think. Hugo used to tease me about it. He wasn't allowed in, no one was. But if the house was empty we'd sit downstairs.'

'So it was an escape from him, that room?'

'Poppet, it was an escape full stop. She was a girl on the run. All her life.'

'Two more things. Firstly, what exactly did she make in her business?'

'Oh, don't ask me. Patchwork quilts? Tea cosies? I really don't know. Next?'

'Could you give me Anthony Littlejohn's phone number?'

'Sure, I'll just get it.'

Agnes reflected on the phrase 'What will Hugo say?' until

Athena came back on the line with the number.

'I'll pick you up Saturday morning – looking forward to it.'

'So am I. See you then.'

Agnes looked again at the scrap of paper: 'NB Athena money Friday (No.2)'. If there was one thing the diaries had revealed, it was that for a scatty person Philippa was very careful about money. Agnes stared in the mirror and plucked a stray eyebrow hair, aware of an idea forming, hanging in the room like a mist. It was still there when she lay down and turned off the light.

On the phone, Anthony Littlejohn was affable. 'Come at once if you like: Old Green Stables, just off the main Stroud road towards Hyde. Can't miss it. I'll put the coffee on.'

Agnes parked in the muddy driveway and closed the gate behind her. A hearty-looking figure came out of the farmhouse to her right and waved. He was wearing aged leather boots and a ribbed navy jersey, and as she got closer she saw a pleasant face framed by sandy hair, now receding. He must be no more than forty-five, she thought, but had all the mannerisms of a much older man.

They sat in his kitchen. He waved vaguely towards the rest of the house. 'Never use the other rooms. Warm in here.' Despite his haphazard domestic skills, his coffee was excellent.

'Why do they call you Arnie?' asked Agnes conversationally.

'Oh, a nickname. After a stud horse I owned for years, called Arnold Pickering. He died, but the name stuck.'

'I used to ride.'

'Round here?'

'No, In France. A long time ago.'

'I can always saddle something up for you if you fancy it.'

The idea suddenly seemed very appealing.

'Have you always had the stables?'

'Took it over from the old man. Lot of work, but I love the beasts, always have done.'

'What do you do?'

'Schooling, these days. And stud. My sister Clare ran a riding school here after the old man died, but when she moved away that was that. Couldn't face the endless schoolgirls.'

'How did you meet Hugo?'

'He wanted a mare covered and he came to me. We went out for the odd drink after that. And then through Athena I came to know them better. Hang on, there's some cake somewhere, I think.'

He rummaged in a huge dresser painted in chipped green gloss paint, and emerged with half a fruitcake, which he divided into two large chunks. 'Mrs Vinny,' he said through a mouthful of crumbs, nodding at the cake. Agnes took a polite bite of hers.

'How do you know Athena?'

'Through some sailing mates of mine. I used to sail, before the horses took over. And her old man, Chris, was doing up boats down at Southampton, and then bought a place here.'

'Her husband – Mr Paneotou?'

'Yeah, that's right. He went back to Greece with someone's au pair, I believe. She stayed.'

'She kept her name.'

'Protection,' said Arnie, looking at his coffee mug. Agnes looked up at him and smiled, and he caught her glance, and smiled too. 'From predatory men. Or something.'

'She seems to like predatory men.'

'Oh, that's all a front.' Arnie laughed in an easy way.

'So, that last lunch. How was it?'

'It was OK. No premonitions of what was to come, if that's what you mean. Good food as ever. If I'd known Marie-Pierre was going I'd have pinched her myself.'

'How did Philippa seem?'

Arnie paused. 'You never knew her, did you? She's

impossible to describe. She was like a child and very sort of world-weary at the same time. Nervous, funny when she wanted to be. Quick at some things and amazingly stupid about others.'

'What was she stupid about?'

Arnie looked at her. 'Hugo, mostly.'

'They weren't happy, then?'

'Don't ask me about marriage. What do I know?'

'Though you'd like to?'

Arnie grinned at her. 'Does it show?' He got up suddenly, and grabbed a waxed jacket from the back of the chair. 'Come and meet the family.'

The stableyard was old but orderly. Wheelbarrows full of straw stood at one side, and as they arrived at a row of stalls Agnes could hear whinnying. A horse greeted them, and Arnie patted his neck and whispered to him.

'Does Hugo have much to do with horses, then?' asked Agnes.

'Now it's just racehorses. But that's for money, not love. He had a lovely hunter. Sold her.'

'So what's his business now?'

'Property mostly. Claims to be surviving the downturn, though you can't always believe what he says.'

A young man came past the stalls. 'Ah, Ben,' Arnie called out. The boy approached, looking at the ground. 'Can you bring in Carlo from the top field? I'd like this lady to see him.' The boy nodded and went on his way.

Agnes said, 'That vicar—?'

Arnie winced. 'The ghastly "Bob"? One of Pip's little performances, I think. Athena said the whole religion thing was just to annoy Hugo.'

'Did she have other religious friends?'

Arnie shook his head emphatically.

'Only, Evans said that she'd turned up at his youth group with someone else.'

'Can't see it myself. She didn't have many friends. Apart

from Athena. Don't you think he got it wrong? She probably just went along one day out of boredom.'

They strolled through the yard out towards the paddock, and watched a young mare being worked on the lunge. From the next field, a pony watched too, wistfully leaning over the fence. 'Smidgely,' Arnie said, 'Philippa's pony. I ought to sell him really, but – all in good time, I suppose.'

Agnes was struck by the pony's childish name. Grazing idly in its field, it looked more like a household pet than a serious riding animal. Agnes turned to Arnie. 'Who do you think killed Philippa?' she asked.

Anthony looked troubled. 'Tricky business,' he mumbled.

'Can I take it,' she said carefully, 'that if they put Hugo behind bars, you wouldn't consider it a miscarriage of justice?'

Arnie turned to her. 'Look, don't quote me on this. But that marriage was troubled. Severely troubled. People say she had bruises on her neck that evening. But you see, she'd provoke him. I've seen her at parties flirting openly whenever he was looking. You don't do that with men like Hugo. And that evening' – Arnie looked out across the field, then turned to Agnes again – 'I'm his main alibi, you see. He wandered up here about seven-thirty that evening, we popped out to the Swan for a couple of pints. He left me about nine-thirty.' Arnie stared into the distance. 'Still gives him time, though he says he walked in and found her. The thing is, that evening, he was going on about revenge. He said he had plans, or something. I asked him, revenge for what? And – he just smiled at me. Gave me the creeps, actually.' His voice trailed off. He shook himself and turned to Agnes. 'Come and see Carlo, he'd be just right for you. Chestnut gelding, lovely temperament, a lot of go in him. I could saddle him up for you Sunday, if you fancied a ride. He needs to be worked.'

They walked into a field where a sturdy chestnut horse came to greet them. Agnes stroked his nose and then brought her face close to his neck. She turned to Arnie and smiled. 'Sunday morning, after mass. I'll be there.'

Tomorrow, however, there was the shopping trip with Athena, which promised to be more hard work and less fun than she had hoped.

# Chapter Six

Every garment in Cheltenham had been fingered, every pair of shoes prodded, every shade of lipstick tested – and Agnes and Athena emerged, at last, with a few select packages under their arms and a huge appetite.

'But that red is just the same as the one you're wearing.'

'Nonsense, darling. My whole life has been a search for the perfect lipstick, and I think this might be it.'

'So now your life has lost its meaning,' laughed Agnes.

'Oh no, not at all,' Athena smiled. 'There's still the search for the perfect pair of black high heels.'

They sat in a bistro and ordered lasagne with avocado salad and two glasses of house white. Agnes thought about all the years she had spent avoiding fun; wasted years, it suddenly seemed to her.

'I wonder what Julius is doing,' she said suddenly.

'Who's Julius?'

Agnes blushed. 'A priest I know. A friend.'

'I suppose in your line of business that's all he's good for.'

'Don't be vulgar, Athena, it doesn't suit you.'

'Darling, it suits me down to the ground.' Athena's giggling was cut short by the waitress arriving with the wine.

'So,' said Athena conspiratorially, 'what was Hugo like as a young man? Was he just as sexy?'

Agnes shrugged. 'I really couldn't tell you.'

'Oh, come on – we don't need to have secrets from each other.'

Agnes took a large mouthful of wine and then said, 'You

know when Philippa paid you, was it regular amounts or a lump sum?'

'Oh, small amounts, cash only. I couldn't have—' Athena's smile faded. She put her head on one side and said, 'Well, you are quick.' Her eyes became dark, like a curtain coming down.

'And what did you tell the police?'

'The truth.'

'Which was?'

Athena's eyes narrowed as she surveyed Agnes. 'It was a loan. Between friends.'

'In instalments?'

'She was like that.'

'And what did you do in exchange?'

'I said it was a loan.' Athena's eyes flashed.

Agnes took a chance. 'Look, Athena. I like you very much. Really. And you might as well tell me. Because I'll find out anyway. There's one person—'

Athena looked sullen. 'He won't tell you,' she said, uncertainly.

'Ex-wives have ways—'

'Not nuns—'

'Ex-nuns,' Agnes corrected acidly.

'You mean you really would ask Hugo?' Athena looked suddenly, surprisingly, crestfallen.

'It's important that I know why Philippa paid you. And why you won't tell the police.'

'I won't tell them because it gives him a motive. It was one of Philippa's games and it must have gone wrong.'

'Look,' said Agnes gently, 'we don't know each other very well, but as you said, the one thing we have in common is that neither of us thinks Hugo did it. So I'm hardly going to shop him, am I?'

Athena narrowed her eyes at her; then took a deep breath. 'Well, it was a few weeks before, you know, the murder. I'd asked Pip to lend me some money, she was rolling in it as you know. And she said she'd like a favour in return. One of her games. She wanted me to seduce Hugo, you know, have an affair with him. I said, is that it? And she smiled, and said yes. She wouldn't tell me why, mumbled something about taking his mind off things.'

'And you were happy to do this?'

'Firstly, it wasn't a loan, and she knew it. Money is something that's always eluded me. Secondly, I'd fancied him for ages. She probably knew that too.'

'So what went wrong?'

'I don't really know. On the day of the murder, she seemed anxious, more than usual. Over drinks, she took me on one side and said, "Stop the affair. Please. It's too dangerous." I said what do you mean, and she said "This afternoon, when he comes to you, tell him it's all over." She was whispering, and pleading. So I did.'

'What happened?'

'That afternoon, after lunch, he came to my place, and I did the "Darling, we have to talk" number.'

Agnes noticed the sparkle return briefly to her eyes, but then just as suddenly it faded. Athena continued, 'You see, he took it rather badly.'

'I can't see Hugo taking it well—'

'He ranted and raved, I'd never seen him like that before. He said, "She put you up to it, didn't she?"'

Athena was now quite pale, and staring at the table. 'And I said, yes, she did. I didn't know what else to say. And then he went rampaging back home.'

'When you told him it was over—'

'Yes?'

'Didn't he – I mean, weren't you worried he'd—'

'You mean, did I think he'd kill Philippa?'

'No. Didn't you think he'd kill you?'

Athena seemed surprised. 'What, just for saying no?' She shrugged coquettishly, falsely. 'The men I know have to get used to it.'

They ate in silence, Athena concentrating on her food.

'By the way,' said Agnes, conversationally, 'did you know all of Philippa's circle? I mean, would you know who'd come to the house?'

Athena seemed relieved at the change in the conversation. 'I think so. She didn't have many friends.' She frowned, and added, 'There was, what's his name, David Mellersh. I never met him. Hugo didn't like him. Probably with good reason.'

'Philippa's lover?'

'Business associate, supposedly.'

'In the patchwork quilts?'

'He did the selling, she did the making. When she ever got round to it. Pin money.' She laughed.

'What other games did you have?'

The girlish giggle returned. 'Oh, silly things. We'd dress as men and go to places.'

'What, really as men?'

'Make-up, wigs, latex, the lot. It would take hours.'

'What places?'

'Pubs, usually. Our favourite was this golfing place over towards Stroud, full of dreadful men discussing their game. "A blinding shot down by the ninth, old boy." We'd dress the part, put on their voices. And no one ever guessed, I swear.' Athena laughed at the memory.

'What other games?'

'Well, gambling – the casino in Cheltenham. We'd go there when we could. And up to London sometimes. Oh, and we once stripped at a dinner party. It was a polite affair over at my house. We both got up to do the coffee, and in the kitchen we just decided to go in as if nothing was different, but wearing no clothes. Except hats. She put on some trilby thing of my ex-husband's, and I wore the tea cosy.'

Athena was convulsed in giggles. Agnes smiled politely. 'And was Hugo there?'

Athena's eyes were wide. 'Heavens, no.'

'So this business, the affair with Hugo, was – different from your usual games?'

Athena looked subdued again. 'Yes. S'pose so.'

They sat in silence. A waitress came and took away the plates. Athena's was still half full.

Agnes got up and had a word with the waiter, and a few moments later a bottle of champagne arrived at their table.

'For us,' said Agnes. 'I've rather spoilt this afternoon, and I didn't want to. Cheers.'

They smiled; but Athena was distant behind the fluted, fizzing glass.

Later that evening, Agnes carefully laid out a collection of bottles and jars on the bare dressing table. She opened a milky bottle of face preparation with the expression of a wine connoisseur handling a rare vintage and, dabbing at her face, was aware of certain doubts floating around her mind.

Firstly, there were these two untraced 'friends' of Philippa's, if they existed – one, the girl who brought her to the church group, the other the underwear handler, who may or may not have been connected to Jimmie. Secondly, why was Philippa 'rolling in it' financially, if she only did the occasional patchwork quilt for 'pin money'? Agnes knew how Hugo was about money: generous with his male friends, mean with his wives. Philippa would never have been given the run of his bank account. Which all pointed to Colin's blackmail story; and how involved was this Mellersh? Thirdly, what was the reason for Philippa's panic on the last few days of her life, that made her call off the affair with Athena; that made her write with such fear in her diaries? And fourthly, Agnes knew with absolute certainty that Athena was holding something back about Hugo. Nothing in Athena's tone had conveyed any real fear of him; but Agnes knew better than anyone the violence that would have been directed towards Athena had she really attempted to deny him what he wanted.

Agnes checked her face in the mirror, then picked up the phone.

'Hugo, it's Agnes.'

'What do you want?'

'I want to share some more of your excellent Scotch.'

'You mean, you want more chit-chat about this blasted murder.' The voice was not altogether unfriendly.

'How well you know me. Tomorrow afternoon?'

'S'pose so,' he grunted, and hung up.


Through the biting March wind across her face, she saw that they were cantering straight towards a gate at the end of the field. Arnie's horse Carlo had been everything he said, willing and spirited.

'Be careful over hedges and walls,' Arnie had instructed, 'but the three gates across the lower fields are OK. Old man Gillies doesn't mind, and at this time of year the ground's good.'

And now Carlo had his ears forward, and his canter was becoming faster as he saw the gate too. In those few brief moments she was twenty-two again, racing across the French countryside as if fleeing for her life, taking blind leaps at the highest fences as if to crash into oblivion on the other side. Suddenly Agnes found her heart was pounding in terror, and she was checking the reins hard in panic, bending the horse's neck away from the jump, trying to gather him back to her; and Carlo was tossing his head in confusion, his mouth pulling against the reins as he fought her sudden restraint.

At last they were trotting along the edge of the field. Agnes was shaking with fear. Real fear. She slowed Carlo down to a walk and tried to calm herself, looking out over the Gloucestershire countryside.

'England,' she thought, 'not France. Not the old life.' But

there was still Hugo; Hugo, whom this afternoon she would challenge for only the second time in her life, whose rage she would be forced to meet head on. She simply wasn't up to it. Her hand went to her throat as a memory stirred in the darkest part of her mind. The thought of what she might unleash made her feel hollow inside. The fact is, she thought, Hugo will always be stronger than me.

But Carlo's even pace had calmed her. She breathed deeply, and looked about and thought of all the years that had passed since she was the half-dead terrified girl on a church doorstep. It was time to be as strong as Hugo.

Carlo had settled into a lazy walk. She took up the reins again, and pushed him into a canter around the field, until they were heading towards the gate again, and again his ears were forward, his stride bold, and the gate was upon them; and with one fine leap they were over it and racing back up the hill towards the stables.

Hugo opened the door to her with a wry grin. She walked ahead of him into the room, then, before he could sit down, turned and faced him.

'How did you expect me to help you when you told me nothing?'

Hugo ambled over to a chair and slumped into it.

'You should wear make-up more often. And the clothes are good too.'

'Are you going to tell me the truth?'

'I've told you everything I know.'

Agnes marched over to where he sat and stood over him. He shifted in his seat, spread his legs and leaned back in the wide armchair, looking coolly up at her.

'OK, I'll tell you,' she said. 'Philippa paid Athena to have an affair with you, and then broke it off. Why?'

Hugo sneered. 'Because she's a whore – there's nothing she won't do for money.'

'Athena?'

'Both of them. Whores. Anyway, so what?' He smiled up at her, all charm.

Agnes tried to keep her voice firm. 'I would have thought it's quite a key point. It gives you a motive, after all.'

Hugo laughed, looking up at Agnes with his easy stance, forcing her to look down at him uncomfortably.

'A motive? Because of two bitches having a silly game?'

'Why didn't you tell the police?'

'None of their business.'

'For God's sake, Hugo, you're a murder suspect!'

'It's still no reason to share details of my private life with PC Plod.'

Agnes sat down in the chair by the window. In her mind she and Carlo were sailing over the gate again. She said, 'You were angry, though.'

He shrugged. 'Yeah. At the time. But then, Philippa often made me angry.'

Watching Hugo closely she said. 'Athena told me.'

'I know. Have you noticed, I've had the room painted?'

Agnes looked around, remembering the blood thrown in great wide splashes. The walls were now a delicate rose colour, glowing in the afternoon light that spilled between the newly hung brocade curtains. She remembered Athena's cool account of rejecting Hugo. Only, of course, it wasn't a rejection.

'Just a game, then,' she said.

Hugo was beaming at her, maliciously. 'A game indeed *ma chère*. But you remember, when I play, I play to win.'

'By killing Philippa?'

He shook his head, and smiled again. 'No, of course not.'

'By – sleeping with Athena?'

'Oh, what delicacy,' Hugo smiled. 'Yes, by fucking that bitch Athena.'

'Still?'

'Still. Jealous, are we? How touching.' Hugo beamed again.

'By the way, next time you want to snoop around my house, just ask.'

Agnes looked across at him at the spittle in his stubble, at the leering grin which tightened his lips without touching his steely eyes. She got up and left without a word.

Agnes strode across the lawns, down the drive to her car, gulping in the crisp afternoon air against a feeling of intense nausea. She started the engine and roared away from the house. In her mind Hugo stood before her, full of revenge bubbling like molten lava, the same today as he was then; as he ever was. She thought of him with Athena. At least in her marriage with him there had been love – cruel, bitter, warped – but still love.

Agnes drove through the countryside in a glorious sunset. The thought struck her that, oddly, Hugo had seemed somehow smaller than she remembered him.

Later, she stood by the open window of her hotel room in the scented dusk, fingering the soft petals of a bunch of irises, Hugo's irises; then suddenly gathered them up, their stems slimy and dripping, and marched out into the corridor, where she deposited them in the large bin by the lift. She returned to her room and emptied it of all its blooms, the roses which were only now beginning to fade, the carnations which still looked fresh, all crumpled heads down in the black plastic bin-bag.

Then she lay on her bed and thought about Philippa. A world-weary, childlike woman with long auburn hair and a body that was too thin. Who was hopelessly vague about everything, but very very organized about money. Organized enough, possibly, to blackmail people. Someone who was deeply unhappy. Someone who would ask her friend, as a favour, to play a game, a dangerous game, with her own husband.

And Athena? She imagined her accepting Philippa's request, shaking her shiny dark hair in mock modesty; inwardly delighted. And, no doubt, expert at being a mistress. The thought of Athena and Hugo together in that way made her uncomfortable. She found herself remembering Hugo's pleasure. For there had been good times, at the beginning. Her breathing quickened at the thought of Hugo's young body – Oh God, that body, she thought. What does Athena know of him? And anyway, he hates her, whereas me—

She sat bolt upright, and caught sight of herself in the mirror opposite the bed. A glamorous woman, wearing a white silk shirt, tailored black trousers and a black, angular jacket; an expensively flawless complexion; lips tinted red. A nun. She rushed to the basin and scrubbed her face clean with soap and water, then, still dripping water everywhere, she picked up the phone and almost wept with relief when it was answered.

'Julius, it's Agnes.'

There was silence at the other end of the line.

'Julius?'

'Yes.' There was more silence.

'Are you busy?' Her voice faltered.

'Only running a stressed-out parish and a project for the young homeless single-handed. No, not busy at all.'

'Julius, my dear, I'm sorry. What can I say?'

'Oh, I'm sure it can wait. It's waited this long.'

'I would have phoned before. I've had a lot to do.'

'So I hear.'

Agnes blinked. 'From whom?'

'From you, now.'

'What do you mean?'

'Listen to yourself.'

'Julius – I need—'

'Agnes, you can't. You can't ask me now. You knew what would happen if you went back.'

'No, that's not—'

'I rescued you once. This time it's up to you.'

'Julius, please—'

78

'I'll pray for you.' He hung up.

'Julius—' Agnes found she was crying. She cradled the receiver against her face while tears rolled down her cheeks and splashed on to her new silk shirt.

# Chapter Seven

Colin paced the kitchen again, then turned to Agnes. 'But Jimmie's a good sort, he is.'

'I know,' said Agnes gently.

Colin walked to the window. 'He'll be all right,' he said, staring out into the distance, as the weary March sun struggled to break through the mist.

'I'm sure he will,' she replied softly. 'But I've come about something different this time.'

Colin waited. Agnes continued. 'Can you tell me where I can find Marie-Pierre and – Jane, is it, the maid?'

As she left the house five minutes later she saw Hugo at an upstairs window, tousled curls and a flash of dark silk dressing gown. He had his arm raised in a brief wave, but to Agnes, looking back across the frosted lawns, it was a gesture full of menace. Last night she had slept badly, and had dreamed of angular, nameless male bodies, of hard muscular limbs encircling her. She had woken exhausted just before dawn, her mind still full of Hugo, her body hot and damp with aching need.

Without thinking, she had begun to move her hands over her body, over her breasts, her nipples which hardened at her touch; her fingers traced the firm lines of her thighs, her hip bones, and then, as if they were not her fingers at all, they dipped between her legs, to the moist warmth of her desire. She heard herself give a long sigh. The noise in the silence startled her, and suddenly she was out of bed and standing in the middle of the room, shivering in her silky pyjamas. She opened the window, allowing the grey chill of the dawn into the room.

'Holy Mary Mother of God . . .' Agnes began to recite, watching dark clouds scudding across the sky. 'Holy Mary Mother of God . . .' She paused, her arms wrapped tight across her chest, thinking about the woman to whom she prayed, a young Jewish girl who had managed to bypass all the confusion and terror of lust, and who had found in that human, real, bloody birth the glorious outcome of her pure desire.

'Blessed are the pure in heart,' sighed Agnes, hoping to hear in the sudden burst of birdsong a chorus of angels, but finding instead just the twitter of her own self-disgust.

She stumbled into her oldest clothes and a pair of boots and went out. Her walk had been aimless, cutting through fields, still wintry in the thin air. The sky became pale, and gradually she was calmed by the dew-soaked ferns and straggling brambles brushing wetly against her legs. The aching lust, that in her room had seemed monstrous, out here became mild and ordinary. She thought of Hugo, still asleep, of Colin sitting by the kitchen range, the windows all steamed up. It was still early morning. She had turned towards South Grove House.

Later that day, Marie-Pierre showed Agnes into the smaller drawing room of Stapleton Hall with a certain pride. Now, as she sat down neatly opposite Agnes, there was no trace of the mockery that Agnes thought she had detected on the phone. 'Come at teatime,' she'd said. '*A l'heure du thé.* I'll have half an hour then.' Now she was a picture of courtesy, sitting straight-backed in her plain Victorian upholstered chair.

The room was dull but comfortable, and its windows looked out on the kitchen yard, where Agnes could see a cat hopping between the dustbins, stalking their contents in the hope of a kill. She turned to Marie-Pierre, noting her fine neat features: a woman of indeterminate age, with dark brown hair streaked with grey pinned back in a plain bun. After a moment, a young woman in a maid's apron brought in a tray of tea things.

'I have a bigger staff here,' Marie-Pierre said with obvious satisfaction, then added, 'What part of France are you from?'

'Oh, it's years since I lived there. My family was based in Paris. Hugo and I—' She broke off. 'It was a long time ago. My life has really been in London.'

Marie-Pierre nodded. 'I know. One becomes . . . how one is. I left a long time ago too.' In the silence, she gracefully poured pale china tea, adding a delicate slice of lemon to each cup. 'And now you want to know about Monsieur Bourdillon. Though you, madame, should know as well as any of us whether he's a murderer.'

'And is he?'

Marie-Pierre sighed. '*Vous voyez* – there can't be murderers without victims, can there?'

Agnes leaned back in her chair and took a sip of tea. 'Go on,' she said.

'It's the psychology of two people that creates a murder, *n'est-ce pas?*' Agnes began to see Marie-Pierre in a new light, as she continued, 'Madame Bourdillon wanted to die. It's as simple as that.'

'You can't believe it was suicide?'

'Not directly, no. You see, she was tired of life. She was someone with nowhere left to go.'

Agnes imagined this neat, correct woman in front of her moving quietly about Hugo's house, observing its inhabitants with keen intelligence; and her respect for her grew.

'Did you like Philippa?'

'She was difficult to like. She was a hidden person. But I felt sorry for her.' Marie-Pierre leaned back a little in her chair. 'Do you know the house?'

'A little.'

'Well, there's a painting on the landing, near the window seat. It's very English. It shows a group of people having a party. Madame Bourdillon used to sit and stare at it, when no one was around. I'd climb the stairs and see her there. She never saw me. It's such an English picture, so precise, with this dull grey English light everywhere, and the people are so miserable—' Marie-Pierre allowed herself to smile at Agnes. 'I can tell you because you know about these things.'

'Of course,' said Agnes. 'The food.'

'Ah, food.' Marie-Pierre shook her head sadly. 'That girl and food—'

'Did she not eat?'

'Mostly not. Occasionally she'd eat everything in the house and then blame someone else. Usually Jane. But I knew.'

'There's a table of food in the painting.'

'Yes. English food.'

Agnes and Marie-Pierre exchanged the glances of exiles, and smiled. Then Marie-Pierre looked at her watch.

'*Eh bien*, this is my country now. And I have a dinner to prepare. I can't trust these *petites anglaises* in the kitchen on their own.' She stood up and smoothed her skirt, then offered her hand, which Agnes took. 'You see, if you're going to commit suicide you need a method. Hanging, razor blades, drugs . . . But with a husband like that, Madame Bourdillon didn't need to lift a finger.'

Marie-Pierre shook hands again as she showed her out. Agnes set off along a bridleway towards her hotel two miles away, reflecting on her words. Even if Hugo hadn't intended murder, might not the housekeeper be right? Might Philippa have deliberately provoked her own murder as some sort of perverted revenge?

The pink sunlight flecked the bare branches of the trees, and it reminded her of Savigny, of a walk with Julius where the snow was thawing around them and their hands had touched. The words 'Madame Bourdillon' with Marie-Pierre's French accent still rang in her ears, and Agnes shivered. Who could say what Hugo might be capable of if provoked far enough? Agnes had a fair idea.

By the time she had arrived back at the hotel to face another lonely supper, she had made a decision to give herself two more days, maybe three. Just time to get one last piece of evidence, to follow up these leads from Jimmie and David Mellersh, and then back to London. Poor Julius. He'd agree with Marie-Pierre. Why do you want more evidence, Julius would say. What are you trying to prove? That Hugo isn't capable of murder – when you know better than anyone that he is?

The dawn seemed a long time ago.

Later, thinking about the painting, she opened her dressing-table drawer and looked at Philippa's diaries; then closed it again and lay on her bed. She flicked through a couple of pages of a book about Julian of Norwich, finally discarding it in favour of the latest edition of *Car* magazine. The phone made her jump.

'Hello?'

'Hello. You don't know me, but I'm ringing with some advice for you.'

'Who is this?'

'My name is David Mellersh.' His voice was deep, attractive and very English.

'Oh.'

'You've heard of me.'

'Y-yes. In fact, I wanted to ask you—'

'There's no point. That's why I'm speaking to you now.'

'But—'

'I'll say this once and once only. Philippa was in danger because she'd put herself in danger. God knows what it was, we'll never know. But anyone who sniffs along the same trail is going to come up against the same danger. I'm sure you know what I mean.'

The calm voice had become suddenly steely. His statement expected no answer.

'Goodbye.'

The line went dead.

Agnes stared at the phone. She lay back on her pillows, picked up her magazine again, turned a page. And another. She got up and poured herself a whisky. The glossy pages slithered off the bed and landed on the floor with a thud. Agnes jumped.

That night she lay awake in the dark, her eyes wide open, for a long time.

Jane had insisted they meet in Chidding Ford, and said she was free at lunchtime. It was a bright morning, and the bustling town restored Agnes's spirits. At the clock tower she noticed a young woman with straight, mouse-coloured hair nervously staring at her shabby trainers. Agnes approached her gently. 'Jane?'

The girl smiled with relief. 'Yeah. Let's go.'

The small café was dominated by the noise from three shiny black computer games machines in the corner. Jane sat down opposite Agnes and arranged on the stained formica a can of Diet Coke and two packets of salt and vinegar crisps. Her lips were painted a cheap red which shone greasily against her perfect young skin. She wore a black skinny-rib sweater and jeans.

'I expect you're glad to have left that job,' said Agnes. Jane opened one of the crisp packets and the Coke.

'Dunno really. I got nothin' else to go to. Me mum's on at me about getting a job.' Her voice had a nasal Gloucestershire whine.

'Did you like working for the Bourdillons?'

Jane shrugged. 'S'all right. The money weren't bad. No one noticed if I skived, apart from old Mary-Pary.' She grinned and took a swig of Coke from the can.

'Why did you leave?'

Jane looked indignant. 'What, with her blood everywhere, and 'im tellin' me to clear it up? I was out the same day. And I got my money. It were like one of them films, with them serial killers, you know. I looked him in the eyes and asked for my eighty-two quid, two weeks notice, I said. Took nerve that did, with the blood still on the carpet. But why should he get away with it just 'cos he's a murderer?'

Jane filled her mouth with crisps and munched sullenly. Agnes noticed a young woman break away from the group around the games machine as voices were raised in argument.

'You've zapped the God Tharg you stupid cunt . . .'

'Piss off, that was Haydar of the Underworld . . .'

The girl was tall and moved swiftly out of range. She wore a large black T-shirt, and Agnes read the words 'One Aim, One Destiny' splashed across it. The boy arguing with her had a shaved head and leaned on a pair of crutches. Jane was saying something.

'Sorry?'

'I said, it's gonna work out OK when I get on my hairdressing course.'

'Jane, can you tell me, who are those kids around the machines there?'

Jane surveyed them. 'Oh them. You see them around here sometimes.'

'Where?'

'Dunno. Just around.'

Jane and Agnes watched as the abuse got louder, someone punched someone's shoulder, and then a group broke away from the machine and left the café. Two young boys were left, beeping quietly.

'So you think Hugo's a killer then,' asked Agnes. She could see into the street and down the main shopping precinct, scanning the crowds for the tall girl in the T-shirt. Jane was saying, 'He was scary. He'd throw her around, you know. It was all right to start with, like watching telly. But then it got too serious.' She glanced at her watch and looked up in panic. 'Gotta go. I told our Steph I'd pick up her kids.'

Agnes walked down the high street with Jane, still searching with her eyes, as if some huge and obvious clue would emerge from the milling groups of shoppers. At the clock tower a toddler was sitting on a wall drinking bright blue fizzy liquid out of a sticky bottle. Near him there was a girl wearing a shabby khaki coat; next to her a boy sat on the pavement with a fat mongrel dog. Agnes turned to Jane.

'Do you know why he might have wanted to kill her?'

'Dunno, something she done, I suppose.'

'But what?'

'Another man? She went out that evening. She was seen with bruises on her neck.'

'So I keep hearing. By whom? Who told you?'

Jane scratched her head. 'I think it was Mrs Wells over at the post office who told me.'

'Whom do you think Philippa was meeting?'

'How should I know? She didn't have no friends. She was always weird.'

They reached a housing estate on the edge of town. There was a distant sound of barking. The school was a modern fifties building, and a crowd of women had gathered by the gates. Toddlers sat in pushchairs munching soggy biscuits. Agnes kept her distance, listening to snatches of the mothers' conversation.

'Isn't it terrible, that kid in Coventry, on the news.'

'Terrible. Only three years old.'

'What would you do, eh?' and the air filled with unnamed dangers as a sudden wave of children hurtled across the playground to be rounded up and taken home.

Out of the corner of her eye Agnes suddenly saw the shaven-headed boy on crutches, now with another boy and a dog. They were ambling across the main road towards a bus stop. She was on her feet, shouting, 'Bye Jane, thanks,' to the girl, now preoccupied with three little girls in pink, and across the road just in time to follow the two boys on to a bus. The boys sat at the back, tearing up sweet wrappers and dropping them on the floor. Agnes sat by the window, watching their reflections. The bus took the ring road, and when it stopped by a deserted industrial estate the boys jumped up and tumbled loudly off. Agnes watched from the window as they disappeared towards a patch of waste ground a little way further back. She peered back towards it, but could see only a clump of trees and a thin column of smoke.

She got off at the town centre, tired and hungry, and headed for the tea lounge at the Feathers. A flash of black hair and red lipstick confirmed her hunch, as a voice rang from the depths of an armchair.

'Darling! This is a surprise. And what a wonderful excuse to start all over again.' A hand with long scarlet nails indicated the empty cake stand. Agnes smiled and sat down. Athena looked at her hard and then said, 'Are you all right?'

'Me? Yes, fine. Just a bit tired. I might go back to London soon.'

'Not yet, darling. Don't leave us when we need you. Anyway, I have a present for you.' She waved, and a waiter appeared from nowhere. 'Assam tea, darling? Keemun?'

Agnes ordered a pot of Darjeeling, while Athena rummaged in her handbag. 'Here it is, look.' She waved a scrap of paper at Agnes. It was a thin, yellow receipt, with the words 'Albion Gallery, Painscombe' written across the top.

'It's where Philippa sold her handicrafts,' Athena was saying. 'Hugo told me, after some coaxing.' She blushed slightly.

'So you've been rifling too,' Agnes laughed. 'Where was it?'

'Oh, in his room. In an ashtray.'

Agnes poured tea, and Athena helped herself to one of the delicate sandwiches which now appeared at their table. After a moment, Agnes said, 'Well, I won't ask you what you were doing in his room.'

Athena seemed to breathe more easily. 'Nothing that would offend a nun, darling. Well, at least, not one like you. Anyway, what I thought was, we could check out this gallery place tomorrow. A drive in the country would do you good.'

'That would be lovely. Athena – do you know anything about David Mellersh?'

Athena leaned slightly towards her. 'That's what's bothering you, isn't it. What's he done?'

'I don't know. He's rather a shadowy figure in all this, isn't he?'

'Honest, I've never met him. Philippa mentioned him from time to time. I don't think she liked him either.'

They munched on cake for a while, until Agnes said, 'I'd better go. I've got to renew my car hire before the office shuts. See you tomorrow.'

On the way back, Agnes popped into the post office and explained to Mrs Wells that she wanted to know about the last sighting of Mrs Bourdillon.

'Ooh, yes, her neck, all black and blue it was.'

'So you saw her then, that evening?'

'Er no, not exactly.'

Agnes sighed. 'So how do you know about the bruises?'

'It was my friend Ivy, the greengrocer's girl.'

'She saw Mrs Bourdillon that evening?'

'Yes. The police inspector said she was the last person to see her alive, apart from the killer, that is.'

'Could I talk to her?'

With a flourish Mrs Wells picked up the telephone and dialled a number. She put her hand over the mouthpiece and said conspiratorially, 'She's a bit tired of the whole business but if I ask her nicely – ah, Ivy, my dear, I wonder if you'd mind . . .'

Agnes browsed around the shop, and a few minutes later an elderly woman with tight white curls and bright blue eyes came into the shop.

'This is Mrs – erm—' Mrs Wells stood with one arm awkwardly extended.

'My name is Agnes. I was Mr Bourdillon's first wife.'

The two women stared. Agnes said, 'I gather you work in the greengrocer's.'

Mrs Wells wandered over to the window. Ivy said, 'Seventeen years ago this June, it'll be.'

'It was under that lamppost,' said Mrs Wells, pointing across the road.

'Seventeen years ago this June, eh, Alice?' repeated Ivy.

'Pardon my dear? Seventeen years already? Goodness me,' replied Mrs Wells.

Ivy turned back to Agnes and smiled warmly. 'Since the greengrocer's closed.'

Mrs Wells was pointing across the road. 'She passed her just there, wasn't it, Ivy?'

'Yes, that one. I was coming home from the PCC meeting, and Mrs Bourdillon stopped me under that lamppost and asked me the time. It was twenty-five to eight, that's how I know. Before they changed the clocks. It was dark.'

'What was she wearing?'

'Oh, you know how these young people dress. Something leather. And a woollen scarf, cashmere I wouldn't wonder.'

'So how did you see the bruises?'

Mrs Wells nodded fiercely. 'The police said they were there. On the corpse. All round the neck.'

'It was dark, and she had a scarf on,' said Agnes.

'The scarf was open, and we were under the lamp.'

'Did it surprise you that she spoke to you?'

'Most definitely.'

'Oh yes,' interrupted Mrs Wells. 'They'd never pass the time of day like that, would they, Ivy?'

'So this was unusual.' In her mind Agnes saw a young woman deliberately stop under a lamppost to engage one of the village gossips in conversation. 'Did she seem frightened?'

'Yes,' said Ivy. 'But then, she was always jumpy when you saw her.'

'Comes of living with you-know-who,' said Mrs Wells, jerking her head in the direction of Hugo's house.

In her mind, Agnes saw the girl ask the village woman the time, in order to make sure her presence was imprinted on the woman's memory; to make sure that she existed at that particular moment in time, because she feared that soon she

91

would cease to exist altogether. Agnes picked up a packet of digestive biscuits and two biros. 'Thank you, ladies,' she said, 'you've been most kind.'

So, she thought, as she made her way home through the dusk, Hugo visited Athena that afternoon, went home and was furious with Philippa, in the course of which he bruised his wife's neck, then went out again, all before seven o'clock. At seven-thirty Philippa went out, determined to be seen. At ten o'clock she was found murdered. But, if she was noticed going out, hadn't she been noticed returning?

Soon it would be time to catch up with Lowry. Then she could go back to London. She was pretty sure she knew some things he didn't. But she needed just a bit more, just one more thing to make it really clear, at least, that whoever killed Philippa, it wasn't Hugo. Whatever Julius might think.

# Chapter Eight

The Albion Gallery, despite being very well placed in the main street of a charming village, was deserted. Athena and Agnes stood in front of a blue glass vase veined with sparkly pink and indigo.

'What do you think, Agnes?'

'I think it's very you.'

'Well, I think that's very you,' replied Athena, pointing to a tall thin jug glazed in dark grey with a molecule pattern of little yellow dots.

'Could be,' said Agnes.

They smiled at each other, trying to disperse the tension that each had felt since they arrived. In the car on the way, Agnes had asked Athena why she'd left it to her to guess that she was still seeing Hugo.

'Perhaps I just knew you would,' smiled Athena.

'Yes, but—'

'Does it matter?'

'No, not really.' Agnes had looked out of the window, wondering why she felt it did. An image flashed into her mind, of Hugo with his hand around Philippa's neck. She turned back to Athena. 'When you heard what had happened to Philippa, what did you feel?'

Athena had suddenly swerved sharply into the middle of the narrow road to overtake a huge tractor.

'It's too late now,' she'd replied evenly, her knuckles white on the steering wheel.

Now in the shop, Athena picked up a brightly painted fruit

bowl, and said in a tone of forced jollity, 'Gosh, twenty-five quid for that? They sold those in my village for fifty p.' Agnes was examining a set of chunky tumblers in recycled glass.

'Why did you betray Philippa?'

Athena replaced the bowl and turned sharply to her. 'I think "betray" is a bit strong.'

'But why?'

'It was a damn fool idea of hers, and I tried to tell her so.'

'You can't have tried very hard.' Agnes's voice was raised.

'Why do you think I betrayed her?' flashed Athena. 'Why does any woman betray another woman?'

Agnes looked around the shop and lowered her voice.

'Not for Hugo? Surely—'

Athena replied, 'My dear, he's just the sexiest man I ever knew. Mmmm.' She gave a little shiver of pleasure, then continued, 'I suppose those convent years have put the lid on all that. Otherwise you'd know what I mean. Or perhaps you do,' she added, looking at Agnes through narrowed eyes, a trace of mockery around her lips. Someone appeared behind the counter, and Agnes bent her head to study a carved wooden box.

Athena continued in a lower voice, 'Anyway, I've told you everything now. I guess he did have a motive to kill Philippa; maybe he did kill her.'

'I thought you said you were convinced—'

'Convinced nothing. There's just no way I'm going to see the best lay I've ever had locked away behind bars for the rest of my life.'

Agnes looked up and studied her friend, who was exquisitely dressed as usual, this time in a houndstooth weave suit with loud brass buttons. Agnes wondered whether Athena had had all normal human feelings removed by surgery or whether she was born that way.

'Can I help you?' a voice said. A tall, smartly dressed woman who seemed to be the owner of the shop smiled at them from behind the counter.

'Oh, just looking, thank you,' replied Athena, then whispered to Agnes, 'So what do we do now?'

Agnes took a deep breath. 'We investigate.'

'Here?'

'This was the shop, wasn't it?'

'But?'

'Do you see any Bourdillon originals?'

'Darling, I wouldn't know one if it was caressing my nipples.'

Agnes smiled thinly. 'All the more reason. This was a cover. The amounts she recorded were more than she could ever have taken from this stuff. She was doing some other business here.'

The two women whispered briefly, and then Agnes approached the counter. 'Hello, I'm looking for a present for my – er – mother-in-law. She's very interested in – er – insects . . .' Agnes wished she'd swapped roles with the effortlessly mendacious Athena, who was even now creeping up the staircase at the back of the shop. Her theatrical, high-heeled teetering seemed suddenly ridiculous, and it took all Agnes's self-control not to burst out laughing.

'Hmm. Insects. I have some hand-printed silk scarves with a spider motif,' the woman said in a deep, English voice. 'Or how about this butterfly candle holder – very attractive.'

'Mmm,' mused Agnes, seeing Athena reappear at the top of the stairs and gesture wildly.

'Or this scarab brooch? Excuse me a moment, please.' An elegant middle-aged woman had appeared at the counter waving a receipt and now embarked on a tale of refunds and damaged goods. Agnes seized the moment and crept away.

''You'll never guess,' whispered Athena breathlessly at the top of the stairs. 'Look.'

It seemed to be a spare bedroom. The bed was bare. Two large wardrobes flanked the window, making the room even darker.

'You were right about the cover,' said Athena, opening a

wardrobe. It was full of women's clothing. Athena leafed through it, picking out pleated skirts, lacy petticoats and black underwear. Agnes was confused.

'You see?' said Athena. 'Look.' She opened the other wardrobe and showed her a hole cut into it, half hidden with clothes, then led her out of the room to a cupboard next door, where, on the floor, amid the dust, lay some sort of electric flex. 'Video leads,' said Athena, as if that summed up her explanation. Agnes stared blankly.

'I'm sorry, I'm lost,' she whispered at last.

'Transvestites, secretly recorded.'

'What?'

'Dressing up in women's clothes. Loads of men will pay good money for a safe place and a sympathetic woman to help with shopping and things. Only this wasn't safe.'

'You mean, Philippa's clients would come here—'

'And be secretly recorded. And then blackmailed.'

'Oh course. Jimmie.'

'What?'

'*Mon Dieu*, I'm glad you were here, Athena. I'd never have worked this out on my own.'

They stifled giggles, but then whirled at a sudden noise behind them. The shop owner stood in the doorway.

'I'm calling the police,' she said firmly.

'I don't think you are,' said Athena, swinging open the wardrobe door with a melodramatic gesture.

'It's not illegal.'

'What, blackmail?'

'It's nothing of the sort. Just some lonely souls needing a bit of kindness—'

'And being videoed.'

'Pip was a nice girl. She wouldn't have done that.'

Athena waved the video lead threateningly. 'And this? Or didn't you know anything about this?'

The shop owner faltered, looked from one woman to another, and then flopped down on to the bed. 'After she was – after she went away, I left it all alone. I just took the rent. It was nothing to do with me.' Her chin trembled. 'They were just lonely old gents most of them. There was no harm in it.'

A single tear ran down her cheek. Agnes gave her a hankie and sat beside her. 'Was anyone else involved?'

'No, just Pip. She arranged the room, paid me rent for it, you know. When the police came here, when they told me she'd been – you know—' She sniffed. 'I'd better get back to the shop.'

'What did you tell them?'

'Nothing. Only that she sold me things for the shop, she always said to say that if anyone asked. I'd better go, really.'

As they went downstairs the woman said, 'You won't tell anyone, will you?'

'No,' said Athena quickly.

'No,' said Agnes uncertainly, then added, 'have you heard of someone called David Mellersh?' The woman looked blank. 'Never mind. Here's my phone number,' said Agnes, scribbling it down. 'If you think of anything, ring me. Just ask for Sister Agnes. And now, there's one thing I must have.'

'It figures, though,' said Athena on the drive home. 'Philippa always had loads of money, and none of it came from Hugo.' She put her foot down hard on the accelerator. 'Do you think she was a man too?'

'Who?'

'Mrs Whatsit in the shop.'

'I've no idea. Mrs Elsworthy,' said Agnes, reading the small print on her receipt for one brightly painted Greek fruit bowl.

'You was robbed,' said Athena.

Back at the hotel, there was a note waiting for Agnes. It said:

Philippa cooked her goose. If I were you, I'd go for the chicken.

There was no signature. As she reached her room the phone began to ring. She hesitated before answering it. It was Mrs Elsworthy.

'I just wanted to tell you, what with the murder and the police and all that – well, I thought you should know that some of her clients were quite, shall we say, top people. High-profile, politicians, media people. And it may be that one of them, if she was doing what you say, with the video machine and everything, one of them might have wanted her . . . out of the way.'

Agnes thanked her very much, and as she rang off wondered again about her deep voice.

The next morning she set out for South Grove House. She was vaguely aware of a grey Vauxhall Astra driving behind her most of the way. Colin was once again ready with a pot of tea.

'I've found out something about your brother's involvement with Philippa. She wasn't having an affair with him at all.'

'Really, he was, he told me himself.'

'I don't quite know how to put this. It's rather tricky. You see, Philippa was blackmailing men who liked to dress up in women's clothes.'

Colin looked completely blank. He went to the window and traced a pattern in the condensation, then suddenly whirled to face her.

'You think you can walk in here talking pigswill like that, dragging our Jimmie's name into this? You're just like them, you are, just like them with all their filth.' He sat down heavily at the table. A dog barked outside.

Agnes said gently. 'Doesn't it make sense?' In the silence the kettle bubbled on the hob.

At last Colin sighed. 'Yeah. OK, it makes sense,' he said wearily. 'Only, when you get 'im to talk, swear you'll keep 'is name out of it?'

Agnes nodded. Colin sat for a while, then looked up. 'There's another thing,' he said. 'I didn't think to mention it before. That gear she was wearing – when the police came – that leather an' that – I'd seen it in Mr Bourdillon's things a few days before. I was hanging clothes in his wardrobe and came upon it all. Surprised me at the time, but with them lot you never asked questions.'

Driving towards Chidding Ford, Agnes was surprised to see the same grey car on her tail again. She tried to catch its numberplate in her mirror, but it was too far away. When she reached the ring road, it had gone. She turned off to the industrial estate, and parked a little way from it. Then on foot she headed for the patch of wasteland where she had seen the two boys go. There was a scrubby patch of trees, and behind that a field full of rubble, and a half-demolished terrace of small houses. Some were still whole, and from behind one came a column of smoke. There was a barbed-wire fence, collapsed and lying jaggedly in the mud, with a sign attached to it saying 'Dangerous Structure – Keep Out'. She could hear voices, and was about to step over the fence when an idea came to her. She went back to her car and drove back to the Cotswold Crest, relieved to catch no more glimpse of the grey Vauxhall.

A quick phone call to Jimmie was enough to get him to agree to meet her that evening.

'It'll have to be Cirencester. Dress smart and look like a customer,' he said tersely, giving her the name of a hotel bar.

She chose her outfit carefully, picking out the black jacket from the Cheltenham trip, a green silk shirt and a pencil skirt. Putting on her lipstick, she thought about clothes: her clothes, Jimmie's clothes; her habit, his dresses.

The Flag Hotel was bland and deserted. They sat down with their drinks in one corner.

'What am I buying?' said Agnes.

'What?'

'If I'm one of your customers, what are you selling?' She smiled at him. He looked up from a handful of peanuts and said, 'Oh. Office furniture,' then took another handful.

'I know this must be difficult for you,' Agnes tried, noticing how weary he seemed. He was wearing a polyester suit in navy blue, and looked about fifteen years older than his brother.

'What will you do?' he asked.

'About you? Nothing of course.'

'But the police—'

'Whatever you tell me now goes no further. I promise.'

He sighed. 'If my wife knew. Or my customers . . .'

'Did you know the name of the person you paid?'

'Only as Pip. She was nice to start with.'

'And who did you make cheques out to?'

'No cheques. Cash only.'

'How much did you pay Philippa?'

'Just a tenner for each session. Then, when the trouble started, a couple of hundred. It would have been more if she hadn't . . . if it hadn't stopped.'

'And there were lots of you?'

'Yes. I mean, always separate, of course. But you'd meet the others in passing.'

There was a pause. Agnes said gently, 'Was it really easier to pay the money than have people know?'

Jimmie looked up. He had his brother's clear grey eyes. 'I'm just an ordinary bloke,' he said at last.

Agnes took a sip of white wine. 'Would any of the other clients be likely to kill her, do you think?'

Jimmie paused, beer glass in hand. 'I passed a man on the stairs once who looked – familiar. Like I'd seen him on the telly or something. But I couldn't place it. Only saw him the once.'

Agnes wrote down her phone number again. 'If anything occurs to you, let me know.' They gathered up their coats. 'And Jimmie – if you told your wife—'

His eyes widened in horror.

'I mean, she might already suspect. It might be a relief to her to know.'

'You don't know our Amy,' said Jimmie, shaking his head.

Driving back, Agnes glanced in her mirror and thought she saw a grey Vauxhall Astra. She fixed her eyes on the blackness of the road ahead, gripping the wheel with shaking hands. When she next dared to look up the car had gone.

# Chapter Nine

'Smidgely?' It was more of a roar than a question. 'SMIDGELY?'

Agnes shrank back in her chair. 'I don't quite see . . .'

Detective Inspector Lowry towered over his untidy desk, his large hands spread flat across the piles of paper.

'You even know the name of the girl's bloody PONY!' Lowry straightened up, reached behind him and took down from a shelf two large box files which he now thumped down in front of him, releasing a cloud of dust into the yellow sunlight. He sat heavily into his swivel chair and rocked to and fro.

Agnes took the tiniest sip of undrinkable coffee and said, 'But Inspector, surely if you'd asked them—'

'It's not that bloody simple, is it, Sister? If I ask someone a question, I get an answer. But the answer I get depends on which question I ask in the first place. Whereas, in your case—' He opened a file and riffled through it. 'I mean, when you came in this morning with your tales of camcorders in the camiknickers, before I got my lads to check it out—' He broke off and leaned across his desk. 'Don't poison yourself with that.'

He took the mug from her hands, then opened a drawer in his desk from which he took out a cafetière, some coffee beans, and an old-fashioned wooden coffee grinder with a little drawer at the bottom. While he talked he measured out some beans into the top of the grinder. He began to turn the handle, punctuating his words with a rhythmic grinding noise.

'I mean, I can ask them, "Did she have a pony?" "Yes, Inspector"' – Lowry mimicked a tight-throated English accent – '"What was its name?" "Smidgely". And how far have I bloody got? Whereas with you it's all, "Oh, do come riding with us, look, there's dear old Smidgely out in the paddock, such a shame, he does miss her even though he's only a pea-brained bloody pony" . . .'

Lowry paused for breath, carefully emptying the contents of the little drawer into the cafetière, then went over to the kettle. He turned, silhouetted against the bright window, its ancient dingy smears highlighted by the sun.

'"And by the way, The First Mrs Bourdillon," they say to you over Après-Riding drinks, "Did you know that The Second Mrs Bourdillon was blackmailing transvestites?"'

Agnes felt it was rude to laugh. 'Inspector, it wasn't quite like that, I mean, without Athena—'

'The biggest bloody snob of them all, that Greek woman. She told us next to nothing. You see, in this country, we're suffocating. You foreigners can't see it. When we say nothing, give nothing away, you think it's our celebrated English reserve. The fact is, we're gasping for bloody air.'

The kettle boiled and he poured water on to the coffee.

'You can hardly say Athena suffers from English reserve,' smiled Agnes. 'And anyway, it's crazy to suggest that these people would tell me things they wouldn't tell an officer of the law.'

Lowry returned to his files and took out a wad of papers which he waved at her. 'Statements – from Mrs Paneotou, Littlejohn, the housekeeper, the maid, Mr Bourdillon, David Mellersh . . . On the computer we've got sightings of bloody everything, from cars to dogs to different kinds of hats . . . We've talked to the woman from the post office, we've visited that arty-farty place which turned out to have the business upstairs. You followed the same paths that I did, only with different results. I'd find it galling, only it's just what I've come to expect from this tight-lipped pack of snobs.'

He unwrapped a clingfilm pack of flapjacks, took a bite of one and then waved them at Agnes. 'Home-made,' he said, blowing oaty crumbs across the table. 'The Missus.' He chewed thoughtfully, then continued. 'It's always like that with these folk; even when they're reporting their bloody BMW's been pinched, you're lucky if they whine more than a couple of words at you, and those are likely to be "portable fax".' A trace of a smile vanished as he looked up sharply. 'It's only when I get my lads to retrace your steps that we get anywhere, Sister.'

'Agnes.'

'Agnes.'

'It's wonderful coffee,' said Agnes.

Lowry passed the statements across to her. 'You might like to look at these.'

'What, now?'

'Well, what are your plans?'

'I don't know. I rather thought I might return to London soon.'

'You don't sound convinced.'

Her gaze wandered across his desk, taking in the pile of evidence: papers, files, reports, statements; all methodically gathered, all within her reach.

'You see, Sister—'

'Agnes—'

'Agnes, if you wanted to go through the evidence . . . We could give you access to the computer too—'

She looked at him wearily and sighed. 'The thing is, Inspector, I'm being followed by a grey Vauxhall Astra. And – look.' Agnes fished in her pockets and drew out the anonymous note that had been left for her at her hotel. Lowry looked at it, then got up, pulled out a file and compared it with some other papers.

'Definitely Mellersh's handwriting. I'm surprised he didn't

try to disguise it,' said Lowry, turning the note over in his hands.

'I think he might be in a desperate state. His phone call was very odd. What did you find out from him?'

'Only that he ran the business with Philippa. Tea cosies and things.' Lowry grimaced. 'We looked at his accounts, it all seemed in order.'

'Did you read Philippa's diaries?'

'Aye. Just schoolgirl jottings, we thought, apart from the end bit which points the finger at the husband.'

'The third set of prints at the house—?'

'Lord alone knows. They're everywhere, must have been someone intimate with the household; but they don't match any other set. Not Mellersh, not the staff. And I've never yet heard of a ghost leaving dabs.'

Agnes thought a moment. 'When Philippa went out, she was seen on her way to wherever she was going.'

'Right. You met our Ivy.'

'But no one saw her return?'

'No. The only odd sighting we had was of a suspicious person in a car which turned out to be stolen driving through the village at about nine o'clock that evening.'

'Towards the house?'

'Aye, but nothing's turned up. It was spotted by a couple of punters from the King's Head. It was reported stolen that evening from Cirencester way. Probably nothing to do with this, happens all the time these days.'

'There's one other thing – you don't know anything about Philippa's religious connections, do you?'

'Only the Reverend Just-Call-Me-Bob.' They both smiled, and Lowry added, 'And I can't say I believe Mrs B. was sincere in her Christian conversion.' He gathered up the empty mugs on to a tray stained with brown rings.

'So what do you – we – do next?'

'I'm sending the fingerprinting lads up to our Mrs Elsworthy's secret room.'

'Oh. Inspector, she hasn't done anything – illegal, has she?'

'From your evidence, probably not.'

'Try not to upset her.'

Agnes noticed that Lowry's smile, when genuine, lightened only one side of his mouth. 'By the way,' he said, 'talking of protecting your sources – which of her clients did you meet?'

'I really can't tell you. We made a deal.'

'I'm not sure the rules of the confessional apply in a police investigation, Sister.'

'Nuns don't hear confession,' replied Agnes, gravely.

'So you mean next time I'm lured into vice and temptation I can't tell you about it?'

'On the contrary, you can tell me anything you like. The more the better. Just don't expect absolution.'

Agnes left the police station with a spring in her step. As they shook hands, Lowry said, 'Well, looks like your ex-old man is off the hook – for now,' and it was as much as she could do not to rush straight to Hugo and tell him.

'Look what I've done,' she wanted to announce to him. 'Look how I've saved you.' She imagined his face lighten as the burden of blame lifted from him. And then after that – after that, she thought, they would be friends, and she could go back to London secure in the knowledge that all that, all that chapter of her life with Hugo, was at last resolved. The thought of Julius flashed into her mind, and she tried to block out his cynicism; because, of course, Julius would say, none of that is true. You just want to be part of the lying, brutal mess that is Hugo Bourdillon. You just can't leave him alone.

She wouldn't let Julius ruin it.

She was still in a good mood when she got back to her hotel at about four o'clock. She smiled as she went, again, to her wardrobe. This time she brought out her habit; poor neglected thing, she thought, as she stroked the fabric, then put it on.

When she'd followed the kids to the patch of wasteland, it had occurred to her that, even if the coincidence with the T-shirt slogans did mean they were connected with Philippa, they might not want to tell her so. Any sense that they were being questioned by authority would probably shut them up altogether. She needed a disguise, she had thought then. And this, she thought, looking at herself in the mirror, although hardly a disguise to her, might do the trick.

She swept into the lift, and out again across the hotel foyer, enjoying the puzzled glances of the hotel staff. She got into her car.

She parked in Chidding Ford's central car park, and then headed out to the ring road on foot. Her habit swished as she walked. She felt it balance her, slowing her pace to a dignified tread. She reached the wasteland, and stepped gingerly over the jagged fence and mud tracks towards the column of smoke, feeling in her pockets for the packet of cigarettes and the two ten pound notes. She picked her way past the crumbling piles of bricks; from out of the corner of her eye she saw something move. She turned purposefully towards the clump of trees and sat at the foot of one. And waited.

She heard a shout, a laugh. Someone emerged from the derelict building, saw her and stood still for a moment, then vanished. There was more raucous laughter, followed by sudden quiet. At last three figures came out and stared at her. She sat still. They came nearer. At last one said, 'Look at fucking Mother Teresa saying her fucking prayers.'

'Jez!' a girl's voice hissed.

'Yeah?'

There was a pause, then the first voice called out, 'Oi. Mother Teresa!'

'Nah,' came another boy's voice, 'Mother Teresa's in fuckin' India, man.'

'So 'oo the fuck's this then, eh? Oi, you, fuck off back to them starvin' Pakis.'

'Jez, I said cut it out,' said the girl.

Agnes raised her head, appeared to see them for the first time, and smiled.

'You wouldn't have a drink of water, would you?'

'We don't fuckin' drink fuckin' water. You from the social then?'

Agnes shook her head and smiled again. She took in their appearance, which was ragged and colourful, layers upon torn layers of denim, huge woollen jumpers and khaki jackets. The one they called Jez had matted hair which was bleached halfway up and very black at the roots. The girl had wild brown curls. All three looked about sixteen at the most, much, much younger than Philippa. Agnes stood up, smoothing the folds of her habit.

'I was hoping you could help me. I was looking for someone, but I doubt you knew her. Philippa Bourdillon.'

She was surprised by their reaction. Glances snapped between the trio like firecrackers. The girl spoke.

'But don't you know?'

'Shut up, Lisa,' Jez hissed.

'Know what?' asked Agnes gently.

'Why can't I tell her? Everyone else knows.'

'No one knows we know, do they, you stupid slag.' Jez punched Lisa's shoulder and she reeled back with the blow, regained her footing and stared at him hard, her fists clenched at her sides.

'What, know that she's dead?' she said, loudly, not taking her eyes away from his. 'Fucking murdered, you mean?'

The other boy stood hunched, staring out at Agnes, his arms hugging his body. Agnes walked towards them, feeling for the money, which she now offered with an outstretched arm. The hunched boy and Lisa looked at Jez, who waited until Agnes was near, then snatched the money with an empty smile. He squared up to her, his eyes level with hers.

'And?' he said.

'When did you last see Philippa?'

'When she was alive,' he grinned, looking to his friends for

109

support. But the boy looked away, and Lisa turned her eyes upwards and clicked her tongue.

'Was she here much?'

Jez was silent now. Lisa answered, 'When she could get away. No one knew. You're the first to come here.'

Jez said suddenly, 'You got a fag on yer?'

The three sat and smoked around the pathetic fire. Lisa brought a plywood pallet for Agnes to sit on. On one side of the fire a tattered canvas half-covered a couple of ancient saucepans and a plastic bottle of water. Through the doorway of the one house still standing, Agnes could see damp squares of coconut matting and a blanket. A supermarket trolley was wedged in the mud, full of dustbin bags which spilled out their contents of old clothes and newspaper.

'Did Philippa talk about her husband?'

Lisa giggled. Jez said, ''E was rich. That's all we knew.'

'An' she liked shaggin' 'im,' said Lisa.

'She liked shaggin' anythin', she did.'

'Piss off, just cos she wouldn't 'ave you.'

Jez aimed a punch at Lisa who ducked and laughed, harsh and loud. ''Scuse him, miss.'

'Miss,' sneered Jez.

'Well, she's a – you know, aren't yer. What do you call 'em?' She turned wide eyes to Agnes.

'I'm a nun. My name's Agnes.'

Jez laughed emptily.

'She used to ride over on Smidgely,' added Lisa.

'Mental cow misses the horse more than the gel,' Jez said.

'Fuckin' don't.'

'She loved that horse. She'd give that horse her last sandwich, she would.'

'Don't be a cunt, Jez. They don't fuckin' eat sandwiches.'

Jez laughed again. 'Like Billy the Rat here.'

The other boy, who up till then had remained silent, produced a large white rat from one pocket and part of an old sandwich from the other, which he fed to the rat, stroking it and murmuring, 'Don't you take no notice of 'im, man.'

'You'll have seen 'im up in London,' Jez said to Agnes.

'Will I?'

'In Piccadilly, eh? He puts the rat in his mouth and gets them tourists to take piccies.'

Billy looked up from his communing and smiled proudly.

'Twenty quid a throw.'

Jez said, 'More'n 'e'll ever get fer his body, eh, Bill?'

Suddenly Billy stood up, his face set, the rat back in his pocket. He went to Jez and stood over him.

'Go on Bill, doff 'im one,' said Lisa.

Jez smiled emptily up at Billy. No one moved. Neither boy even blinked. Then, just as suddenly, Billy turned and went back to his place, retrieving his rat from his pocket. 'Don't you take no notice of 'im,' he murmured, stroking its head.

Jez got up and stretched. 'Well, well,' he said loudly, 'I smell our dinner.' As he spoke, there were voices and laughter and a small group approached the fire. Agnes recognized the tall girl from the computer game and the boy on crutches. Behind them there was the boy with the dog. They carried polystyrene boxes and cans of lager. Jez bounded towards them.

'I hope you've got enough for our guest. Mother Teresa. She's been working wiv the poor for so long she's fuckin' starvin'.' He laughed loudly.

'We only got seven,' said the girl.

'Well, what we fuckin' goin' ter do?' shouted Jez. 'She's our bleedin' guest, in't she?'

Agnes said, 'I think we are seven.'

Six faces stared at her blankly. At last the boy with the dog said. 'This is Norm. Norm the dog. People sometimes forget.'

Jez stepped in. 'Back off, Smoke. She can share mine.' He extravagantly divided his burger unevenly into two and insisted she take the larger half. The others all settled around

111

the fire, making space for the boy on crutches, whose name seemed to be Den.

'No, really, it's your dinner.' Agnes smiled.

'Well, you have more chips then.' He grinned at her, his mouth oozing red ketchup, then took a slurp of lager and said to the assembled company. 'Mother Teresa wants to know about Cuntface.'

'Who?' said the girl.

'Fip.'

'Dead, in't she,' said Smoke. 'Her old man done it.' He patted Norm, who was wrestling gamely with his burger.

'How did you know about us?' said Lisa.

'I saw your T-shirt,' Agnes said to the tall girl. 'She had one the same.'

'She flippin' nicked it off me,' said Lisa.

Everyone ate noisily. Jez shouted out, 'Oi, Latoya, fire's goin' out.' The tall girl got up and poked at the smouldering wood with a stick. Agnes asked, 'Were any of your friends – religious? Would they have gone to a church group?'

Jez sneered. 'Nah, not us. What's God ever done fer us, eh?'

'Ignore 'im, 'e's a mental bastard,' said Lisa.

Agnes ate a chip. 'Have any of you heard of David Mellersh?'

Six people and a dog continued to eat. Jez shook his head. Agnes ate another chip. 'What does it mean, then?'

'What does what mean?'

'One Aim, One Destiny?'

Again, six blank looks. Latoya said. 'Our friend Angie did them. She got a training scheme grant thingie to do T-shirt printin'. Went up to London in the end, we ain't seen her since.'

'Mind you,' said Lisa with her mouth full. 'She were religious, weren't she. Kept goin' on about Jesus and that.'

'Well, at least God got her a bleedin' grant,' sneered Jez, licking ketchup off his fingers.

It was nearly dark when Agnes left. 'I'll see you out,' said Jez, walking with her to the fence.

'Could I visit again?'

'Yeah. If we're still 'ere.'

'I'll give you my phone number. Just in case.'

Jez turned the scrap of paper around in his fingers. 'Bet that's posh, eh? We'll come and visit and you can buy us all cocktails in the bar.' His smile suddenly died and his eyes went steely. 'Just 'cos you've been bleedin' clever – you see, no one else knows we knew her. And it better bloody stay like that, OK?'

Agnes met his gaze. 'OK.'

'No offence an' that.' He smiled again, reached out and shook her hand, then was gone, bounding over the barbed wire, back towards the fire which glowed sullenly in the twilight.

There was another note waiting for her at the hotel. Agnes's hands trembled as she opened it, but instead of the nervous biro she found a broad italic sweep of black ink:

Am in the bar. H.

Agnes raced up to her room, flung off her habit, put on a knee-length button-through black dress and a hasty smear of lipstick, and hurried down to the bar. Hugo was smiling wryly. 'What's with the habit, eh?'

'What habit?'

'I watched you arrive.'

She blushed. 'Just something I needed to be today.'

'You chameleon thing, you. Though I prefer you like this.' He allowed his gaze to travel up and down her body, coming to rest on her eyes. He smiled. 'Let me buy you a drink.'

She watched him saunter to the bar, looked at him waiting to order, broad-shouldered in his ribbed sweater, his dark curls at his neck. She felt suddenly at a loss – why was she here, now, drinking with this man as if it were the most natural thing in the world? Even more confusing, why did she feel so happy? Watching him banter with the girl behind the bar, it struck her how he'd changed; how the good looks of his youth had given way to a distinguished, mature sexiness. In that moment, she saw him for what he was: the man she'd married, for better or worse; in some way, for ever. She wondered how she'd lived all these years without being aware of his presence, as real as anything else in her life. 'As real as your Faith?' she heard Julius ask. She couldn't think of an answer.

And now here was Hugo returning to their table with a chilled bottle of Sauternes. 'I believe, my dear, that we're celebrating. I had a little chat with my lawyer today, and he said the heat is off though not to get too excited yet. And that I owe it to you.'

'He said that?'

'Something like that, yes.'

'We've found nothing new, really.'

'We? The Gloucestershire police force plus Sister Agnes?'

'All I mean is, the evidence suggests that other people might have had motives to kill your – to kill Philippa. And that there was a third person in your house that evening.'

'Lovers. Loads of them. And that Mellersh is louche, a nasty piece of work. He phoned the house the other night. I'm sure it was him, said it was a wrong number. Anyway, enough of him. It's you I came to see.'

They clinked glasses. 'I trust you still prefer Sauternes at this time of day?' Agnes smiled and nodded. 'Though why I should think so when everything else has changed . . .'

'Ah, but not that.'

'So the Sauternes is still favoured even though I've been cast aside?' His eyes flashed grey. She wanted to trace the angles of his face with her fingers. 'You can't know what it's meant to me, your being here.'

'Of course, it's not for much longer,' she said hastily.

'You need to be cared for, Agnes.' Hugo's voice was low. Agnes tried to laugh.

'Hugo, I'm a nun.'

# Chapter Ten

The phone rang rudely. Agnes stretched out a languid arm and picked up the receiver.

'Yes?' Her voice was a decadent whisper.

'Agnes?' Lowry sounded uncertain.

'*Bonjour*, Inspector. You start work early. And on a Saturday.'

'Eleven o'clock?'

'It can't be.' Agnes sat up, pulled the covers around her and smiled. A flash of sunlight peeked through a gap in the curtains and then exploded across a huge vase of fresh daffodils that had appeared on her dressing table overnight.

'What can I do for you, Inspector?'

'I fail to see the joke, Sister.'

'No, no, it's not you. Just something here. Right, I'm serious now. What's new?'

'Two things that might interest you. Firstly, the stolen car's turned up, and we're taking fingerprints now. Secondly, the prints in Mrs Elsworthy's little boudoir – they're the same as the mystery ones up at the house.'

Agnes ran her fingers through her hair. 'Get grinding those beans, Inspector, I'll be right there.'

She lay back on her pillows and stretched. She smiled. She wondered if Hugo was awake yet. Probably not, given the time they'd left the bar last night. He must have ordered the flowers at reception after kissing her goodnight. No, Julius, she answered the voice in her head, the goodnight kiss was a mere brush of the lips. I did nothing of which I need be

117

ashamed. My actions were pure, as were my words. My thoughts, on the other hand – but my thoughts are private. Even from God? Julius would ask. No, she answered. But God knows as well as I do just how charming, how beautiful, how bloody sexy, Hugo Bourdillon can be.

Lowry shifted down into third gear for a bend in the road.

'So this is the Rover 216 then. How do you find it?'

'Pardon? Oh, fine.'

'It's the 1590cc sixteen-valver, isn't it?'

'I'm sorry?'

'The engine?'

'Mmm.'

'Nought to sixty in nine point five seconds. And I hear they've solved the chassis problems they were having with the 200 series. Cornering's pacey, is it?'

'Sorry?'

'The grip?'

'Oh, yes, fine.'

'It's just, the way you took that bend . . .' There was a silence filled only by the hum of the engine.

'Or maybe you're not interested in cars, Inspector?'

Lowry turned to Agnes as far as his driving would allow. 'I don't think, Sister, it would look good for a Detective Inspector to be caught doing a wheelie on the A504 just outside Cirencester, do you?'

Agnes smiled. 'I'll drive us back then.'

'You'll do no such thing. Police property, this car.'

'It's a shame to see it wasted,' she replied. Lowry glanced at her sharply, but she was gazing out of the window, humming a few bars of the Kyrie from Bach's Mass in B Minor. When he turned back to the road, she said, 'So, why is this stolen car we're going to see so important?'

'All I know is, Driscoll said I'd find it interesting. We'll see.'

'And then what?'

'I think it's time you sat down with the files.'

'Are we going to talk to Mellersh?'

'Do you think that's wise?'

'Well, at least I can ask him why he's following me, Inspector.'

'Call me Jim. I think it's time we had another chat with Mellersh down at the station – and you're welcome to be there.'

'Thank you – Jim.'

They turned on to a dual carriageway which was signposted 'To M5'.

'No wonder your wife makes flapjacks,' said Agnes suddenly.

'I beg your pardon?'

'I mean, if you spend Saturdays driving around in search of evidence the whole time. What else is there for her to do?'

Lowry did his half-grin. 'Baking's her relaxation. If she's not making flapjacks she's writing endless reports about her delinquent clients. She's a psychiatrist, does social services stuff.'

'So if her workload's really bad, do you get a Victoria sponge?'

Lowry laughed. 'Oh yes, and chocolate éclairs when it's nervous-breakdown time. Here we are.'

They pulled up on a layby near the dual carriageway. There was a dull roar of traffic from the M5 which lay a little way beyond. A shabby beige Ford Escort was parked crookedly on the verge, surrounded by orange sticky tape and men in dark suits, with the occasional uniformed policeman. Lowry got out.

'Morning, Driscoll.'

'Glad to see you, Inspector.' The Sergeant gave way to a tall, smartly dressed man, whom Agnes took to be part of the forensic team. He was carrying a small polythene bag which he handed to Lowry. Lowry peered at it and then passed it to Agnes. Inside the bag were several long, wavy, auburn hairs.

* * *

'Does it have to be smoked salmon?'

'Is there a problem?'

'The local shop does ham or cheese. Anyway, I thought nuns were supposed to live simply.'

'Oh, all right then, ham.'

Lowry picked up his phone and instructed someone on the other end to fetch two rounds of sandwiches, then settled down with the files.

'The car had Philippa's prints in the back, round the floor, and the mystery ones in the front. Plus some glove prints and one other lot, probably the owner's. I've asked him to come in, it might help.'

'Do you think there was violence?'

'There is a lot of hair. More than you'd normally get. But no blood. We'll see what the labs come up with.'

Agnes flicked through a file. 'Did you have a statement from the drinkers in the King's Head?'

'Let's have a look.' Lowry riffled through the sheaf of papers she handed him. He looked up as the door to his office opened, and a young constable appeared with a plate of sandwiches which he put down on the corner of the desk. Agnes saw thick-cut white sliced bread with a thin, moist, pink line between the slabs. The young policeman nodded at Agnes and left again. Lowry returned to his papers.

'Here we are. "Appeared to be driven by a young white man wearing a thick dark coat and a flat cap." These things are always unreliable. And it was dark.'

'Did they see a passenger?'

'No.'

'And yet, all the hair . . . ?'

'Lying down. That would go with the prints being low in the car.'

'It does suggest violence, doesn't it?'

'Mmmm. But we know she died at the house. Shortly before ten o'clock. And we know from the blood splashing that she was active at the time of the murder.'

'Was the car seen leaving after that?'

'No one's reported it. We'll have to ask around. Though you could take B roads to that slipway. No one need see you at all. And Mr Bourdillon's drive was gravel, all churned up, not ideal for leaving evidence.'

'What did the murderer do after dumping the car, then?'

'Probably switched cars and got on to the motorway. We'll look into that too.'

'Do you think the killer nicked the car himself?'

'Maybe. Maybe got some kid to do it for him. These days, if you slip any of the local youth a fiver, they'll find you a car.'

Agnes thought of Jez, and wondered how long it would be before she'd have to break her vow of silence. She reached across and took a sandwich. Lowry suddenly said, with his mouth full, 'I wanted to ask you one thing, Agnes. Your friend Athena – she jumped to conclusions about videos and things very readily, didn't she?'

'Yes. But why not? She's a woman of the world.'

Lowry chewed thoughtfully. 'And in her world it's normal for people to have little business set-ups like that one?'

Agnes took another bite of sandwich. 'It's the same world as yours, Jim – or mine.'

Later that afternoon Agnes was pacing the streets restlessly. Phrases of evidence tossed around in her head like the fragments of litter whirling round the clock tower in the spring breeze. 'I left South Grove House at seven that evening, maybe eight—' 'I'd known the couple for two years, maybe three—' 'It must have been dark by then, or getting dark anyway . . .' 'It was a white man, young – yes, definitely young . . .' 'It was definitely Mrs Bourdillon I saw—' 'I am absolutely certain—' 'I could swear to it—' 'Without a shadow of doubt . . .'

Certainties. Julius ought to be proud of me, she thought, confronting the paradoxical relation between doubt and certainty – isn't that how he'd put it? Only, of course, he wasn't impressed at all, because rather than struggle with such concepts in the course of strengthening her faith, she was merely using them to find a murderer. A worldly, villainous murderer.

She waited to hear her inner voices surface in their shrill chorus of disapproval, listing her shortcomings, highlighting her sinfulness in a punishing litany. From within there came only silence. All the noise was exterior; traffic, people, a dog barking. To Agnes the silence was the worst there could be. Deserted by her inner voice, she was alone, deaf to the will of God. Her legs felt weak, and she looked round for somewhere to sit down.

Suddenly an empty juice carton whistled past her ear. She turned sharply to see Jez sitting on the wall by the bus stop, grinning at her.

'How nice to see you,' she said, joining him. 'Aren't you going to pick up that litter?'

'It was meant for the bleedin' bin. Ain't my fault if it missed.'

'How's the gang?'

Jez smiled. 'The gang,' he mocked. Then he looked at her more closely. 'You OK?'

Agnes felt a sudden urge to confide in him, this lithe, spotty, colourful youth. Instead she heard herself say, 'Er – yes, fine.'

They sat on the wall, swinging their legs. Agnes asked, in a conversational tone, 'Nicked any cars recently?'

He grinned again. 'Yeah. Do it all the time.'

'It's just, Pip's murder – there was a stolen car involved.'

'Yeah, well, we're bound to twoc a car to murder one of our mates in, ain't we.'

Agnes swung her legs, then stopped as she felt her tights snag against the rough Cotswold stone of the wall.

'If I were to ask your friends about it—'

'Listen 'ere, Mother Teresa – that crew, 'alf of 'em weren't around when Pip was bumped off. We come and go, us lot. They'll tell yer nothin'.'

'Do you think her husband did it?'

'No idea, man.' Jez picked thoughtfully at one nostril, then added, 'Prob'ly not.'

'It's just, it's getting a bit difficult to keep silent about your connection with her. I don't want to tell the police about you, but the more they need to know the likelier I am to have to . . .'

'You can fuck off then.'

Jez's expression shut down. He made no attempt to move, but stared morosely across the square towards a crowd of foreign students jostling along the narrow pavement, watching them as they made their chaotic way past the Feathers. He turned back towards Agnes with a leering grin.

'Rich pickin's there, man.'

'Jez, who was around when Pip died? Who was she hanging around with who isn't here any more?'

Jez looked at her, still leering. 'You see, thing is, Mother Teresa, it's the fuckin' drugs, innit. Do yer brain in, don't they. If I did know once, I don't know now.' He pointed theatrically at his head. 'Memory? All fuckin' gone, innit. Wiped out. Chemic'ly destroyed.' He stared into her face and giggled.

Agnes stared back evenly. 'Names, Jez. Friends of Philippa. Come on.'

Jez sighed. 'Well . . . Angie.'

'Angie the religious one who went to London to set up a T-shirt printing business.'

'Yeah, that's right. She was 'ere the whole winter. And Sinead. They went to London together.'

'Before the murder?'

Jez looked irritated, and scratched a spot on his chin.

'Yeah, must 'ave been. Sinead was good mates wiv Fip.'

'Does she know?'

'Prob'ly, by now. Someone'll 'ave told her. Taff went to

London after, he'd 'ave found Sinead.'

'Will she come back?'

'Dunno. She did last time.'

'What do they do in London, your mates?'

Jez looked at her. 'Oh, you know. Get rich. 'Ave a ball. Tea at the Ritz, shoppin' at 'arrods. Take in a show, see the sights.' He looked at the ground, swinging his legs. 'They survive. Mostly. And some don't.'

Agnes stared at the ground too. An image flashed through her mind, of desperate, scattered, lost young people – of Julius, alone, trying to reach out to them. She looked up again at Jez.

'Do you know anyone who'd have a motive for killing Philippa?'

Jez laughed harshly, and shook his head, his bleached locks bobbing with the exaggerated movement.

Agnes continued. 'There was this man David Mellersh.' She noticed Jez suddenly seemed pale. 'She had a business with him. A dangerous business. Do you know anything about it?'

Jez suddenly flung himself off the wall and burst out, 'S'nuffin' to do with us, right?' His feet in their huge trainers were braced, legs apart, his shoulders flung back with hostility. 'You're sad, man. Way off it, right? An' if you blow about us, you're dead.' His face flashed cold menace, then he turned and slowly sauntered away up the hill of the high street, not looking back.

Agnes watched him go, wondering, as she felt the rough wall on the back of her knees, where she could buy a new pair of tights. It was funny, she thought, that all the kids had looked blank last time she'd mentioned Mellersh to them – whereas now the name was capable of producing an effect like that.

Her head was spinning. It was time to take stock. She turned and headed for the car park, looking forward to an evening off; a hot bath, a drink in the bar, a Chabrol movie on the television, an early night.

The Sunday morning sunlight filtered through the high windows of the church. Agnes sat in the soft darkness of the confessional, calling to mind her sins.

'Bless me, Father . . .' The words soothed her as she sat shut away behind the curtain, amid the familiar scent of old, damp wood, feeling the anonymous, attentive presence behind the grid. Her voice was low, and her words tumbled out in an anguished sigh. 'I have turned away from God, I have deliberately blocked my ears to His voice, I have grasped at illusory, worldly things. I have deserted my calling, preferring instead to dabble in vanities . . .' She thought of her black silk jacket; red lipstick; Athena. 'I have been tempted . . .' She saw a powerful, male body; smouldering, laughing eyes, and she stopped short. Tempted by what, she wondered. 'I have sinned against my fellow men in thought and word and deed . . .' With relief she settled for the old familiar words, with relief she received her penance and her absolution.

Later she walked out of the church into the brightness of the day. Her shoulders were straighter, her tread was light. It was simple. She would return to London, to Julius. Soon. Just a few more days.

'Shall I expect you back this side of Tuesday?' asked Arnie drily. He grinned up at her. 'You look set to gallop into the sunset, never to return.'

'That seems to be Carlo's plan,' she replied, feeling the horse step jauntily under her as they turned to the gate. 'If I have any say in the matter, I'll be back for coffee.' Arnie watched them trot out on to the road and turn towards the woods.

Agnes leaned over Carlo's neck to avoid the overhanging trees, aware of the speed of the horse under her, checking him gently with her hands to keep the canter steady. She saw fresh streaks of green; felt budding branches whisking past her, wet ferns and brackens brushing her knees. There was only the horse's neck against her cheek, the sunlight dappling the trees, the dewy caresses of the branches, the steady pace of the hooves. The moment was a gift from God; and she smiled.

Arnie greeted them in the yard on their return. Behind him Ben was parking a barrow of hay. 'How did he go?'

'Fine. Wonderful.' Agnes's face was flushed, and her jodhpurs were streaked with mud.

'Good. Good. He's been a bit off recently. Had a novice on him earlier in the week, bit of a mistake it turned out.'

'I won't hear a word said against him.'

Agnes dismounted and buried her face against Carlo's neck, who nuzzled her affectionately. Arnie patted the horse's side and handed the reins to Ben, then turned towards the house. 'Come in for a while.'

They sat in the homely kitchen. Agnes picked at the burrs on her jacket. A huge number of woollen socks hung crookedly from the old ceiling airer, most of them single, occasionally a matching pair.

'How's the investigation?'

'The plot thickens.' She laughed.

'The heat's off Hugo, then?'

'Almost certainly.'

'I'm glad really. Despite what I said. One doesn't like to think one knows a killer.' Arnie got up and put the old kettle on the range with a clatter.

'Arnie – why did he marry Philippa?'

'Often asked myself that.'

'They seem – somewhat ill-matched. Not that I can talk.'

'Well, she was a beautiful woman, and Hugo would overlook most things for that. But only up to a point. She always seemed – phoney, in a way. I always felt there was some kind of performance between them, and he was going along with it. Reluctantly. Yes,' he added, nodding, 'that was it. When he talked about revenge in the pub that time, I had this impression – you know when you're asking something of a horse that it doesn't want to do, a big, powerful, spirited horse – the way it fights back? That was what he was like. And I was surprised, because I'd always felt Hugo had the upper hand in his dealings with women.'

'He was in debt in France when he met her.'

'Perhaps that was it then. She bought him. Though God knows what with, she was always broke.'

'And what did she want from him, do you think?'

'That's easier. I mean, think about it. She was a local Gloucestershire girl, from an ordinary family. The parents split up, she ends up in France, working bars or something. When she comes back she's married a wealthy foreigner and settles here in fine style. Cuts herself off from her family. They've all moved on or died since, anyway.'

'So the mystery is, did she bail Hugo out, in France – and if so, what with? And did he resent her for it?'

Arnie shrugged, and drained his cup. 'It's all hearsay in the end, isn't it. Gossip. All I know is, Hugo tired of her.'

Agnes stared into her empty cup and shivered. 'When Hugo tired of me . . .' She blinked, shook herself, and smiled up at Arnie. 'I must be going.'

In the doorway, Arnie hesitated. 'Seen – um – Athena recently?'

'I'm having dinner with her tonight, actually.'

'Oh. Send her my – um – regards, won't you.'

Agnes was unsure she'd got the right house. Sparkbrook Terrace was an unprepossessing row of early Victorian houses on the edge of Chidding Ford, standing forlornly as if it had been left there by mistake, an afterthought of nineteenth-century development. Number 7 had a peeling blue door and dirty windows. As she rang the bell she was reassured by hearing it tinkle a hollow rendition of the last few bars of 'Big Spender'. Athena opened the door in a flurry of red silk.

'Darling! How wonderful.'

Agnes smiled. She was glad she'd dressed up too.

Sunday evening, thought Lowry. He wished he was sitting on his patio with a pint of Tetley's bitter instead of watching the sun set over the Superstore car park. He wondered, not for the first time, whether he'd work more efficiently if his office had a better view.

Agnes tried hard to admire Athena's living room. 'Gosh,' she said, taking in the expanse of dark golden shiny floorboards, the steel tubes of the dining table, the black angular lamp which was suspended over the table by a curly flex.

'I knocked down a few walls,' said Athena over her shoulder as she stood by the huge marble breakfast bar pouring drinks. 'I like space and light.'

The walls were the colour of bare plaster. A few white shelves cut cleanly across one corner. An ethnic-looking rug in woolly terracotta colours hung on the wide wall above the table. The last of the daylight streaked rosily through a glass-panelled french window, beyond which Agnes could see a wild mass of rose bushes in bud and a scruffy hydrangea.

'Here we are.' Athena handed her a glass of delicate pink liquid. 'Kir. I waved the cassis over the top of yours.'

'How thoughtful,' smiled Agnes, noticing Athena's own drink was a sugary purple in colour. '*Santé*,' she said, raising her glass.

'*A la votre*,' replied Athena. 'We're having Kleftiko. I hope you like Retsina.'

'Lovely,' said Agnes, perching on a black leather bar stool. 'We can have my Chablis with the dessert.'

Sunday evening. No different from any other, thought Jez as he wandered back to the Bunker. He wondered why they called it that. In the twilight it looked like home as he stepped over the debris, seeing the fire glow, the familiar shapes hanging around it. Lisa seemed to be trying to cook something. The idea made him laugh out loud, and they all looked up as he approached, their coarse shouts of welcome blurring his thoughts. In his mind he was trying to hold on to a memory of Fip talking to him urgently, telling him something of such importance that she took hold of his hand. But then someone passed him a can of lager, and the satisfying fizz as he opened it cleared his mind of everything else. He flung an arm round Lisa and she grabbed the beer can that was now level with her cheek and took a large swig, laughing up at him.

Agnes sat down to a table spread with little dishes. Olives in coriander and garlic, houmous, taramasalata, yoghurt. In a basket, sliced pitta bread nestled warmly in a linen cloth. Athena settled opposite her and poured wine.

'Tuck in,' she gestured.

'You've done us proud, Mrs Paneotou,' laughed Agnes.

Sunday night. He sat over his desk, writing another note, his hand illuminated in the anglepoise light. He could hear his wife fussing in the next room. He wrote in scratchy biro, 'Athena P. 7 Sparkbrook Terrace. Chidding Ford.' He wondered whether to find out the telephone number, but as he looked at the phone on his desk, it rang loudly.

Agnes watched admiringly as Athena stood at her breakfast bar and served tender joints of lamb from a huge earthenware casserole, adding rice and salad from white porcelain dishes. 'I've just realized how hungry I am,' she said. 'I was riding Arnie's lovely horse again this morning, and I hardly ate any lunch. He sends his love, by the way.'

Athena brought two plates to the table. 'How sweet of him. I haven't seen him for absolutely ages.'

'He's a nice man. Though I don't think living alone entirely agrees with him.'

Athena paused, her fork at her lips. 'Whereas for me, poppet, it's ideal.'

Agnes took another mouthful. 'This is absolutely delicious.'

Athena continued. 'My dear, where's your usual subtlety? What you mean is, poor old Arnie still has the hots for me and wouldn't it be nice if I fell for him too.'

Agnes laughed. 'Well, wouldn't it?'

'And leave you the field free?'

'For – for what?'

Athena was still smiling. 'For you two star-crossed lovers. Still crazy after all these years.'

Agnes put down her fork. 'Must we have this again?'

Athena put down her fork. 'I was right in the first place. Your marriage never ended.'

A blaze of yellow daffodils flashed across Agnes's mind. 'Athena, *ma chère*; we're divorced. I'm a nun.' She hesitated. 'It's over, our marriage. It was over a long time ago.' She remembered how real Hugo had seemed that night in the hotel bar. 'Even though . . .'

'Even though what?'

'Nothing. Sometimes it's all so confusing. I'm going back to London soon.'

'Do you think that will solve anything?'

Agnes sighed. 'There's nothing to solve. It's much better that he's with you, really it is.'

'You don't sound convinced. And anyway, he isn't "with" me, so to speak.' Athena's eyes flashed behind the golden prism of her glass. 'As far as I can see, you two are inextricably bound together. Inextricably.' She took a large gulp of wine, then grinned and shrugged her broad shoulders which were smooth against her low red neckline. 'I'm growing very fond of you, Agnes. But you must admit I'm right.'

Sunday night. Lowry dialled Mellersh's number. It was answered at once, the voice at the other end abrupt and harsh. Lowry's conversation was brief. At the end of it,

Mellersh had agreed to come to the police station the next day. Lowry hung up, marvelling once again how compliant people can be when threatened with the prospect of several burly policemen escorting them from their homes while the curtains in the surrounding windows twitch furiously.

Agnes pushed her plate away and sighed. 'That was wonderful, Athena,' she said. 'If you opened a restaurant in Paris, you'd have people queueing round the block.'

'It's a pleasure. I don't get the chance to cook for people much.' Athena jumped up and drew heavy white muslin across the dark windows, switched on tiny black spotlights here and there. While she fetched the Chablis from the fridge, Agnes went upstairs.

Athena's bathroom was huge, with a square sunken turquoise bath and silvery dolphins everywhere: holding the soap, embellishing the towel rail, and supporting the toilet roll. Agnes noticed several shelves were packed with hair products: dyes, sprays, setting gels, shampoos and conditioners. Coming back down the open-plan staircase, she said, 'Did you leave any structural walls intact?'

Athena laughed. 'I knocked a bedroom through into the bathroom. I only need two bedrooms. Well, one really.'

'Do you do your hairdressing here?'

'Uh-huh. I have so few clients, it's not worth having a salon.'

'What do you live on, then?'

'You really have lost your subtlety.'

'Call it friendship.'

'If you must know, my ex-husband is generous. Sometimes, anyway. Precarious but generous. I survive.'

They settled back at the table over cheese and grapes. Agnes took a sip of wine. 'So,' she said. 'Hugo.'

Athena spat out a grape pip into the ashtray. 'Hugo,' she said.

'Was he into – bondage?'

Athena laughed. 'You should know.'

'He might have changed.'

'You mean, the way Pip was found? It surprised me, too. I mean, leather?' She made a face. 'Speaking personally, props have never been my thing,' she added, then giggled again.

Agnes took another sip of wine. 'How is he?' she asked.

'Don't ask me, poppet. I hardly see him these days. He's like a damn teenager at the moment. No, more like one of those classical paintings, called Eros, or something, and he's some naked god – only better endowed than those classical ones—' She giggled coarsely. 'And there's a twee little cupid in one corner, and arrows flying. And he's smitten. With you.'

The feelings this statement provoked in her made Agnes uneasy. She answered quickly, 'Athena, he can't be. And anyway, I'd much rather be friends with you than have all this Hugo business hanging over us.'

Athena shook her head slowly, smiling.

'If only, darling. If only. I appreciate your intentions are honourable, but—' She sighed and took a sip of wine. 'The fact is, Agnes, and you're being a teensy bit reluctant to face up to it, darling – the fact is, Hugo is the only man you've ever fucked. He's bound to live on in your mind. You've known nothing else, and believe me, there's no reason why you should want to.'

Agnes took a large mouthful of wine. 'It wasn't like that.' Her voice shook. 'He was vicious and brutal and he hated me most of the time. Probably all the time. It was a very, very unhappy marriage. A terrible time in my life. There's nothing there I want to return to. You see, Athena, I am enjoying seeing him now, you're right. I'm enjoying it very much. But the point is, it's the opposite of how it was. We've found a new way of being together. Because I'm free of all that; free of him, in a way—'

Athena was looking at her hard. 'Who're you trying to kid?'

'Athena, for God's sake. You're the one who doesn't

understand. He tried to kill me once. In fact he very nearly succeeded.'

Athena's eyes widened. 'Tried to kill you? You mean, while you were . . . ? Wow,' she breathed. 'What was that like?'

The two women stared at each other. 'No, Athena,' Agnes stammered at last. 'It wasn't how you think. It was for real. He hated me, that's all. And now he doesn't. It's a resolution. It means I can go back to London soon and you and he can—'

Athena got up suddenly and came and stood behind Agnes, her hands on her shoulders. 'My poor dear,' she said, her voice nearly a whisper. 'You really don't see, do you. People like Hugo don't change. He still thinks he owns you. You were his prize possession – I'm just a cheap trinket by comparison. If I didn't like you so much, I'd hate you.'

Agnes reached up and took one of the hands in hers. Athena leant over the table and with her free hand plucked two grapes from the bunch. She placed one in Agnes's mouth and one in her own. The two women munched in silence.

Sunday night. Lowry arranged the chaos of papers on his desk into haphazard piles. He picked up the phone and dialled. Eventually it was answered. 'Yes, I know,' he said at once. 'I'm sorry. Yes, I know sorry isn't good enough . . . It is? Well, bless you for saying so . . . Toad in t'hole? You're baking chipolatas in t'middle of t'bloody night? I don't deserve to have such affection lavished on me . . . Yes, I can see you might be hungry too, but let me enjoy my illusion of wifely devotion.'

He rang off, looked at the phone and smiled. Outside, the floodlight beams of the Superstore car park cut through the darkness. Lowry's office door banged shut behind him, and the noise reverberated in the night.

# Chapter Eleven

'Right, let's go through what we've got so far. The owner of the stolen car, Mr Killick, is coming in this morning, Mellersh is coming in this afternoon and – you all right?'

Agnes put her hand up to her head, again. 'Yes, yes of course. Just a bit of a headache, that's all.'

'More coffee?'

'Not at the moment thanks. Maybe a drop of water.'

'Or hair of the dog? I've got a half-bottle of Scotch here somewhere.'

Agnes shook her head. 'What makes you think it's a hangover?'

'Copper's intuition, Sister.' He stood up and went to the door, grinning, returning a moment later with a polystyrene cup of water. He settled down opposite her.

'Right. Let's say someone has a motive; someone involved with the wardrobes and the video camera. Someone who's had enough of paying out to Philippa.'

Agnes was writing notes in her book. She looked up. 'It may be someone who knows nothing about Mellersh – else why didn't they try and kill him too?'

'Right. Or, it might be someone connected with Mellersh. So, that Sunday night, they arrange for Philippa to meet them. She goes out, after the row with Hugo. She deliberately stops on the way to make sure she's seen – scared, presumably. An hour or so later, probably about eight thirty or nine o'clock, she's driven to her own house in the back of a stolen car, leaving large amounts of her hair. Between arriving at the house and about ten o'clock, our mystery guest – wearing Hugo's clothes – murders Philippa and goes, leaving very little traces apart from prints.'

'They wore gloves for the killing but not for anything else.'

'Yes. Strange.'

'Perhaps they wanted to implicate Hugo, by making sure only his prints were on the knife. And by dressing in his clothes.'

'They succeeded for a while.'

'And all the prints in the house?'

'Might have been searching for something. Though there are so many, it suggests they were already intimate with the house from previous visits.'

'Was Philippa immobilized?'

'No signs of rope burns or anything on the body.'

'And why did she go willingly to meet them?'

'Perhaps she was collecting money—'

'No,' interrupted Agnes, 'she wouldn't have drawn attention to herself. Have you managed to trace any of their clients?'

'Almost impossible. Mrs Elsworthy's told us all she can, but it's all just faces. No names. Nothing written down. And you say your source knows nothing either.'

Agnes thought of Jimmie's words. 'Only that he remembered seeing someone well-known, he thought.'

Lowry stared out of the window, then looked back at Agnes. 'Why do you think Mrs Bourdillon got involved with Mellersh in the first place?'

'Money. She must have met him somehow, he proposed this business to her, and an independent income would have appealed to her.' Agnes sipped more water. 'She was probably desperate to get away from Hugo.'

Lowry looked at her closely. 'You seem to know a lot about it.'

Agnes's voice was flat. 'Men like Hugo don't change.'

As they went downstairs to meet Mr Killick, Lowry took

her arm. Perhaps it was the headache, but she seemed oddly vulnerable this morning.

A lunchtime pint in the local seemed to lift Agnes's spirits. She was almost gleeful as they paused at the door of the interview room, where Mellersh waited inside. 'I'm getting a taste for this,' she whispered to Lowry.

As they opened the door, Mellersh jumped to his feet. 'There's no need for this, no need at all,' he cried. He stood awkwardly with his back against the wall. He was a stocky man, quite tall, with thinning grey hair. He wore glasses for long sight, and his dark eyes were large behind the lenses. His suit was well-cut. Agnes noticed he had surprisingly long, delicate fingers.

'No need for what, Mr Mellersh?' said Lowry, genially, sitting down across the desk from him.

'Treated like a criminal. Left to stew in here—'

'We're sorry to have kept you waiting a few minutes, Mr Mellersh. Do sit down. You'll know Sister Agnes, won't you?'

Mellersh stared at Agnes, dropping heavily into a chair without taking his eyes from her. At last he said, 'Yes,' and then abruptly turned to Lowry. His face took on an odd, thin smile, and he said, 'So. How can I help you, Inspector?'

'Firstly, why have you been following my colleague here around?'

Mellersh looked at Agnes as if he had never seen her before, then back at Lowry and shook his head.

'Your car is a grey Vauxhall Astra, numberplate K599 AME?'

'That is so, Inspector.'

'Well, it's been spotted on several occasions trailing my friend here.'

Mellersh shrugged. 'Just checking. What else?'

'Well, there's your business connection with Philippa Bourdillon. Blackmailing transvestites. And you've been very clever at hiding behind Philippa, haven't you, Mr Mellersh?'

'We sold handmade goods—'

Lowry stood up suddenly. 'Come on, Mr Mellersh, we've progressed from there, I think. The figures in your accounts show more profit than you'd ever make from tea cosies. We've found evidence of video leads in your secret room. Mrs Elsworthy—'

'Who's Mrs Elsworthy?' Mellersh's face was open, a picture of a sincere wish to know. Lowry glanced across at Agnes.

'Surely if you sold her quilts, you'd know who she was?' said Agnes quietly.

Mellersh flashed her a hostile look, then turned back to Lowry and asked, politely, 'She ran one of the – galleries, then?'

'That's right,' Lowry replied, sitting down again.

'Only, Philippa dealt with that side of things.'

'And what side of things did you deal with, then? Eh? Who wrote the wheedling letters – who made the menacing phone calls, explaining that if certain money wasn't forthcoming, to be paid in cash to your charming assistant, certain video tapes would be made available – to wives, employers – the press?'

Mellersh got up suddenly. He leaned across the table and fixed Lowry with a stare, drumming his long fingers on the formica surface for a moment. Then he turned abruptly and stood facing the wall. Above him two windows, set high in the grimy concrete wall and barred, let in the dingy sunlight.

'Am I here because you think I killed her?' he asked at last, his back to them, his voice very quiet. No one spoke. 'Because, if so, you're wrong. Very wrong. There were people—' He whirled, and once more leaned over the table, breathing hard, his knuckles white as they supported his weight. 'There were people—' he repeated. Then, just as suddenly, he sat down in his chair again.

'You mean,' said Agnes, quietly, 'there were other people who'd want her dead?'

This time Mellersh smiled at her with some warmth. 'Oh yes. What motive, after all, can you attribute to me? Our business, which you allege to be so – so, sordid – was doing very well. Why would I get rid of my partner? Whereas, there were men, very important men—'

Now Lowry stood up. 'Listen, Mr Mellersh. If you have information about her killer, I think you'd better give it to us, if you want to avoid criminal charges yourself. Perhaps there's someone, one of your – clients – who'd had enough, eh? Perhaps, rather than the frightened little chaps you were used to, this one proved to be made of sterner stuff – eh? Turned nasty, eh? Very nasty. Put the wind up you as well? What d'you think?'

Mellersh stared at the table, drumming his fingers. 'That doesn't make me a murderer,' he said quietly.

'No one's saying it does,' said Agnes.

'I didn't do it. I didn't. Now she's gone, it's all much more – it's impossible really.' His fingers kept up a relentless rhythm. When he did look up, his eyes seemed wide and frightened, distorted by the lenses. 'I was glad when they got the husband. She was frightened of him. Good riddance, I thought. Then you came,' he said, turning to Agnes, 'and I found out who you were. Ex-husband and all that. Better keep tabs, I thought, better keep tabs.' His voice trailed off and his fingers began their work once more.

'Well,' said Lowry, conversationally, 'shall we have some names, eh? Clients? Particularly, dangerous ones?'

Mellersh smiled agreeably. 'But that's just the problem. Philippa kept the names. It was only when we needed to – release – a name that she gave it to me. And this one – this dangerous one – it's all anonymous, you see. Only, he's on to me now. If he thinks I'm going to – I mean, even this interview—' The smile left his face and again his eyes seemed dark and pleading. 'You understand, don't you – I'm under a certain amount of pressure at the moment.'

\* \* \*

Lowry and Agnes walked slowly back up the stairs. 'What d'you make of that?' said Lowry, gruffly. 'D'you think he's telling the truth?'

'A desperate man, I'd say,' said Agnes as Lowry opened the door of his office. 'But it seems quite clear that Mellersh knows no more about all this than we do.'

'Except that he's getting anonymous threats, from an ex-client, and he won't tell us more because he's scared.'

'Why would a client keep up the pressure if the blackmailing's stopped?'

Lowry flung himself into his chair. 'Good question, Sister. Perhaps it hasn't. Or perhaps it got too far – incriminating evidence already circulating. How's the headache, by the way?'

Agnes smiled. 'Do you know, Inspector, I'd completely forgotten about it.'

That evening, Agnes walked past the Bunker again. She could see a couple of people near the fire, and went to join them. Jez was sitting on a box. Smoke and Norm the Dog were playing with a bone some way off. Lisa was walking around the fire. Her arms were tucked inside her jacket and she was flapping the empty sleeves.

'You're fuckin' mental, man,' Jez was saying to her.

'I ain't. In'I?' she said, turning to Agnes. 'What's mental about sabbing, eh?'

Agnes looked blank. 'Hunt saboteurs to you,' Jez said, putting on a posh, sneering voice. 'Stupid cunt. Some rich bastard'll 'it you over the 'ead and then go and kill a fox or two. So bleedin' what?' He took a swig from his can.

'Poor little fox. I 'ate them bastards,' said Lisa.

'Poor little fox,' sneered Jez. 'If I was rich, I'd be out there wiv 'em. Watchin' them doggies tear the ol' fox ter bits, eh? I'd laugh, I would.'

'Well, that's just like you, innit. I'm still fuckin' goin', OK?' She walked off to join Smoke and Norm.

Jez looked up at Agnes and grinned. "Ow's Inspector Mother Teresa Morse, then, eh?'

Agnes grinned back. 'I've been questioning your friend David Mellersh this afternoon.'

'What d'ya mean?'

'You seem to know him.' Agnes sat on the box next to him. Jez shook his head vaguely, then drank some beer.

'Come on, Jez, you might as well say. Has he threatened you?'

'Look,' said Jez suddenly. 'Until you come along, no one knew nothin' about us, right? Then you come fussin' about. Then, next thing, this Mellersh cunt appears, saying not to say nothin' about Philippa. To anyone.'

'He's a desperate man. He's scared. But he's not dangerous. The police have got their eye on him—'

'Oh well,' sneered Jez, 'if the Law's out to get 'im, everythin's all right, then, innit.'

It occurred to Agnes, in a wave of remorse, that Mellersh could only have found out about the Bunker by following her there. 'Had any thoughts, then? Anything emerge from what was left of your memory?' she asked.

Jez looked at her hard, took a swig of beer, wiped his mouth and passed her the can. She took a swig too, and met his gaze levelly. 'Whatever you say stops with me.'

''Til you need to tell the cops,' he said dully.

'Please trust me.'

Jez gazed at her for a long moment. He took a deep breath. 'All right then. I consulted my one remainin' brain cell, and I remembered. Fip were telling me somethin', some time ago, not long before she died. She said she had somethin' that were dangerous. I thought she meant gear or somethin', I couldn't see the fuss. She said she 'adn't realized it was dangerous, it looked ordinary. But she was scared, I reckon.'

'Did she show you this thing?'

'Nah. She said she'd 'idden it at 'ome. It'd all gone too far, she wanted out.'

'Did she often confide in you?'

'Sometimes. If she was in trouble, like with her ol' man –
you know . . . And I think Sinead had already gone. So she
couldn't talk to 'er about it.'

'On the night she died someone may have searched the
house.'

'Maybe it's gone, then, whatever it was.'

'Maybe. Jez, you're quite something, you know.'

'Piss off.'

As she looked back, she could see him still sitting by the
fire. He raised his can to her, and she waved.

On Tuesday morning, Agnes phoned Hugo. He answered
warmly. 'If I can help the forces of law and order in any way,
my dear, just ask.'

'I wondered if I could come and search your house.'

'Again? What secrets am I concealing here, unbeknown
even to me?' He laughed.

'It's just a hunch at the moment.'

'You detectives, eh? *Ecoute, ma belle*, I'll cook you dinner
this evening. Come early, in time to do your stuff, and when
you're ready, we'll eat.'

'Sounds lovely.'

'Oh, and Agnes—'

'Yes?'

'I particularly like you in that green silk shirt.'

Agnes replaced the phone with a little shiver. She hoped
the hotel dry-cleaners did a two-hour service.

She arrived at the house just after five, clutching Philippa's
diaries in a plastic carrier bag. Hugo let her in and offered to
take her raincoat. As the light fabric slid off the silk
underneath, he smiled; and the expression on his face made
Agnes catch her breath.

He looked at her, amused. 'Tea?' he said. 'And then I'll
leave you to it.'

Half an hour later, Agnes was sitting on the landing, in the little window seat from which Philippa used to stare at the painting. The house was silent. She looked up at Philippa's 'English' picture. Marie-Pierre was absolutely right. The light was grey, the people were tight-lipped. The table of food was set out like a penance, its detailed lushness and colour a reminder of unpleasant necessities rather than pleasure. She looked at the figure of a young woman painted at one side of the canvas, facing away from the food. A memory jolted into her mind. She looked quickly in her bag for Philippa's last diary, and flicked through the pages, until she came upon the entry:

Look at them eating, eating, eating.

And, before that:

The thin one looks on. They all hate her.

She sat and thought about this for some time. If the 'she' in the diary described not only Philippa but also the painting, perhaps it could describe other people too. Or perhaps, just one person who felt torn in pieces. She checked through the diaries to see when Philippa ever called herself 'I': 'I lost two pounds . . .' 'I lost three pounds . . .' and the very last entry:

I'm frightened of him. I think he wants to kill me.

Something about this struck Agnes as odd. She looked at the painting again. Who was the 'she'? Philippa's fragmented self? And who was the 'he'? Did she fear Hugo then? God knows she had reason to. Or was it another man?

Agnes closed the diaries and packed them away, and then walked quietly along the corridor to Philippa's room. If Pip had kept this mysterious, dangerous object, it wouldn't be anywhere else. The room was exactly as she had last seen it, clothes piled in chaotic heaps, spilling out of drawers, the open wardrobe. The shiny surface of the chest of drawers was thick with dust. Afternoon sunlight streamed through the window, and dust particles floated brightly in the musty air.

Agnes wondered where to start. She lifted the lid of the desk, stared into it and closed it again. She wished she had confided in Lowry, who at least would have some experience of searching for something when you had no idea what you were searching for.

She sat on the bed and tried to recall Jez's words. Something ordinary that turned out to be dangerous. Something that might identify someone? A personal possession? Clothing? A tie? Agnes riffled half-heartedly through the clothes in search of something masculine. Everything was lace and satin, and even the denim and leather was small and girlish. A video tape? A photograph? She scanned the bookshelves, which were mostly empty, and then went through the desk again, which held only a schoolgirlish pencil case and some empty notebooks. She searched under the bed, feeling as she lay down and fingered the dusty carpet that it was all completely hopeless. A white quilted dressing gown lay on the bed, and Agnes idly went through its pockets. She stood up and went over to the wardrobe, where she looked for jackets and jeans, and went through their pockets too. Apart from old tissues, she found nothing. She reached a well-worn leather jacket, and as her hand dipped into its torn lining, she felt something flat and round. She drew out a shiny circle of plastic. It seemed to be a compact disc, but was entirely anonymous. It came with no case; there was not a mark of identification upon it.

Agnes remembered with sudden clarity that Hugo's only source of recorded music was a chunky old record player that she was sure was the one from Savigny. She gazed briefly out of the window, wondering whether she had found what she was looking for. The sun had almost set, and the garden was bathed in pinkish, indigo light. Then she heard Hugo call her, faintly, his voice muffled by the solid ancient stone of the house. She made a cursory search through the rest of the clothes, pocketed her find, and descended to dinner.

Hugo was waiting for her in the hall. He took her arm and smiled down at her. 'Shall we go in, madame?'

The dining table was laid with a white cloth that looked vaguely familiar. Heavy silver candlesticks threw a golden light across the silver cutlery, catching the crystal glassware and the gold rim of the plates. Hugo pulled out a chair for her. He paused for a moment behind her as she sat down, and his fingers brushed the nape of her neck.

'All your own work, Hugo?' asked Agnes, trying to keep her voice light.

'You just can't get the staff these days.' Hugo sat down and they smiled at each other across the table, which seemed suddenly intimate despite its size. A crab mousse, exquisitely set in a tiny ramekin with a single leaf of mint on top, was laid in each place, a roll, still warm, by its side. Hugo poured white wine into one of the glasses beside her plate. 'Do start, my dear.'

Agnes tasted the buttery, salty fish across her tongue. She felt cherished, cared for, in a way she hadn't known for years. Her eyes smiled as she looked at Hugo.

'I don't suppose it was like this in the convent,' he said.

'It's not what convents are for,' she replied.

'And did all that mortification of the flesh do you good?'

'It's a comfortable old order,' she replied. 'Hardly sackcloth and ashes.'

'But you must have missed – certain comforts.'

'No. Not particularly.' Agnes concentrated on her mousse, which she finished methodically. *'Délicieux, mon ami,'* she said.

'The deli in the High Street, I'm afraid. I can't take the credit.'

'Athena gave me a fine dinner the other night.'

'Did she? How is she, the old flirt?'

'Strangely unflirtatious,' replied Agnes, looking at him hard.

'Hmmmm.' Hugo went to fetch the steak.

Later, Agnes found it difficult to remember the details of the evening, although perhaps that was hardly surprising. She remembered rare Châteaubriand steak with new potatoes, and an excellent old Bordeaux wine. She remembered Hugo's smile, open and appreciative. Looking back, the delight of sharing that meal with Hugo came to seem false, and yet in time little glimpses of pleasure emerged through the blur: of delicate compliments, fragile jokes, careful reminiscences about their shared past, shared friends, shared possessions.

After dinner she went through to the lounge while Hugo prepared coffee. She stood by the window, staring out into the blackness of the garden. She was aware of Hugo coming into the room and putting down the tray, and as he came to stand next to her she experienced a subterranean rush of feeling, like the rumblings of a long-dormant volcano. Hugo touched her waist.

'Come and have a brandy,' he said conversationally.

She was relieved to find space around her again as she chose an armchair across the room from him.

'You know, you haven't really changed.' His tone was still light.

'I can hardly have stayed the same,' she said.

'Fundamentally, *si*. You know, you were a remarkable young woman.'

Agnes stared into her glass, turning the cognac round and round.

'I made terrible mistakes, Agnes.' She looked up. He was leaning forward, his expression one of urgency.

'It was a long time ago, Hugo,' she said quietly.

'Yes.' He sat back in his chair and sipped his drink. Agnes felt as if the volcano were now outside her body, as if the room itself were growing warm, molten, explosive.

'God, I loved you in those days.'

'Hugo, all that has passed. I might seem the same, but I'm not.'

She felt as if she were pouring a single tiny bucket of water on to a blazing fire. Hugo uncrossed his legs and looked at her. 'Are you sure? You seem exactly the same to me.'

'And anyway, if you loved me you had a strange way of showing it.' She was surprised at her boldness.

'I regret all that so much, my dear. I can't tell you . . .' He sipped his drink, and his eyes seemed dark with emotion. 'I squandered everything.'

He got up and came and stood in front of her. His eyes seemed to lock into hers. The room seemed much too hot. She stared into his eyes, afraid of seeing only molten lava.

'With you it was always a surrender. Always.' His voice was thick. She could feel his rapid breathing, or perhaps it was hers. He knelt in front of her, leaning against her knees. She shook her head. 'No.'

He took one of her hands and kissed the palm. 'No,' she repeated. 'We can't go back.' But part of her already had, and as he began to whisper to her, his lips brushing her ear, she closed her eyes and sighed out loud, an exhalation of yearning.

'You see?' he breathed, caressing her neck. 'You see?'

Her head was against the back of the chair, her eyes were closed. She felt his hands reclaiming her; she felt her body respond. Only then did his lips touch hers, and her body arched with desire, returning his kiss, losing herself. Was this how it had been? This pleasure, this need?

'You see?' he whispered again as she sighed against him.

He lowered her gently to the floor and she felt a kind of terror, but it was so familiar and so mixed with wanting him that she abandoned herself to it. She heard someone sigh, someone whispering, 'Hugo.' Hugo too was whispering, 'God, I loved you, I've never known anything like you . . .' His body was on hers, and she wanted to bury herself against him.

She heard him say, 'And my virgin bride became a nun?'

and opened her eyes. He was staring down at her. 'No one else but me – ever?' She realized with a jolting wave of terror that he wanted an answer.

'No, Hugo, no one else,' she whispered, suddenly frozen, her eyes wide. He smiled down at her, and his hand moved slowly down her body, resting on her breasts, smiling as her nipples hardened at his touch.

'Madame, I am honoured,' he said, and she shuddered. He watched her. 'You haven't changed at all,' he said, tenderly, and then his lips were hard against hers, his mouth burning, his tongue forcing and penetrating, and she seemed unable to move under him. She felt his hands pulling and ripping at her clothing until he found bare flesh which he explored hungrily. He adjusted his own clothing, and she felt him hard against her. In that moment all desire left her. She felt only ice-cold fear. And suddenly, she remembered. Like a floodgate opening, like a dam bursting, she remembered. In a cascade of dazzling clarity, she remembered; this was how it had always been, like this. Cold, vicious, brutal; an act of possession, of destruction. Nothing to do with love. For all these years she thought she had been trying to forgive him, but instead she had simply locked it all away. And now it was too late.

'I've never fucked a nun before,' he laughed, absorbed in caressing her body, which was still and cold, oblivious of her lack of response. 'You've worn well, you know.'

Her mind was steel, icy sharp. She saw suddenly that Hugo had only abused her all that time because she had allowed him to; not because of his physical strength, but simply because of his will. Like a mouse caught by a cat, she had stayed frozen in his grip for year after year, powerless because she believed herself to be powerless. Now it was different. She had grown up.

She felt him move against her. She looked slowly around the room, taking in the lamp stand (too far away), the paper knife (too small), the poker by the hearth (not heavy enough)

– until she saw a large terracotta pot beside the fireplace. Hugo had one arm heavily across her body, the other hand by his crotch, preparing himself to enter her. She summoned up all her strength and heaved at him, at the same time rolling from under him, seizing the pot as she stood up. She felt ridiculous, holding the huge thing above her head as he too got to his feet, his towering height making her feel suddenly insubstantial. He grasped wildly at her – 'What game is this, you little whore? I'll have you begging for it . . .' He lurched towards her, his clothes awry, his face ugly with desire – and she brought the pot down hard over his head. She watched in horror as the fragments of clay settled gently on the carpet like feathers; as he, completely unscathed, continued to advance towards her, his arms outstretched. She stepped out of his way. He reached for her, his expression glassy, his lips drawn back; and then his eyes flickered whitely as he too floated to the floor, followed by a loud crash as his body landed.

Later, she could hardly remember the drive back to London. She recalled going to the hotel, packing everything into her suitcase, leaving behind the clothes from Cheltenham, all the spoils of her shopping trip, taking only what she'd arrived with. She remembered, somehow, reassuring the night porter on the desk, who had raised his eyebrows to see someone checking out at two in the morning. Then it was a blur of black night, black road, empty black thoughts.

She drove along the Thames embankment as a thin grey light spread over the water, and at last she saw the spire of St Simeon's against the hazy sky of a London dawn. The car pulled into the drive of the church and stopped. She got out and went round to the side of the building, fumbling in a new growth of nettles for the key. She let herself into Julius's office. And there she sat, staring blankly into space, until Julius found her two hours later.

149

# Chapter Twelve

Julius took in the glassy stare, the ashen face. 'My God. Agnes. What's happened?'

She was silent.

'One of these days I'll condemn myself to Hell for the sake of killing that man—' Julius began.

'I'm so cold.' It was barely a whisper.

'Agnes – my only—' He knelt in front of her, staring into her face. She struggled to speak again. 'Julius – I'm sorry. I'm so sorry.'

Julius helped her to her feet, and led her gently to her lodgings. She leaned against him. He lay her down on the bed, took off her shoes, and covered her with blankets. He took in the ripped tights, the crumpled silk shirt with its missing buttons. He sat down heavily on the bed, feeling suddenly cold and weary, and took her hand, and stayed there quietly until she appeared to go to sleep.

'I'll be back,' he said gently, then bent and kissed her forehead. As the door shut behind him her eyes opened wide in the dim light.

She is in the elegant sitting room at Savigny. She looks up as Hugo comes noisily into the room. He is waving something, a piece of paper. She recognizes it, and a chill runs through her body. He comes over to where she is sitting. '*Qu'est-ce que c'est?*' he says, waving the paper across her face.

'A train ticket,' she stammers.

'To Lille.'

'Yes.'

'Where there's some kind of convent, *n'est-ce pas?*' The look in his eyes makes her feel sick.

'Yes.'

'All arranged by your little priest, eh?'

'Yes. How – how did you find out?'

'My servants are loyal, my dear. You can't really have thought you'd leave me, can you? You're my wife, after all.' He laughs.

Of course he's right. She can't leave. Ever.

'So, this jerk of a priest has been trying to screw up my marriage? This Julius. And he screws you too, of course?'

'No, no, *mais non*, he's a priest.'

Hugo laughs again, an ugly laugh that seems to go on and on for ever. 'As if that would stop you. Little whore . . . Do you know what it's like being married to a whore? It's boring, that's what it is. Fucking you is boring. One cock's just like another to you, isn't it, my dear? Whereas other women – take my current mistress, for example – perhaps you know her, Mathilde Gayral, from across the valley, a charming and delightful woman. You see, she wants only me. Everything I do pleases her. She comes calling my name and then wants more. That's a real woman. You, on the other hand, you could be fucking anyone.'

'Hugo, you know that's not true,' she whispers.

He hits her hard across the face and she falls to the floor. The old, polished wood is cool against her cheek. She is tired. Very tired. She lies there where he's left her, her eyes closed. Of course she can't leave him. She was silly to try. Silly of Julius to think it was possible. And now it's too late. She feels Hugo place his hands around her neck. This is the only way out. This was always how it would end. It was only a matter of time.

'Look at me,' she hears him say.

With a huge effort she opens her eyes.

'Do you think I'm going to kill you?'

She wonders what the right answer is.

'Do you?' he repeats, harshly.

'Y-yes,' she whispers.

He laughs. 'Good,' he says. 'But not yet I'm not. If that little priest can fuck you, then so can I.'

A long time later she is aware of light. She wonders whether she can open her eyes. She thinks that perhaps if she's thinking about opening her eyes, she isn't dead after all. Or perhaps she is. She tries to remember all she has been taught about the afterlife. Harps and angels; obviously not for her. Purgatory. She opens her eyes and closes them again.

More time passes. She dreams of a fox, hunted beyond endurance, creeping through the night to find a safe place to die. She decides to follow it, and so she too crawls, bleeding, from the room, down the stairs, through the huge, echoing house, out of the door.

Agnes lay in bed, staring into the darkness. She was remembering a church door in France, one which had sheltered her on a very dark night. Even now she could remember the detail of the wood grain, the curves of the stone carvings, the heavy brass latch which had reflected the moon in tiny flecks as the night passed and she had realized that she wasn't going to die after all.

At lunchtime, Agnes appeared in the office. Julius helped her to a chair and made her a cup of tea. She sat and stared at the floor.

'Agnes, are you hurt?'

She shook her head. He sat at his desk, watching her. She took a sip of tea, and then said, 'I have to go away.'

Julius touched the crucifix at his neck. She went on, 'It's obvious to me I can't live with myself like this.' Outside a wood pigeon cooed, a gentle counterpoint to the constant traffic rumble.

'Have you slept?' Julius asked.

'I don't know. I think so. A bit.' She gulped some more tea and then said, 'You were right. And he was right. Sniffing round – round – the dung heap. I am without hope, Julius, I welcomed it . . .'

'Agnes, tell me what happened. What did he do to you?'

'Him? Oh, nothing, really. It's what I've done to myself.'

The image of a half-dead girl in a church doorway floated briefly in the air between them.

'Agnes.' Julius used the French pronunciation, carefully. '*An-yes.* Please tell me.'

'He tried to rape me. But it was nothing—'

'Tried?'

'Yes.'

'And failed?'

'Yes. I knocked him out with a pot.'

Agnes looked up in time to see the corner of Julius's mouth twitch. She looked down again.

'It's not really that, you see. It's because I wanted . . . I wanted him to—'

The pigeon had been joined by a mate, and now they both trilled loudly outside the window. Julius waited. Agnes continued.

'I've kept up a pretence for a very long time. All those years away from him – I was just running away. He and I belong to each other, simply because—'

'No—' interrupted Julius.

'Simply because I'm as bad as he is. That's all. Within me there lurks all the badness, all the warped, perverted desires – however bad he can be, I respond with worse. I stayed in Chidscombe because I wanted – I wanted—'

'But you didn't want it enough, did you?'

She looked up, startled by his tone of voice.

'If you'd really wanted it, you wouldn't have hit him with a pot, would you? What I mean is, you saved yourself.'

'Saved?' Agnes shook her head. 'I'm beyond saving.' She

laughed a brittle, empty laugh. 'You'll never understand, Julius, you're too good. You can't know what it's like. Red lipstick, silk shirts, dinners out, admiration. It was wonderful. I loved it. You can't know how bad I am.' She paused. 'This morning I took my habit downstairs and threw it in the dustbins.'

Again there was silence in the room, disturbed only by the courting pigeons.

Julius said at last, 'Agnes, you've always wanted the world. You've always been hungry for more. But that's what makes you human, makes you what you are. Don't tell me I can't know. Yes, it leads to sin, human sin, sin that makes you whole. Better that than never knowing—'

She stared at the floor.

'Please don't go away, Agnes.'

They sat in silence again. The revving of nearby lorry engines drowned out the gentle cooing. Julius's face took on a far-away look as if he were listening to a celestial choir, then he suddenly jumped up and fled from the room. Agnes, bemused, stumbled after him.

Out in the street she saw a wiry figure, cassock flying, hair awry, vaulting the church railings to the street. Beyond, she could see a huge yellow dustbin lorry, its attendant workers emptying the tall bins outside her block. She saw the white-haired figure remonstrate with the men, then he climbed a bin and rummaged through it. At last he jumped down clutching something, and shook the bin man warmly by the hand. He turned and walked back towards her, his face pink with triumph, and handed her a crumpled filthy mass of grey and white fabric.

She took it from him and smiled.

'You see, Agnes,' he said. 'We can all sniff round dung heaps when we have to.'

That afternoon Julius took Agnes to see the temporary accommodation they had arranged for the young runaways project. On the way they passed the house that would be theirs, now spiky with scaffolding, minus its roof, and peopled with men in hard hats. They went a little further down Borough High Street, where the Council had made available two flats in a new housing block.

'We can sleep six between both flats.' Julius showed Agnes into a bright, newly fitted kitchen diner. Two tins of baked beans stood by the cooker, the only clue that anyone might have used the room at all. In the office she met the day shift, Liz and her assistant Daniel, who was on the phone and whom she recognized from the soup run. Daniel put down the phone as they arrived and turned to Liz.

'There's two boys on their way over from Vine Street. Caught shoplifting. One's thirteen, one's fourteen. Come from Dundee, been living rough in London for days, maybe weeks. Hi,' he said to Julius.

'Hello,' Julius said. 'This is Sister Agnes. She's part of the – er – Diocese Team for the project.'

As they walked back half an hour later, Agnes took Julius's arm.

'You don't have to cover for me. You know I shirked my responsibilities, and they must know that too.'

'How about we start with a clean slate, from today? That is, if your conscience can bear to keep quiet for a while?'

Agnes grinned. 'It's a deal. Though I can't speak for my conscience.'

Over the next few days Agnes threw herself into the Southwark Teenage Project. She slept at the hostel for a couple of night shifts, and met some of its here-today, gone-tomorrow residents: a thirteen-year-old girl picked up by the police for soliciting – 'And she's one of the lucky ones,' said the WPC who accompanied her; a thin and pale fifteen-year-old boy who had fled his home, but who wouldn't say why; a large and cheerful girl from South Wales who claimed there was no room for her back in the Barry council flat as she had sixteen brothers and sisters. The two boys from Dundee were sent back home, disappointed to find that their Social Services department budget would only stretch to the single train fare each – 'Oor mates wha' came doon got the plane back.'

One day Agnes put on her newly washed and ironed habit, took a bus up to the West End and walked the streets. She walked aimlessly, past designer clothes shops and burger bars, mingling with the busy lunchtime crowds, but gradually aware only of the youth: pale faces in shabby clothes hanging round Piccadilly Circus subway, sitting in shop doorways on piled old blankets; some asking for money, some looking away. In Leicester Square a tall young woman in a mini skirt and bright T-shirt brushed past her. The shirt proclaimed 'Jesus Saves', and Agnes thought of Angie and wanted to follow her, to ask her – to ask her what, exactly?

Agnes sat on a bench. A few feet away from her a couple in identical leather outfits stood entwined against a litter bin, kissing passionately. It was over, Agnes told herself. Even if she knew what Angie looked like, or Sinead, or Taff, how would she find them? And what was there to ask? She got up and smoothed down her habit. I am Off the Case, she thought.

'There was a phone call for you this morning,' said Julius, handing her a folded scrap of paper. 'Rose took it while she was cleaning here.'

Agnes read, 'Hugo Bourdillon phoned.'

Julius looked up. 'You didn't kill him, then?'

'Apparently not,' said Agnes, screwing up the paper and throwing it in the bin.

'Probably just as well, given our line of business,' said Julius, concentrating on trying to force open a brand new ring binder. The phone rang and he picked it up, then handed it to Agnes.

'Hello?' she said.

'No need to sound so worried, poppet,' tinkled Athena at the other end. 'Aren't I clever, tracking you down.

What happened? Where did you go? Tell me everything, darling.'

'There's nothing to tell. I'm off the case, that's all.'

'It's that Hugo, isn't it? He's been looking terrible you know—'

'I'm not interested. Listen, Athena, it was great fun but it was just one of those—'

'Something's got you badly, hasn't it, my dear. Well, if you're ever passing, you know where I am.'

Later in the afternoon the phone rang again. It was Inspector Lowry.

'Ah, Sister, there you are.'

'It seems that all of Gloucestershire knows where to find me.'

'I can't speak for the rest of your fan club, but we in the Force have ways and means.'

'I'm sure you do.'

'I know it's your prerogative to disappear just when we need you, but might I ask why?'

'Personal reasons, Jim.'

'Your ex-husband, perhaps?'

'Copper's intuition, eh, Jim? But it's none of your business, I'm afraid. Have you phoned me for a reason?'

'Well, I've had a lad who calls himself Jez come to see me.'

'Jez? You?'

'Yes. Not my usual sort of visitor, at least, not willingly, as you can imagine. He's in a bit of a flap about something, wanted to talk to you. I gave him this number, I hope you don't mind.'

'No, not at all. What did he say?'

'Something about a stolen car, and people called Angie and Sinead. And he said there was more. He seemed quite frightened, odd for a lad like that. Wouldn't tell me the whole story, and I didn't want to push it at this stage.'

'I wish you had. The problem is, Inspector, I'm off the case. I've done my bit. Gloucestershire, it turned out, was bad for me. All that country air. I'm healthier in the London smog, Jim, believe me.'

'Oh. OK. Right you are, then.'

'If I hear from Jez, I'll let you know.'

She replaced the receiver, and Julius looked up.

'Agnes, if you want to go back to your investigation—'

She shook her head. 'No, I'm better off here. Thank you, but – being there was all about something else. And it's over now.'

All the same, Julius noticed as Agnes went about her business that she lacked her usual energy; there was a dullness about her eyes, as if her mind were on other things.

Sister Katy noticed it too. 'So, how was Gloucestershire?' she asked, beaming, as she settled down to a packet of Bourbons in Agnes's room one afternoon. 'Did you catch a murderer? It wasn't your villainous ex-husband, was it?'

Agnes smiled distantly and helped herself to a biscuit.

'I say, I haven't put my foot in it, have I, old girl? Oh dear, Sister Katy does it again. Do forgive me.'

'No, no, it's fine, Katy, really. It was just rather – tiring, that's all. It's taking me a while to get over it.'

Katherine munched another biscuit. 'Tonic wine,' she said suddenly. 'Sister Phyllida swears by it. You look as if you need a pick-me-up. Of course,' she added, stirring her tea, 'we all thought it was him. We thought you'd been lucky to get out alive the first time – and then to go back into the lion's den, as it were—' Katy shook her head, and Agnes saw a little group of such heads shaking in unison, as her every exploit was carefully mulled over in the convent lounge after tea. She wondered how it had ever seemed possible to confide in Katy, this plump, fresh-faced woman sitting opposite her, her hair neatly tied back in the short pony-tail that, apart from a few grey hairs, had probably remained unchanged for the last thirty years. Agnes felt as if there were an abyss between them; any attempt to describe the events of the last month would be met with kind attentiveness and blank incomprehension.

'Nice to have you back,' said Katy, patting her arm at the door. 'I'll drop round again soon. And don't forget the tonic wine – Phyllida gets hers from the Co-op.'

Her neat black shoes echoed faintly on the stairs, then there was silence. Agnes sat on her bed. How successfully she had locked her true, bad, self away, for all those years of convent life. Even Katy – dear, sweet Katy – had never seen through her.

'It's a form of gross egoism,' said Julius, pacing his room. 'You should know better.'

'I don't know what you mean,' said Agnes sullenly.

'Suddenly to declare yourself a terribly bad person, much worse than any of us could ever know—'

'You did ask what was wrong,' said Agnes quietly, staring at the pattern of the carpet.

'You're feeding this huge, greedy conscience of yours with every breath you take. Wallowing in guilt is just as sinful as wallowing in pride. Do you think God would love you more if you'd never sinned?'

'God? Me? No one can love me.'

'Don't you believe it, Agnes.' Agnes looked up as he left the room, and blinked as he slammed the door behind him with uncharacteristic force.

The next morning, she went over to the church early to catch up on some paperwork. As she approached, she noticed a solitary figure dressed in black, sitting in the doorway.

'Latoya? What are you doing here?'

'Jez sent me to find you. He's in a state. It ain't like 'im. He's lost it, you know?'

'What's happened?'

'Can we go somewhere and talk?'

They went to a transport café near London Bridge, and

Agnes watched as Latoya ate eggs, bacon, sausages, mushrooms and three rounds of fried bread.

'Been travellin' all night,' she said through mouthfuls.

'How did you get here?'

'Thumb, didn't I?'

Agnes sipped her tea.

'Where's Jez now?'

'Gone to ground,' replied Latoya with a sense of drama. 'Says 'e's in danger. Lisa knows where 'e is, but she ain't letting on. Thing is,' she said, wiping her plate with the last of the bread, 'he knows somethin' dangerous, he says. Somethin' about Fip and why she was killed. Somethin' she 'ad. And there was two other things. 'E says that Smoke said Fip was going on to Angie and Sinead about nickin' cars. Then they went up to London. After that Fip was killed. And the other thing was, I had to describe Sinead to you. 'E says this is the most important bit. You 'ave to know what she looks like. So's you can track 'er down 'ere. She must know somethin'.'

'Did he say what?'

Latoya frowned in concentration, then shook her head. 'Nah, just what I told you. 'E said, to tell you what she looked like. And – oh yeah, 'e said 'e'd tell you the rest 'imself.'

'So – what does Sinead look like?'

'She's got long hair, dark brown, no, sort of mousy brown. It's all plaited with false locks mixed in. Bright pink, you can't miss 'er. Thin, pale face. Pretty. Green eyes. Kind of Irish lookin', I s'pose. She always wears white make-up, like a Goth, only not. She wears black lipstick. Black round 'er eyes, but not much.'

'And her clothes?'

'She's really thin. Black mostly. She used to wear leggin's but last time I saw 'er she'd gone into dresses, long floaty things. And more pale colours. She's got a leather jacket she really loves. It's kind of ripped. She had some Doc Martens too.'

'Anything else?' Latoya shook her head. 'And where might I begin to find her?'

Latoya shook her head again. 'She could be anywhere.'

'The problem is,' said Agnes, as they walked back towards the church half an hour later, 'I'm not really doing this any more. On the other hand, for Jez – I'll keep my eyes open. And he really ought to go back to Inspector Lowry, particularly if he really is in danger. I wonder why he hasn't. Julius, this is my friend Latoya,' she said, as they walked into the little office. 'She's from Gloucestershire, and she counts as homeless in London, and she's under sixteen, aren't you – so I thought she might sleep at the hostel tonight, if that's all right?'

Julius smiled. 'I hope there's space.'

Agnes turned to Latoya. 'I'll be there too, tonight. Then tomorrow I can pop you on a train at Paddington.'

In the small hours of the morning, Agnes was woken by the duty phone.

'Southwark Teenage Project,' she mumbled.

'Ah, Agnes, it's Jim Lowry here.'

'I told you, I'm off the—'

'The thing is, it's bad news I'm afraid. Your young friend Jez – he's been found dead. Asphyxiation from glue sniffing, inhaling vomit – not very pleasant. We wouldn't normally treat it as suspicious, but given what he said the other day—'

'Jez?' Agnes's voice was faint. 'No . . .'

'I wondered whether you'd be kind enough to visit us again, Sister. If you don't come of your own accord I can always arrange for Sergeant Driscoll to pick you up – but knowing what you're like as a passenger, I imagine you'd rather drive yourself.'

# Chapter Thirteen

Agnes replaced the phone receiver. She lay on the little single bed, absolutely still, her eyes wide open. Jez. Dead. Jez who had just found something out, who had got half a message to her – dead. Why hadn't he phoned her? Why hadn't he gone back to the police? Hiding out indeed. Silly boy. To think you can hide from a killer when you know something they don't want you to know.

Jez. Dead. And who had led the killer to him? Who was the only person to have made the connection between Philippa and the Bunker kids? Who persistently visited them even when she knew she was being followed by a grey Vauxhall Astra? It was all very well for Julius to talk about wallowing in guilt, but what did he know of it? If it wasn't for her, for her total bloody stupidity, one sparky, intelligent, desperate, funny boy would still be alive.

Hours passed. Agnes remained immobile on the bed. The light became grey behind the cheap new curtains. The lorries rumbled down the high street. Agnes blinked. She got up slowly, dressed, and went to wake Latoya.

At nine o'clock, Latoya was on the Swindon train, red-eyed, with promises that Agnes would be in Chidding Ford by the end of the day. Agnes hurried to the church. Julius's little door was locked, and she was just wondering where to find him when she heard a loud bang from the overgrown churchyard. She hurried round to see Julius standing in a cloud of black smoke, apparently reloading an ancient-looking pistol.

'Julius, what on earth are you doing?'

He nodded to her and went to a plank of wood which he had balanced between the stonework of the church and the railings. He placed three empty Coke cans on the plank, paced a distance away of about ten yards, cocked the pistol, aimed and fired. There was a bright flash and a loud bang, and when the smoke had cleared Agnes could see the middle can was missing.

Julius was grinning. 'Can't have fired this thing for years,' he muttered, unable to keep the pride out of his voice.

'Julius, what is going on? One of the kids in Gloucestershire has been killed, and I have to go back,' she said.

'I know,' he replied quietly, delicately ramming gunpowder into the gun, then reloading it.

'Well, it seems a funny time to practise your shooting.'

In answer, Julius cocked the pistol and handed it to Agnes. 'Don't do anything yet,' he said, walking back to the cans and arranging another three. Then he paced the distance back to where she was standing. 'You need to be a little bit nearer – these have a very short range.' He positioned her, then stood back. 'Go on then.'

Agnes was bemused, but she concentrated on the cans, took aim and fired. At first she could see nothing through the smoke, but when it cleared the can on the right had gone. Julius ran to retrieve it.

'A mere graze, I'm afraid,' he laughed, showing her where the bullet had caught the edge of the can. 'You'll have to do better than that on the day.'

'Julius, what are you on about?'

Julius took the pistol from her, and held it lovingly in his hand. It was beautifully carved, with a finely chequered butt. 'Eighteenth-century, French, made by Boutet. Muzzle-loading flintlock pistol. I'll have to teach you how to load it and prime it too.'

Agnes stared at him, exasperated. He raised his eyes from the pistol to look at her. 'Well, my dear, if, as it appears, this murder business has become more dangerous than you realized, you're going to need to look after yourself. And this is all I have. Ungainly with all this loading business, I know, and you only get one chance in a tight corner – but at least it's beautiful to look at, which is just as important, don't you think?'

Julius was aware, as Agnes flung her arms around him and kissed his cheek, that it was the first time he'd seen her laugh, really laugh, in a very long time. He extricated himself at last, pink in the face. 'Yes, well,' he said, 'I don't suppose we need bother about firearms certificates. I did have one somewhere, but it's not as if you intend to fire the thing, is it. I mean, not in our line of business.'

Agnes placed the beautiful mahogany box containing the pistol in the glove compartment of her hired 7-series BMW. From time to time she would take her eyes off the fast lane of the M40 to glance at it and smile.

Back in his office, Julius smiled too. That afternoon, as they had worked together making arrangements for her departure, Agnes had been her old self, quick and incisive. When she said goodbye she had taken his hands in hers, and he had noticed how the light had returned to her eyes. Well, he thought, it didn't take much to cheer her up. Just a murder for which she could blame herself, and a shiny new car. He smiled again.

Just outside Burford, Agnes stopped for a cup of tea. As she walked away from the car she patted her raincoat pocket. She could feel the neat plastic circle of the compact disc tucked away, and then wondered whether she shouldn't sew it into the lining itself for safekeeping. Whatever it was, someone was prepared to kill for it.

Once more back in the car, and winding along the A roads to Cirencester, Agnes put Bach's *St Matthew Passion* into the cassette player and allowed herself to think about Jez. With the opening notes of the Chorale No. 10, she concluded that whoever killed him must have thought he knew more than he did. Either that, or Jez knew more than he'd managed to tell her. She became aware of the words of the Chorale, '*Ich bin's, ich sollte büssen*' – It is I, I who should do penance . . . '*Und was du ausgestanden*' – For what you have endured . . . and a cold chill descended upon her. The sky seemed bleak and wintry over the rolling Gloucestershire fields. The music spoke of suffering and salvation, and all she saw was an image of Jez, his body twisted, his youth squeezed out of him. And what was the point, she thought in anguish. In what sense could that be God's will? It was random, futile, absurd.

She tried to listen to the message of redemption in the ancient words, but it seemed suddenly feeble, a mute cry in a maelstrom of evil. As she drove, she watched the storm clouds gather over the countryside.

She arrived in Chidscombe at half past five in pouring rain, and went straight to the police station. The duty sergeant called Lowry down for her. She heard him clattering down the stairs, his voice booming behind the frosted glass of the door.

'Sergeant, tomorrow isn't bloody good enough . . . So they're not answering the bloody phone, go round to the house now. NOW, d'you hear? Well, I don't care if there's no one there, you just wait till there is. Take a bloody picnic and have tea on the lawn if you must, you soft bugger—' The door opened, and he was standing there. 'Ah, Sister Agnes.' He grinned broadly. 'Ee, it's just like old times.'

They walked slowly up to his office, and took up their customary places, Jim at his desk, Agnes in the chair opposite. He switched on his desk lamp against the dark drizzle of the afternoon.

'So – Sister. What now?'

'I was hoping you'd tell me, Inspector.'

'Well, what have we got? A dead kid, found with a placcy bag, blue in the face, more lighter fuel than oxygen in his bloodstream. His clothes have been searched, and that place they hung out—'

'The Bunker.'

'Aye, the Bunker. All turned over too. We've had one of the girls taken into care, she's only fifteen – the other reckons she's staying with friends, and the rest have gone – skedaddled.'

'It's my fault. If only I'd used my brain properly, worked it out – I just came blundering into Jez's life without a thought for the consequences.'

Agnes saw once again the image of Jez, laughing, mocking, sneering – and now dead. She drooped suddenly in her chair, and her fingers began to work on a scrap of paper from Lowry's desk, folding it over and over into a tiny roll.

'I'll get us some tea.' At the door Lowry paused. 'I learned a long time ago, Sister,' he said quietly, 'there's no room for guilt in this game.'

Agnes sat alone in the room, aware of the sky darkening outside, listening to the rain against the window. Lowry came back with two cups of tea.

'So, what have you got to tell me?' he said, handing her a cup.

'Firstly, I believe the killer was looking for this.' Agnes brought out the compact disc. 'I found it in Philippa's things last week.' She handed it to Lowry. 'I think Mellersh is being threatened over it, Pip might have been killed for it, and Jez certainly was – the stupid bloody thing being, he didn't know about it. All he knew was that Pip had something that someone else wanted. "Something dangerous", he told me.'

Lowry was turning the disc over in his hands. 'Are you sure? I mean, this is a music disc. Anonymous, which is odd, but hardly incriminating.'

'That's what I thought at first. But there's nothing in Hugo's house that would play it. Philippa must have acquired it in an unusual way. And I haven't had a chance to test it out – or rather,' she added, fiddling with a biro, 'I couldn't really be bothered.'

'Ah yes, you were Off the Case. Well' – Lowry looked at the disc, frowning – 'all we have to do is stick it in a machine. We'll soon find out. I can play it at home if you like.'

She nodded, and said, 'Secondly – I assume Mellersh is high on your list of suspects?'

Now Lowry nodded. 'The only problem is, Sister, he's altogether vanished. We've had the wife on the phone again, she's worried sick.'

'Where do we start, then?'

Lowry played with his empty cup between his large hands. 'Well, tomorrow, I, er – I thought you might like to visit the mortuary. Your friend Jez is there. Pay your last respects.' He looked up at her sharply, questioningly. She nodded.

'Right,' he said, getting up, suddenly business-like. That's the morning then. And we'll go on from there.'

He showed her out into the rainy evening. 'You have a nice rest now. Back at the Cotswold Whatsit, are you?'

'Actually, I had other plans.'

'Ee, you're a woman of mystery, Agnes. See you in the morning.'

Twenty minutes later Agnes was standing by a shabby door in Sparkbrook Terrace listening to a tinkling rendition of 'Big Spender'. Nothing happened. She tried the bell again, and was aware of someone moving about within the house. At last there was the drawing of bolts, and the door opened a crack, held by a chain. Agnes glimpsed Athena, and in that moment she saw a nervous, lonely, ageing woman. The unmade-up face seemed drawn and lined, then it suddenly cracked into a charming smile, and the door was opened fully.

'Darling. What a lovely surprise.'

'I hope I'm not imposing.'

'No, not at all. Though you must excuse the *déshabille*. I

wasn't expecting anyone. Come in, come in.'

Agnes sat on a bar stool while Athena tinkered with her vast collection of alcoholic drinks. 'So, to what do I owe this unexpected pleasure?' she gushed, selecting a bottle of wine.

'It's just – I wondered if you'd ever thought about taking a lodger. Only temporary. Just while this case is on.'

'The hotel not up to scratch then?'

Agnes sighed. 'I'm tired, Athena. I just couldn't face it. Having to keep myself going . . .'

Athena handed her a large glass of white wine. 'I know that feeling. What you need is a wife, my dear. But I suppose I'll have to do. And I suppose you nuns never pay rent either.'

'I promise to cook the odd meal.'

'In every sense a marriage then.' Athena laughed and came to sit next to Agnes on a stool. 'You know, poppet,' she said, 'I'm tired too. I'm tired of spending evenings sitting here staring into the fire. I don't like what I see. A woman of my age has too much past to be left alone to brood upon it.' She stared into her wine glass for a moment, then jumped up again. 'Come on, I'll show you to your room and then fix us some supper.'

Later they sat in front of Athena's fire, a pile of burning logs stacked on a rough brick hearth in the wide chimney breast.

'Do you think it'll work out?' asked Agnes sleepily. 'I mean, we've both been alone for a very long time. Maybe sharing living space is a bad idea.'

'Oh, I'm sure we'll manage. Anyway, it's not for long. Only till you find a murderer or two.'

Thursday morning was bright and spring-like – 'Hardly a suitable day for viewing corpses, darling,' Athena had said as she made coffee. The Coroner's Court was tucked away in a neat Georgian terrace. Agnes wondered whether the residents minded having the ghoulish evidence of murder cases stored so near their homes. Mind you, people get used to anything, she thought. Jim Lowry greeted some old friends amongst the Coroner's officers, and then they were led down to the mortuary.

'We've had prettier corpses than this one, I'm afraid,' said the officer cheerily, opening the door.

Agnes was aware of a clean, cold smell; of harsh fluorescent light and a shiny floor. They were led down a narrow aisle containing stacked drawers. The officer paused beside one and drew it out. Jim pulled back the sheet, and Agnes was looking at Jez.

'Poor kid,' said Jim. Agnes stared down at the body. His head lay at a strange angle from the rest of his body, which seemed to be naked apart from the sheet. His eyes were closed. Jim lifted one eyelid, and revealed a heavily bloodshot eye.

'Petechial haemorrhage. Consistent with suffocation.'

He let the lid fall shut again and then wandered off to read the notices on the wall.

Agnes looked at Jez; or what had been Jez. His face was white. Deathly white, thought Agnes. She was struck by the finality of death; all that human life, all that bundle of activity that was Jez, all that rudeness, quickness, humour and pain, all come to this. And yet – and yet despite the violence of his end, his brow was smooth, his face composed. He was at peace.

Jim looked across in time to see Agnes murmur over the body and then make a cross on the forehead before covering it gently with the sheet. She paused for a moment, then came and joined Lowry by the noticeboard.

'When did he die?'

'Between seven and eight on the evening of Monday the twenty-sixth.'

'That was the day you phoned me to say he'd been in,' said Agnes. 'Where was he found?'

'His girlfriend – Lisa is it? – found him. Poor kid. About

170

eleven that night, in their hide-away. A shack in the woods over towards Brimscombe. She thought it was glue at first.'

'Might it be? I mean, might it not just be coincidence?'

Lowry was shaking his head. 'The plastic bag he'd been using for sniffing was held over his head for some time, we think. Death by asphyxiation. It left no marks, apart from a sheen to the face, but there are signs of a struggle. Grip marks to the arms, that sort of thing.'

They wandered towards the exit. At the door Agnes paused. 'Is – is Philippa here too?'

Lowry gave her a sideways glance, then set off along another aisle marked 'Deep Freeze'. He paused by a row of drawers, then pulled one out.

The first thing Agnes saw was the hair, curling out from under the sheet cover, still red and shining. Lowry pulled down the sheet to reveal her face and neck. Agnes was unprepared for the difference between the newly dead Jez and this corpse of several weeks.

'How – how dead she looks. Very dead. Barely human.'

'She's frozen. But it's true, bodies still change. Her bruises have faded – see the neck? You can hardly tell it was marked.'

'Was that a cut on the left cheek?' asked Agnes.

'Mmm. Probably a false blow with the knife, glanced off the face.'

They stood for a moment in thought. Lowry said, 'It's hard to believe she was a beauty once.'

'All this earthly life is transient. Man came from dust, and to dust he shall return,' said Agnes.

'Cheering thought, isn't it?' said Lowry. 'I'll wait while you pay your last respects.'

But this time Agnes didn't say a prayer. Instead, on some strange impulse, she took a pair of scissors from a nearby bench and cut off a lock of Philippa's hair, wondering, as she twisted it carefully and wrapped it in a scrap of paper, why she had done so.

Outside the clouds were clearing, allowing the late March

sun to break through. Agnes and Lowry breathed deeply and headed back to his office.

'What news of the compact disc?' asked Agnes.

'I'll tell you over lunch.'

'I suppose I can have any sandwich I like as long as it's ham,' said Agnes.

'Or cheese,' said Jim. 'Don't exaggerate.'

'The thing is,' said Lowry over coffee, 'the disc just didn't play at all. Fitted the machine and everything, but nothing happened. I even got our Steven – that's my older boy – to check I was doing it right. Then Madge said you can store anything on compact disc, she said, text or pictures or computer programmes, and a man in my position really should be up on all this, and what did I think I was doing, next thing I'd be holding it to my ear and tapping it – and so I phoned a mate of mine who works in computers, and we're going to see him tomorrow. I don't see what's so funny, Sister.'

'When do I get to meet Madge then?' said Agnes, and giggled into her cup of coffee.

Lowry pointedly ignored her, picked up his phone and punched an internal number. 'Driscoll – do you have a moment please, Sergeant?'

Driscoll popped his head round the door.

'How're we doing on the Mellersh search?'

'Nothing so far I'm afraid, sir.'

'Wife had any news?'

'No, she thinks he's been bumped off.'

'I hope you reassured her.'

'Did my best, sir.'

'I think we should visit her this afternoon, Agnes and I. Pop in for a friendly chat. Car not been sighted then?'

'Fraid not, sir.'

'Well, it can't have just vanished into thin air. Maybe we should book the helicopter from Cheltenham – and no, you can't drive it,' he said to Agnes, who had looked up from the last of her sandwich with a gleam in her eye.

The Mellersh home was a modern detached house on a newish housing estate. Smooth crazy paving provided a wide parking space in front of the fake Georgian front door, which featured discreet brass carriage lamps either side. Agnes rang the bell. There was no response. She tried again. She stood with Lowry, aware of someone peeking through a spy hole, and then the door opened. A thin, slight woman, in a shabby dress with dark brown hair awry, stood in the doorway.

'Mrs Sue Mellersh?'

'Yes?' her voice was faint.

'Detective Inspector Lowry. We've spoken on the phone, you've met my Sergeant Driscoll. And this is Sister Agnes. Sorry to intrude upon you. No, we have no news as yet' – as Mrs Mellersh tried to speak – 'we just thought we'd pop by for a chat.'

With an air of extreme weariness she let them in and showed them into the front room. A neat blue three-piece suite was arranged in front of a large television, next to which was a fireplace in fake marble which housed a set of plastic logs. Over everything, Agnes noticed, was a thick layer of dust. Mrs Mellersh sat down and said suddenly, 'Sister? Nurse, then, are you?'

'Actually, I'm a nun.'

'I'm sure he's dead anyway, you know.'

Lowry began to speak, but Agnes leaned forward. 'Might he have wanted to die, do you think?'

'Suicide, you mean? Oh no, not him. I meant killed. Murdered. They've been after him, you know.'

'It's just, taking his car and everything. Did he take clothes too?' Agnes got up, and began to walk around. Mrs Mellersh followed her nervously.

'His best suit. And some pyjamas.'

'So it's quite likely he meant to go.' Agnes went into the hall, followed by Mrs Mellersh, who was clasping and unclasping her hands. 'He'll have gone off to reason with them. And then they got him.'

'What did they want from him?' asked Agnes gently, going into a room which was obviously Mellersh's study. She noticed a computer with various drives attached to it; a separate phone line; a broad desk with a single, stark anglepoise lamp.

'It was all a mistake,' Mrs Mellersh was saying, her hands working away.

'He's gone to stop their menaces, then?' Agnes led her little party back into the hall again.

'We're so tired of it all.'

'Were there letters as well as phone calls?'

Mrs Mellersh stopped still in the doorway of the lounge. Lowry cast a warning glance at Agnes.

'Can we see them?' Agnes's voice was soft.

'He said not to. Not to tell—'

'They might help us to find him.'

Mrs Mellersh crossed the room with a sudden, birdlike movement, and opened a drawer in a reproduction bureau. She took out a small stack of papers which she passed to Agnes. They were white sheets of notepaper, and the messages were made up from letters cut out of newspaper.

'People really do that?' said Agnes quietly, handing them to Lowry.

'They frightened him.' Mrs Mellersh stood in the middle of the room, stooping slightly, her hands clasped together.

'And the video tapes?' asked Agnes, gentler still.

Mrs Mellersh's voice was suddenly loud and shrill. 'Oh, take them, take them. Much good they've done us, only harm,' and she fled from the room and up the stairs. Agnes and Lowry exchanged a glance and followed. At the foot of the stairs they stopped as a cascade of VHS tapes clattered down towards them.

'Have them all,' Mrs Mellersh was shouting from the top of the stairs, letting loose another armful. Then she slumped down tearfully on the top step. While Lowry gathered the tapes together, Agnes went up to her.

'Come on now. We'll find him. You've done very well, I'm sure we'll find him now.' She helped her down the stairs. 'It'll be all right, I'm sure it will,' said Agnes, offering her a tissue.

'Let me show you something,' Mrs Mellersh said in a small, calm voice. She led them out to the garden. 'Look, all this, the new patio, the extension over the garage, the barbecue—'

The grass was overgrown, encroaching on the neat, pale-grey crazy paving of the patio. Against the wall of the house stood a barbecue, shiny and unused. Weeds ran riot over the flower beds, and the rockery had partly collapsed, scattering earth and stones across one edge of the patio.

'It paid for all this,' Susan Mellersh was saying. 'Things I only dreamed about when he was working for the Post Office. Then he started his – his business, and we were able to move here, to have all this. I only bought that recliner and sunshade last summer . . .' She stood there, wringing her hands. 'It brought us no good,' she said.

Her voice tailed off. Agnes saw a garden recliner turned over on its side amongst the debris from the rockery, its pink candy-stripe damp and mildewy, its frame rusted at the joints and smeared with earth. Mrs Mellersh was staring towards it, unseeing, her eyes blank with some other fear. Gently, Agnes took her arm and led her back into the house.

# Chapter Fourteen

'That's some haul. Fifteen video tapes and three nasty-looking letters.' Lowry signalled left to turn on to the ring road. 'How did you get on to the letters so fast?'

'That's what we were there for.'

'But how did you know about them?'

Agnes craned her neck as they sped past the Bunker site, trying to catch a glimpse. Of what, she wondered. A column of smoke? A scraggy blond youth? She was aware of Lowry, awaiting an answer.

'Sorry? Oh, hunch. Didn't Mellersh mention letters and calls and things when we interviewed him?'

'Hmmm.' Lowry changed gear.

'She's in a state, isn't she, poor woman,' said Agnes.

'Aye. And the problem is, even when we do find him, it's not going to be good news.'

'Some women forgive their husbands anything. Even the worst, they'll forgive.'

Lowry glanced at Agnes, but she was staring out of the window again.

'Right, Driscoll,' boomed Lowry as he marched through the police station. 'I need a video-tape machine. I need some poor bugger to watch fifteen hours of bad-quality video tape in the hope of catching a glimpse of something or someone, we don't yet know what or who – and get on to the fingerprinting boys, we've got summat as needs a good look.'

'Right-o, sir. By the way, sir, while you were out, your wife

177

biked this fruit cake over for you.'

Lowry gave Driscoll a hard stare. 'My wife what?'

'She sent this cake over, by courier.'

Lowry took the sultana sponge in its clingfilm wrapping and weighed it in one hand, frowning at it.

'This must mean she's finished her big report for the Probation Service. That's a relief. Though it's no excuse for extravagance. Pop your head round my door in a few minutes, Driscoll, you may get a slice. If you've been good.'

Half an hour later, Lowry put the last of Mellersh's letters into a plastic bag.

'There we are,' he said. 'All copied out. D'you want to see?'

Agnes nodded, her mouth full of cake. Lowry passed her the copies, and she read:

GIVE IT BACK NOW OR ELSE
THE GIRLS DEAD YOU WILL FOLLOW GIVE IT BACK
LAST WARNING GIVE IT BACK OR YOURE DEAD

'Clear enough, aren't they?' said Lowry. 'Another slice?'

'The thing is,' mused Agnes, 'the author of these letters assumed that Mellersh would know how to return "it", whatever it was. I mean, there's no instructions.'

'Hmmm,' said Lowry. 'And whoever wrote these knew that Philippa had been killed.'

'Does that make them the murderer?'

'Not necessarily. It seems odd not to mention it till the second letter. We must check dates with Mrs Mellersh.'

'And if they're not the murderer,' Agnes continued, 'then they'd have to be intimate with Philippa to find out she was dead. If she didn't turn up when they were expecting her, or something. Though,' she added, 'it was in the papers too.'

'Maybe he was asking around people she knew. In which case, one of her friends might remember him.'

'Mmm,' mused Agnes through a fresh mouthful of sponge cake. 'By the way, do you have an address for the survivors of the Bunker – Jez's friends?'

Early next morning, Agnes slipped out before Athena was up and drove across town. She passed the school where she'd waited with Jane, Hugo's maid. It all seemed a long time ago. Beyond the estate was a row of condemned Victorian houses, all boarded up. Agnes went up to one and knocked loudly, the sound reverberating in the early sunlight. She knocked again. From behind the makeshift door came frantic scuffling noises, and a sleepy voice said, 'Who is it?'

'Sister Agnes.'

'Bloody 'ell, it's seven o'clock in the bleedin' mornin',' came the reply, and Latoya opened the door furtively to let Agnes in, bolting it sharply behind her.

'Lisa, it's Mother Teresa,' she called up the stairs. Agnes peered upwards into the gloom. In a sudden shaft of sunlight Lisa appeared, puffy-eyed, her hair dishevelled, small and child-like in a huge white shirt.

'It's the middle of the fuckin' night,' she said, and then disappeared.

Latoya showed Agnes into the front room. The bare floorboards were littered with beer cans. A worn sofa, its springs showing, was the only piece of furniture. Agnes sat down carefully on one edge of it.

'A good night, was it?' she said, gesturing to the cans.

Latoya grinned. 'Tea?' she asked. She went into the squalid back kitchen to put the kettle on, then began to scoop beer cans into a dustbin bag. Agnes noticed that the odd strand of old wiring was visible through the gaps in the skirting board. Lisa appeared, still wearing only the huge shirt and clutching a pillow. Latoya handed her a mug of tea, and she settled down in one corner, curled up on the pillow, her fingers wrapped around the mug.

'I had no idea you were only fifteen,' Agnes said to Lisa.

'Bastard cops tried to 'ave me locked up,' Lisa replied. ''Ave we got any food?'

Latoya shook her head. 'Not yet.'

'I ran away,' Lisa said to Agnes.

Agnes sipped her tea. 'You must miss him, Jez, I mean.'

Lisa's eyes clouded. 'Yeah. Yeah, I do. Stupid bastard.' She stared at the steam rising from her mug. 'Who d'you think dunnit, then?' she asked suddenly.

Agnes sighed. 'I've a fair idea, I think. Do you remember someone called David Mellersh?'

The two girls exchanged glances. 'Yeah,' Lisa said. 'That's who 'e were afraid of. This bloke Mellersh came and talked to Jez, couple of times. Then Jez went into 'idin'. He told me it was about something Fip knew about. 'E were dead scared.'

'Do you know any more than that?'

Latoya said, 'Only what I told you in London. 'Is message to you.'

'If you'd come back, 'e might have told you more. An' then 'e wouldn't of—' Lisa's eyes filled with tears. 'Stupid, stupid bastard,' she muttered into her mug.

Agnes stared at her hands, swallowing hard. After a moment she said, 'I think Sinead knew a lot about all this.'

'Sinead?' both girls echoed.

'They were close, weren't they?'

'Yeah, best mates,' said Lisa.

'Got God together, didn't they? Around Christmas it was, bloody baby Jesus rubbish, remember?'

Lisa laughed. 'Sinead got fed up. They went to some church thing and she didn't like the bloke. Fip stayed with it though.'

'Reverend Evans?' asked Agnes.

'Dunno.' Lisa shrugged.

'It seems odd he didn't remember Sinead, if she had pink hair. Even if she went only once.'

'Pink hair?' said Lisa. 'Oh no, it weren't pink then, were it. It were dreadlocked, all matted. Just looked a mess.'

'She weren't no Christian, were she, Fip,' Latoya said. 'Too much of the devil in 'er.'

'So where is Sinead now?' asked Agnes.

'With Angie in London.'

'When Angie got 'er grant, Fip made Sinead go too, d'you remember? 'Cos she weren't sure, it were after Christmas and Fip 'ad her troubles, didn't she? Angie said she'd give Sinead work, and Fip said it were too good a chance to miss. So she went.'

'Do you think she ever visited Philippa's house?'

'Nah. None of us ever saw it. Fip was scared of 'er old man.'

'Did Philippa see her again before she was killed?'

'Nah.'

'And has Sinead been in touch?'

'Nah. But she was never close to the rest of us, really. Too wild. Out of 'er head a lot of the time. She's probably spent the last few months E'd out of her face in London.'

As Agnes left twenty minutes later she emptied her purse of notes and pressed them into Lisa's hand. 'Take care – stay out, eh?'

Lisa nodded, standing in the doorway in the bright spring sun. Agnes kissed the top of her head, then turned sharply and strode to her car. As she got in, she looked back to see Lisa still standing there, flapping her huge sleeves like a baby bird trying to fly, before Latoya appeared and hustled her inside.

Jeff Cox was a tall, affable man, whose floppy blond hair and large, fluid movements made him seem more like an enthusiastic schoolboy than a managing director of a successful software business.

'Nice to see you Jim, and er—'

'Sister Agnes.'

'—Agnes. Come into my lair,' and he set off, striding through airy glass corridors, nodding at members of his staff as he passed.

'They're a good team,' he said, and the sweeping gesture of

his arm seemed to include every person in the building. 'Coffee?'

Agnes nodded thirstily, aware that it was only ten o'clock and she'd been up for four hours with only Latoya's tea for sustenance. Just like convent life, she thought.

'Ah, Stella,' Jeff was saying to a plump, attractive woman. 'Could you be an angel? Three coffees in my office.' He put his head on one side as he spoke, with a pleading look in his large brown eyes. Agnes was suddenly reminded of a puppy dog, an impression confirmed when he strode off again and bounced into his office. He flopped into a large swivel chair, and gestured his guests into two more opposite him.

'Right. This disc?'

Lowry opened his briefcase with some ceremony and produced the disc. He held it between thumb and forefinger. 'Before we begin, Jeff – this really is very very sensitive. We don't know what's on this, but whatever it is, it's summat dangerous. Someone wants it back, very badly. So, not a word.'

Jeff nodded, and Lowry handed over the disc. Jeff looked at it, then placed it carefully on his desk. He picked up his phone. 'Nick? Care to join us?' He replaced the phone and picked up the disc. Sunlight streamed through the delicate venetian blinds and Agnes, used to the gloom of the police station, blinked. Another young man in a crisp shirt appeared in the doorway.

'Nick, this is Inspector Lowry and Sister Agnes. And this is our little mystery,' he said, waving the CD at his colleague.

'Mellersh had one of those,' said Agnes suddenly.

Jeff followed her gaze. 'A modem? For linking into the phone network. Everyone has them.'

They clustered round the screen, and Nick loaded the CD. 'Wait for it,' he said. 'It'll probably turn out to be the Bee Gee's Greatest Hits.'

'Sort of thing my wife would say,' murmured Lowry.

'Sorry?' said Jeff.

'Nothing,' said Lowry.

On the screen it said:

> Logos Primus Software Ltd
> All rights reserved
> Load program now

Nick moved his mouse. The screen said,

> Program Loading
> Drive D

'That's further than I got, anyway,' said Lowry. There was a beep. Jeff moved his mouse again, and clicked on a box in the corner of the screen which said, 'Continue'.

'Hmm. Progress,' said Jeff. The screen filled with lists of words and numbers, then stopped.

'Right. What shall we look at? Let's try HARENG.001.' He moved and clicked his mouse. Nothing happened.

'Hang on a mo,' Nick said. He moved and clicked the mouse again. There was a beep and the screen said:

> Drive C Not Ready
> Cancel operation

'I thought so,' Nick said, returning to the directory. 'This needs to run with another program to access the data on the files.'

'Great. Any ideas on which program?' asked Jeff cheerfully.

'I think we're looking at something fractal. Look,' he said, scrolling through the lists of files. 'There's loads of information there, more than you'd get on an ordinary CD. Whoever programmed this has crunched the data down – clever bastards.'

Jeff turned to Lowry and Agnes. 'Fractal mathematics. It's based on chaos theory. Everything's reduced to equations.'

'Sounds like my life,' said Lowry drily, and Agnes smiled.

'Absolutely fascinating,' Jeff was saying. 'We're only just getting into it ourselves, eh, Nick?'

Nick was staring at the screen. 'Mmm,' he said. 'I'm glad you're the sort of bloke who likes a challenge.' He looked up at Jeff and grinned. 'Because we've got to look for the decompression program to un-crunch this. And it could be anywhere. A world-wide rummage, I reckon.'

Jeff grinned back. 'He means, we'll start with the bulletin boards. You network into all available programs, world-wide. You can check out what programs have been written by other people, advertise for information, that sort of thing.'

Lowry walked round the desk and sat down in a maroon swivel chair. 'Do you mean whoever wrote these files would make available, on your world-wide electronic networks, the data to read it?'

'It's very unlikely. But we might find something. And it's our only chance.'

'Or we could write our own,' Nick added.

'Yeah. Just give Nick two years to do his Ph.D in Chaos Theory first.'

'Make it three,' Nick called back cheerily as Jeff led his two guests out.

Jeff bounced back along the corridors as if someone had just promised him a very large bone. When they got to the smart reception area, Agnes said suddenly, 'That list of files?'

'Yes?'

'Can you print it out?'

'What, as it is? Just the names?'

'Yes. There might be a clue.'

'Sure. I'll just see to it.'

Jeff picked up the phone and spoke into it, then turned to Agnes. 'Someone'll bring it through in a minute,' he said. 'I'll be going, then.'

'One more thing,' Lowry said. 'How good's your security here?'

'Pretty good. We have people on at night and everything.'

'It's just, be careful,' he said, shaking Jeff's hand, 'that's all. I appreciate this, Jeff, I really do. The only alternative would have been the boys in London, and I'll be damned if I have to go scurrying down to them to ask their advice.'

Ten minutes later, Lowry's Rover pulled out of the curved concrete drive of the car park. The sunlight flashed blue behind them against the low glass building.

'Pub lunch and then dirty videos, I think,' said Lowry conversationally, as they headed back towards Chidding Ford.

'If only,' sighed Agnes. 'Those videos'll be dull as anything, I bet.'

Lowry looked at Agnes. 'You know, for a nun you say some pretty surprising things.'

The man was stripped down to his underwear. Agnes could make out something black and tight stretched across flabby buttocks.

'Another bloody G-string,' muttered Lowry. 'Why is it that half the men in bloody Gloucestershire seem to be wearing G-strings under their business suits?'

'This one's going for the mumsy look,' said Agnes.

They watched as the man picked out a floral blouse with a neat, high collar. He put it to one side while he arranged his padded bra in front of the mirror. Lowry pressed the Pause button, and the man was frozen mid-action, one hand pressed against his bosom, the other reaching for the blouse.

Lowry ran his hands through his hair. 'How much more?' he said, wearily.

'We've done six hours. What did Driscoll say?'

'It's all the same. Endless men preening in front of that mirror. Poor buggers.'

'They're all right,' Agnes said. 'Look.' She forwarded the tape until the man was fully dressed and applying the finishing touches to his make-up. 'Look,' she said again, and pressed Play. The man checked his lipstick in the mirror with obvious pleasure.

'If only it were that simple for us all,' Agnes said. 'To shed the outer person and reveal our inner self, the one we really like.'

'Aye, but in a while it's all got to come off, hasn't it. And then he's back down those stairs, back where he started. I mean, me, I might be a difficult old bugger but at least I don't go leaving bits of my inner self littered around the place, let alone recorded for all time on a cheap video tape.'

Agnes laughed. 'It might do you good. Develop your feminine self—'

'Join the G-string set you mean? I think the wife might have views. Talking of which,' he added, looking at his watch, 'I'm already later than I said I'd be. And if the dinner's ruined, it'll take more than a padded bra to placate our Madge, that's for sure.'

In the silence of the evening, as the sun set outside the window, Agnes fast-forwarded through more video tape. Every so often she stopped, rewound and watched the screen carefully, looking for something. At last she found it. One man, going through the usual ritual, which she watched only for as long as it took her to recognize him.

She checked through the rest of the tape, took it out of the machine and slipped it into her bag. 'A debt repaid,' she murmured to herself.

She switched off the machine and turned to the list of file names that Jeff had printed from the disc, settling down at Lowry's desk in the pool of light thrown by his anglepoise. She flicked through the pages. There were about eighty names, she reckoned. Some caught her eye, and she read them off.

ARUNDEL.001
AUXILIA.001
BRECON.001

CATFIGHT.001
DIPLODOC.US
DISCOBOL.US
ELEPHANT.90
FAIRYTAL.E
HARENG.001
HYBRID.001
QUERULOS.001
RHINOCER.OS
RENEGADE.90
SIBLING.001
XANADU.90
XENOPHON.001

Agnes stared out of the window into the night. They could mean anything, these names. But if someone with the right program, the right know-how, found them, they would acquire a significance. Something worth killing for. And would any global screen-hopper who happened upon these names also be in danger? It seemed harmless enough, she thought, that little shiny disc. And yet she was more and more certain it was the clue to murder.

She stared at the Superstore car park, at its great floodlights which made her think of prison courtyards and refugee camps. All this time, she thought, under our very noses, the nature of crime has been changing. All this time we've been thinking it's still a matter of blunt instruments and forged banknotes, it's evolved into this, this jumbled collection of electro-magnetic particles, which when put together in the right order becomes something menacing – and dangerous. She put her head in her hands. And whatever it is, she thought, it's out of our reach.

It was after midnight when she let herself into Athena's house. On the marble breakfast bar was a note, written on thick notepaper in a bold, flourishing hand. It said:

Isn't this just like a marriage? Your dinner's in the microwave – ruined, I hope.

Agnes opened the microwave and removed a dish which was filled with slimy, curdled sauce and something grey and spongy that might once have been a fish. Smiling, she spooned it carefully into the bin, then fetched a ripe Stilton cheese from the fridge, which she ate with some Bath Oliver biscuits and a fine claret. She leaned back in her armchair and stared into the embers of the fire, swirling the dark, blackcurranty liquid around in her large glass, savouring the salty cheese upon her tongue. In her mind she saw Jeff and Nick again, in their crisp white shirts and smart hair-cuts, their pristine, sunny, hi-tech offices. It was almost impossible to believe that the disc she had found might be a part of their world; that even now, locked away in one of their shiny chrome filing cabinets, lurked something dark, dangerous – and possibly evil.

# Chapter Fifteen

Athena stumbled downstairs at half past ten on Saturday morning to an uncharacteristic smell.

'Bacon?' she mumbled, appearing in the kitchen, rubbing her eyes.

Her living room was tidier than she'd ever seen it, the breakfast bar shone, and Agnes was standing at the stove fussing over a large frying pan.

'Bacon. And eggs, kippers, fried bread, tomatoes, mushrooms. Also croissants and honey, coffee and orange juice. What would you like?'

Athena took a mug of coffee and slumped into an armchair, her white towelling bathrobe revealing large areas of tanned, naked body.

'But I don't eat breakfast.'

'You do now.'

'And what's this?' Athena screwed up her eyes and peered at the half-empty bottle of claret. 'My best Château Margaux – how could you, you selfish beast?'

'Darling, the '83 is excellent right now. If you'd left it any longer it'd be past its best. Breakfast's up.'

Athena sat on a bar stool and picked at a tomato.

'The fact is, Athena,' said Agnes, tucking into a large plateful, 'neither of us is cut out to be a wife.'

Athena pushed her plate aside and took a bite of croissant instead. Flaky crumbs scattered down her bathrobe, and a trickle of honey appeared on her chin.

'It's something I've always suspected,' she said mournfully.

'And it's taken a nun to tell me.'

'So, the deal is, no wifely behaviour. If we're both in, we cook. If one of us is in, we cook for ourselves. That way we get no grudges and no rude notes left on the kitchen table, OK?'

'It's a deal, Sister,' laughed Athena. 'And bags I first in the bathroom.'

'But you take ages,' wailed Agnes as Athena, giggling, fled up the stairs in a cloud of white towelling. Agnes poured herself more coffee and then methodically started on Athena's untouched plate.

An hour later, she was sitting in front of the video machine at the police station again. Driscoll was pacing the room.

'Where is he? Just when I've got something real to report, and the Inspector's late.'

'Not very late,' grinned Agnes, as a booming voice resounded through the building, and a few moments later Lowry appeared in the room.

'So, Driscoll. You called. It had better be summat worth while.'

'Oh, it is, sir, it is,' said Driscoll, hurrying to the machine. He pressed a button and everyone watched the screen.

A man was combing a long blond wig in front of the mirror. 'Not him, sir, just a minute—' The screen went blank, there was a moment of scratchy blank tape, and then the picture came on again. It was the same room. A man in a suit and dark glasses was sitting on the bed, in profile.

'This is the one,' whispered Driscoll.

The man sat still. Suddenly a woman with long red hair appeared and knelt down in front of him, then almost immediately jumped up again, and left the picture. A second later the screen returned to the white noise of blank tape.

'That it, then, Sergeant?'

Driscoll nodded.

'It must be him,' Agnes said. 'He's different from all the others.'

'Oh yes?' Lowry turned questioning eyes on her.

'Yes. He's confident – he's in command. He's – he's a Mr Big type.'

'Well, I'm glad you're so sure,' said Lowry. 'Though how you can tell from this . . . Is there any more, Driscoll?'

The Sergeant shook his head.

'By the way, sir, I noticed this morning there was one missing. A tape, I mean.'

'Ah yes, that was me,' said Agnes. 'I've er – borrowed it. I hope you don't mind.'

'Oh, no, Sister, not at all. Just help yourself to the evidence whenever you like. After all, you've drawn conclusions most of us can only begin to feel our way to, on the basis of three seconds of video tape of a fellow in sunglasses sitting on a bed.'

'There's no need for sarcasm, Inspector. I think Sergeant Driscoll has helped us take a huge step forward. Thank you, Sergeant.'

'I'll thank my staff when thanks are due, Sister. Perhaps you'd like to tell me what we do, now we've taken such a huge step forward. Whom are we about to arrest, then?'

'You know it's not that easy – but now we have an image we can show to people. I can think of at least two people who might help us. And Sergeant Driscoll has spoken to Mrs Mellersh again, too, about dating the letters.'

'Grand. What did she say? Any more huge steps forward?'

'I've written the dates down here, sir.'

'You see,' said Agnes, 'the first one was received on Thursday, February the eighth. So it must have been written before Philippa was killed on the Sunday.'

'And?'

'And the second one wasn't received until Monday the twenty-sixth, a fortnight after the murder.'

'So?'

'It implies that whoever wrote the letter didn't know about the murder. If they'd done it, they could have written the threatening note earlier.'

191

'It implies no such thing, Sister. Remember, they're looking for summat, perhaps our disc. They might have killed Philippa, and spent a fortnight searching for the disc before they next contacted Mellersh. Anyway, how sure is Mrs Mellersh of these dates?'

'She said she wrote them down in her diary once her husband had told her about them, sir.'

'And when was that?'

'Er – not at once, sir. Some weeks later, she said. But she'd worked out the dates because she thought we'd want to know.'

'Grand. Surefire evidence, if you ask me. Stand up in court no trouble.' Lowry stood up. 'So much for huge steps forward. If you ask me, we're no further on than we were yesterday. And I've wasted my Saturday for this.'

He strode from the office, the door swinging wildly behind him. Agnes exchanged a glance with Driscoll and then followed him out, catching up with him on the stairs.

'Jim – is there any reason why you should be quite so awful this morning?'

Lowry paused, one hand on the cast-iron banister rail. He sighed.

'Sister, if you knew anything about married life, you'd understand what it feels like to wake up in your marital bed next to the only person you've ever loved on a morning with the sun streaming through the windows and all the time in the world. And both boys away staying with their mates for the weekend. And then that idiot of a Sergeant decides he's got summat important to tell you and drags you from your bed. When I get home now, there'll be a selection of iced fancies – maybe even a Battenberg – but that precious moment will have gone. For ever.'

He took two steps down the stairs, then paused again. 'But I can't expect you to understand, Sister. See you Monday.'

Agnes stood on the stone steps and watched the huge figure descend, until he disappeared altogether. She slowly went back up the stairs, and, as Driscoll was leaving the office, asked to borrow the tape with 'Mr Big' on it. She sat at Lowry's desk with the tape next to her, and made two phone calls.

At one o'clock, Agnes was sitting in the bar of the Flag Hotel, Cirencester, watching the few solitary guests. All were men, all seemed to be wearing grey suits, all had their heads buried in their newspapers. Agnes recalled Lowry's comments about half the men in Gloucestershire wearing black G-strings under their business clothes, and surveyed the bar with renewed interest.

'Ah, there you are.' The voice was low and hurried, and Agnes looked up to see Jimmie standing over her, out of breath.

'Jimmie. Thanks for coming. It won't take long.' She got up. 'I've booked a room with a TV and video, you'll see why.'

Agnes led the way down a dark, oak-panelled corridor carpeted in shabby maroon. She unlocked a door and showed Jimmie to an armchair.

'I hope I didn't disturb your Saturday,' she said, switching on the television.

'Oh, no, it's fine. Amy's taken the kids for a break at her sister's.' He sat on the edge of the chair, and Agnes noticed the tension around his mouth, the sadness in his eyes. She pressed Play, and the man in dark glasses appeared on the screen, sitting confidently on Mrs Elsworthy's hired-out bed. Agnes Paused the image.

'Do you recognize him?' she asked.

Jimmie shuddered. 'I recognize the room all right.'

'And the man?'

He shook his head. Agnes pressed Play again, and Philippa appeared and disappeared.

'That's her, though. I thought she was so nice when I met her.'

'But the man rings no bells? You didn't pass him on the stairs?'

'Nope. Difficult to say, mind you, with those dark glasses. But I'm pretty sure not.'

Agnes retrieved the tape and they both stood up to leave.

'One more thing, Jimmie.' She brought out another tape. 'This is for you.'

Jimmie took the tape and stared at it.

'It's the only existing copy of you – in that room.'

Relief lit up his face as he looked at Agnes.

'You mean—'

'I doubt they made copies. And I'm the only person to have seen it since we seized it. It's yours.'

'Won't the police – won't they need it?'

'Oh, bugger them,' said Agnes, and then laughed at hearing Lowry in her voice. 'I've had enough of the police for today. Take it.'

They walked back to the main entrance of the hotel.

'How's Colin, by the way?' asked Agnes.

'Oh, OK. Still there with that miserable old bastard.'

'And Amy?'

Jimmie stared at the worn red carpet. 'OK. Yeah.'

'Have you worked things out?'

'How can I?'

'That tape might help.'

'This? This'd finish us. This is going in its own personal incinerator just as soon as I can organize it. Then maybe I can patch things up with Amy.'

They shook hands on the hotel steps.

'Well – thanks,' Jimmie said.

'I don't suppose we need see each other again.'

'No. Suppose not.'

'Good luck then.'

'And you. Hope you catch your murderer.'

Agnes watched him go, his step lighter, his head held higher. She wondered what would become of him. Perhaps he'd already found another safe place for dressing up – she hoped it was a truly safe place this time.

Athena was watching the television sports coverage, still wearing her bathrobe. As Agnes walked in, she yawned.

'You can tell I'm bored out of my tiny mind, can't you. I'm sitting here utterly fascinated by Sam Torrance's perfectly struck thirty-foot birdie. It was at the four-five-one yard eighteenth, apparently. Amazing.' She yawned again, reached out an elegant foot towards the television, and switched it off with her bare toe.

'Well, I'm glad you're bored, Athena. Because I was hoping to amuse you this afternoon with a little jaunt back to the Albion Gallery.'

'Darling, how delightful,' said Athena, jumping up. 'We can stock up on Indonesian butterfly mobiles. And if you're driving I can wear my new red suede platform wedges.'

They arrived at the shop as Mrs Elsworthy was closing. 'Ah, there you are dear,' she said to Agnes. 'I've set up the video like you said, in the back room. Come through.'

She led them into a tiny office which was almost totally swamped by a large television set.

'Ready when you are,' she said to Agnes, and sat down in front of it, next to Athena. Agnes let the image of the mystery man run its course and then stopped it.

'Well, that's Philippa,' said Athena emphatically.

Mrs Elsworthy looked at her. 'You know, I've always thought of her as Pip. Never thought it was short for anything.'

'And the man?'

Mrs Elsworthy stared at the frozen image on the screen.

'Yes, he's familiar, I'd say. It's those dark glasses. The gentlemen would often arrive in them, but there was one who I never saw without them. And that's a smart suit, isn't it?'

Athena was staring hard at the screen. 'The jacket hangs well.'

'Look!' Agnes suddenly exclaimed. 'I didn't notice it before.' She pointed at the man's neck. There, nestling at his collar, was a tiny crucifix.

'Your type, then,' Athena remarked. 'Religious, well-dressed—'

'Most of Pip's clients didn't dress that well,' Mrs Elsworthy added, 'not really being so interested in their – outside clothes. Yes, I definitely remember him. There were a couple of occasions which I connect with him, now I come to think of it, when I'd say something odd was going on up there. There'd be – noises.'

'What sort of noises?' asked Athena, leaning forward, all agog.

'Well, let's just say it sounded more reminiscent of a brothel than a ladies' dressing room.'

'How often?' asked Agnes.

'Only occasionally. Once or twice, maybe. That's why I never thought to mention it before.'

'When did it stop?'

'Some time ago – probably soon after Christmas.'

'And you think it was him?'

'It's that smart suit. And the way he's sitting. At ease in his clothes. You see, usually when they come down again, they look unhappy with themselves. But this man, he was like you see him there. Sure of himself, I don't know how else to put it.'

It was drizzling when Agnes and Athena emerged from the shop. They walked back to the car deep in thought.

'I bet he's foreign,' said Athena suddenly.

'I was just thinking the very same thing,' smiled Agnes. 'The smart suit—'

'The air of confidence, despite – unusual – goings on. I mean,' Athena added, 'have you ever seen an Englishman leaving a brothel looking smart and happy and self-assured?'

'How many Englishmen leaving brothels have you seen –
on second thoughts, I don't need to know.'

'How do you know he's the same as the man with the
compact disc?' asked Athena after a moment.

'I don't. Not for sure. It's just all I've got so far.'

'So we've got a well-dressed non-transvestite foreigner, for
whom Philippa is providing a different sort of service – which
she doesn't tape – and from whom she acquires a compact
disc.'

'And,' added Agnes, as they reached the car, 'she hides it in
her jacket, he wants it back desperately, threatens Mellersh
for it, and maybe kills her for it, if not Jez too – if not
Mellersh too.'

'Wow,' said Athena. She got into the car. 'But if he killed
Pip, why didn't he check out the jacket?'

'Perhaps he did try to search for it. The police missed it,
didn't they? Maybe he did too.' Agnes started the engine. 'By
the way, after mass tomorrow I'm riding over at Arnie's
again, and staying on for lunch. He said you'd be very welcome
too – you could have a nice easy lesson on something quiet,
and he's an excellent cook.'

Athena giggled. 'Heavens, poppet, I only have to be
downwind of a horse and I come out in blotches and sneeze
for two days. Still, lunch might be fun. As long as I can stay
in the house.'

As they drove out of Painscombe, Athena said, 'Are we
allowed to talk about Hugo now?'

Agnes stared fixedly at the road ahead. 'Hugo? There's
nothing to say. Why? Are you still seeing him?'

'No,' said Athena, studying her nail varnish. 'He went
rather odd after you left. I gave up trying.'

'Oh,' said Agnes.

'That's that, then,' said Athena, giving Agnes a sidelong
glance.

'Yes. That's that.'

A moment later Athena said, 'You took that last bend, the

one with the sheer drop, at fifty-five, you know?'

'Did I?' said Agnes. 'What fun. I'll do the next one on two wheels if you like.'

# Chapter Sixteen

Detective Inspector Lowry was sitting hunched at his desk, absorbed in reading a file, when Agnes arrived at his office on Monday.

'*Bonjour*, Inspector. Did you have a nice weekend?'

Lowry did not look up. 'Eventually,' he replied, turning a page.

'I had a great time,' Agnes went on. 'I interviewed two people about our mystery man, and one of them recognized him.'

Lowry continued to read. 'And,' Agnes continued, 'I spent yesterday with an old friend of Hugo's who reckons he met him too.'

Lowry raised his eyes at last from the file. 'Aye, well, if I was doing this as my little hobby, and if I could spend my time discussing murder over the claret like some bloody parlour game, I expect I'd be quite happy to spend all weekend doing it too. As it is, Sister, it's my job – no more, no less.' He closed the file shut. 'And we're out of coffee beans – so if you want to be really useful you can run along down the corridor to the machine.'

Agnes smiled at him. 'Promise me you'll never change, Jim,' she said, going to the door. 'I don't care what they say, you're adorable exactly as you are. Two sugars, isn't it?'

'Right, Sister,' said Lowry, when she returned a few moments later with two steaming polystyrene cups, 'I've ordered a helicopter from Stabberton Airport to circle the Forest of Dean. I expect they'll take a picnic and make a day of it. Secondly, they found no fingerprints on those Mellersh letters – nothing at all. Someone really knows what they're doing. Oh, and Jeff's running a couple of likely programs this morning and asked us to pop over later on. What about you?'

'Me? Oh, I was just playing, you know. I did find out that Mrs Elsworthy had seen our mystery man a couple of times at the gallery – and that he visited for – unusual – services. We think he might be foreign, French or Italian or something.'

'Just your type, eh? I knew I could trust you with the sleazy stuff.'

'And Arnie, Hugo's friend, reckoned that a man who looked like our man came into the pub on the night that Philippa was killed, about half an hour after Hugo left it. Arnie said he looked like he was looking for someone.'

'It's not much to go on, is it? He could be nothing to do with this. I suppose you could ask Hugo about it.'

'You ask him.'

Lowry looked carefully at Agnes, then picked up the phone. 'I will then.' He dialled and waited. 'Ah, Mr Bourdillon. Detective Inspector Lowry here. Just one little question, if you don't mind. We've had reports of a man spotted around the village on the day of the murder. Tall, dark, well dressed, tendency to dark glasses and sharp suits – maybe foreign? Ring any bells? No, OK, well – sorry? Yes, she is – er – yes. Right. I will. Thank you, Mr Bourdillon, sorry to trouble you.'

Lowry replaced the receiver. 'He sent you his kind regards.'

'I think perhaps you missed the biting sarcasm,' Agnes replied.

Half an hour later, Lowry and Agnes drew into the car park of Logos Software Limited. The building was sleek and bright in front of them, a blue flash of light against the Cotswold hills. 'So, what do we think then?' Lowry asked Agnes.

Agnes took off her sunglasses and polished them. She sighed. 'Well, we have Mellersh. And we have someone else who owned the disc and wanted it back. Badly.'

'Badly enough to kill for?'

'I don't know. Perhaps Pip and Jez were killed by the same person who then threatened Mellersh; but then, Lisa and Latoya only saw Mellersh around Jez, no one else. In which case, perhaps Mellersh killed Jez, and someone else killed Philippa. Someone who left their fingerprints all over the house. Which means Mellersh is hiding out either because he's afraid of Jez's killer, or because he is Jez's killer.'

'Well, we'll just have to ask him, won't we. Meanwhile, let's learn some more about the modern world, Sister.'

Jeff greeted them somewhat wearily. His puppy-like bounce seemed to have diminished. He was sitting at his desk staring at the screen, his hair awry, his left hand fiddling constantly with his fringe. He waved towards two chairs.

'Hi. Thanks for coming. Take a pew.' He buzzed the intercom on his desk to summon Nick, who appeared a moment or two later. Jeff leaned back in his chair, his fingers still working through his hair.

'Well, I'm afraid there's very little to report. We checked out a couple of likely-sounding programs from the bulletin boards, but nothing bit. One simply didn't work, the other didn't allow us into the CD. Nick's been struggling with a program of his own, but it's a tall order even for a brain like his.'

Nick grinned. Agnes had got up and was gazing over Jeff's shoulder at the screen. 'Is this the bulletin board?'

'One of them.' He scrolled through it, and names flashed before Agnes's eyes.

'It's a whole correspondence?'

'People communicate anything they like this way.'

'Sort of pen pals?'

'Sort of. Anything from serious information about computing, to teenage sex fantasies.'

Lowry smiled to himself as he saw a light come into Agnes's eyes. 'So,' she was saying, 'people just talk to each other this way?'

'Yup,' Nick said.

'And if you wanted something in particular – you could ask for it this way?'

'Oh, people advertise all the time. Look—' An instruction came up for a key word, and Nick said, 'For example—' and typed in the word RAVE. 'You have to wait a while for the system to come back to you,' he said. A few moments later, the screen said:

Conference 'raving' is closed. To gain access to this conference, mail the moderator with a request for membership. Type SHOW raving to see who the moderator is.

'So – if we advertised,' Agnes asked, 'someone who knew about our disc might come back to us?'

Lowry spoke up. 'Given the danger – that would be foolish, wouldn't it?'

'Or if we tracked down these moderators – couldn't we look for likely people that way, without advertising? I mean, what's this . . . "Alt. Sex. Stories". . . ?'

Nick and Jeff exchanged glances. 'When I said teenage sex fantasies, that's what I meant,' Jeff said. 'You can have a look if you want, but it's harmless stuff. If this disc were serious the owner of it wouldn't bother chatting on the phone with a few lonely blokes.'

'What would he bother with?'

'Your mind,' said Lowry drily. 'Like a sewer.'

Agnes turned to him. 'Think about it,' she said. 'Someone's gone to lots of trouble to distribute some form of information this way. And it's visual. What other form of visual information is going to be worth so much to someone?'

'On the other hand,' said Jeff, 'you won't find your villains by scrolling through publicly available conferences. Various well-meaning authorities try from time to time. But your people strike me as more intelligent than that.'

'That one,' Agnes said suddenly. 'There. HIPPOPOT.US. That's like some of the file names on the CD, eight letters, then the ending .US.'

'Shall we call it up?' Jeff moved and clicked his mouse. There was some whirring, then nothing.

'Not that one. Though it's a good thought. To go by related names rather than what the file says it does. That way they could hide the data in these lists and only the right people would know what names to look out for. Like a code. Hmm. Look, leave it with us, can you? I'll correlate lists of names, we may well have something by tomorrow.'

They all walked along the bright corridors back to reception. Jeff was hunched and quiet.

'Needles in haystacks, eh?' said Lowry.

Jeff sighed. 'What I don't understand is, why go to all this trouble? If it is porn. You could just trade videos or discs privately.'

'But if you wanted to maximize your – your audience,' said Agnes. 'Make your services available to new people – internationally—'

Jeff nodded. 'S'pose so. Mmmm. We'll keep looking.'

Back at the station, Lowry was informed that Mellersh's car had been spotted in the Forest of Dean, and he instructed Driscoll to drive out and take some more details. 'Go carefully, mind you. Just the general picture. I don't want him sprung from his lair just now.'

Agnes and Lowry went up the stairs wearily and collapsed in a couple of chairs. Outside Lowry's window they could hear cars coming and going from the Superstore, children shouting, trolleys rattling. Agnes yawned.

'I think I might go back to London soon. There's quite a lot to do there.'

'Like what?'

'Well, there's Angie and Sinead, Pip's friends. I'm sure they know more about all this than Lisa and co. And from what Jez said, Sinead may be connected to this disc business. Also—' She stopped suddenly, and fiddled with a piece of scrap paper.

'Also what?'

'Nothing. Is there a phone somewhere I could use? I'd just like to tell someone I'm still alive.'

Julius sounded rather cheerful. 'Oh, don't worry about me, Agnes. I'm sure if you did meet with an early death they'd let me know eventually. How's my pistol?'

'Oh, fine. I polish it lovingly every night and think of you . . . Julius?'

'Mmm?'

'Oh, you're there. I've never known anyone before who could blush on the phone.'

'I wasn't blushing.'

'Hmm. How's the project?'

'Fine. Just fine. The house is nearly ready. So, what did you really phone me for?'

'Sorry?'

'Why did you phone? I know you too well.'

'Well, there is something, actually. Stop laughing. You see, we think our number one suspect is some kind of businessman. It's just a hunch, but going by how he looks, we're convinced he's not English – probably French or Italian or something. And possibly religious, which makes him one of us, I mean, Catholic. And then I thought, anyone who earns his wealth the way this man does would be generous in donating it to worthwhile causes.' She sighed. 'It's all rather a long shot, really. But I wondered, given the circles you move in, the Catholic fund-raising establishment and all that—'

'I save your life, I find you a job, and now you want me to find you a murderer too.'

'Just keep your eyes peeled, as they say?'

'I wouldn't do it for anyone else, Agnes. But seeing as it's you—'

Agnes hung up, grinning. Then, remembering that she'd promised Athena steak *au poivre* for dinner, she spent the rest of the afternoon scouring all the butchers in Chidding Ford for the right cut. When she returned to the police station, she found Driscoll talking to Lowry.

'We found the car, sir. Abandoned at the end of a dirt track. But you'd have to proceed on foot anyway, from there. There were tracks leading away from the car, and the dogs picked up a scent. And the Forestry bloke said there was an old cottage further up there, derelict. We saw smoke coming from it. But then we came away, like you said, sir.'

'Good. Good work, Driscoll. You might as well get home now.' The door swung shut as Driscoll, murmuring goodbyes, headed for home.

Agnes looked out of the window. 'You know, there isn't a single butcher in this town who knows how to cut a Châteaubriand steak.'

'You'll just have to get it flown in from Harrods as usual, then.' Lowry's grin was cut short by the phone ringing.

'Lowry. Yes. Good. We will. Fine. Right away.' He hung up and turned to Agnes. 'Jeff. They've done it. Matched up names, got a program which works.'

Lowry stood up and took his raincoat from its hanger. 'It's odd, he sounded terrible on the phone. He said he wasn't sure we'd want to see it.'

The building looked bluer in the evening light. Agnes and Jim were ushered past the security man on the reception and found Jeff at his screen again. Nick was sitting next to him. They both looked pale, dishevelled and ill. Nick looked up as they came in and tried to smile.

'You'll soon understand why someone wanted this back so badly.'

'Get them some tea, Nick. Extra strong, lots of sugar.' Jeff appeared not to be joking.

'How did you find the program?'

205

'It was the endings, like you said. We tried a few, the USs, different dates. Then we went for the single E. What was it, Nick, ZAPODIDA.E? XANTHIPP.E?'

'Something like that,' said Nick wearily. 'It was the most amazing outside chance. But honestly, when you've seen it you'll wish you hadn't.'

Agnes and Jim drew chairs up round the screen, and Jeff set the disc to run. Images appeared on the screen, at first dark and fuzzy, then getting clearer. Moving images. Unthinkable images.

The security man was doing his rounds. He'd been told that Mr Cox would be working late – but then, he was always working late. As he passed his office, he glanced inside to see four people staring at the computer screen. He was taken aback by the looks on their faces – a universal expression of horror. He wondered what on earth they were looking at, when it was only computers, after all.

Agnes broke the silence first. 'Do you think – do you think those kids – survived?'

Three white, drawn faces turned to look at her. 'Does it seem likely?' asked Lowry at last. He shook his head. To Agnes he seemed suddenly old. 'Jeff, I'm sorry. I should never have dragged you into this.'

'I've always known it was possible. You read stuff in the trade press about porn exchanges through micromail, but that's just consenting adults. You don't think it extends to—' He gestured with his head to the screen.

Nick took the disc from the machine and handed it to Lowry as if it were burning his fingers. 'No wonder someone wanted it back.'

'And if they can do that – film – film that stuff – the odd extra murder of a homeless youth isn't going to seem difficult is it?' Lowry turned the disc round in his fingers. 'It makes my blood boil,' he went on, the colour returning to his face. 'These filthy porn merchants. I mean, in the old days, you had great tins of film rolling through Customs. Difficult to hide a thing like that. And even if it said Snow White and the Seven Dwarves on the can, all you had to do was pull a few feet out of the roll and hold it up to the light, and you'd soon get a fair idea of what Snow White was doing with her Seven Dwarves – whereas this . . .' Disgust was etched across his face. 'And you say this can be zapped across the world to anyone in a few seconds? No Customs, no borders, no risk of seizure. It makes me bloody sick.'

'It could have been filmed anywhere,' Jeff said.

'Anywhere where life is cheap and people are disposable.' said Lowry. 'And these days you don't have to go far for that.'

'Brazil or somewhere,' said Agnes suddenly. 'No one's going to miss them, are they, street children like that.' She walked over to the window and gazed out into the darkness, blinking.

'We should go,' Lowry said gently.

They all four walked in silence along the corridor. Lowry turned to Jeff and said, 'There's nothing to say that our man had anything to do with the making of that, though, is there. Just the – receiving of it.'

'It could be done anywhere in the world with the right technology. Then they've just got to distribute the CD and the code names.'

They came out into the car park. The night seemed to have a chill about it. As Jeff went to his car, Lowry stopped him. 'Look, I'd be wary if I were you. Step up security if you can – and for you and Nick personally too. And not a word to anyone, OK?'

Jeff nodded, and the car door closed behind him. Nick got into the passenger seat, and a few moments later the engine revved and the headlights cut across the tarmac as they drove off into the night. Lowry and Agnes went to their car. They got in and sat, silent in the darkness, unwilling to move. Agnes shivered.

'I should have thought,' Lowry said, 'before submitting you to all that. It must have been really tough – I'm sorry.'

Agnes shook her head wearily. 'No, Jim. It's probably worse for you, having kids of your own.'

Lowry looked at her. 'If you don't mind my asking, how does all – all that – square with your belief in a God who's supposed to care?'

Agnes sighed. 'Well, that's it, isn't it, the Big Question. The problem of Evil. I could go on about it for days, but given the circumstances . . .' She ran her hand through her hair. 'You see, Faith is just that – Faith. Knowing that we can't possibly know the true will of God. Holding out for Redemption just the same.'

'Believing in something you know can't possibly be true?'

Agnes smiled briefly. 'How do we know what True is?'

'Aye, well, all I know is, if I was some omniscient being up there, I'd strike these villains dead with a bolt from heaven. So, why doesn't He, eh? And He still expects me to believe in Him? I'd rather trust my own judgement, thank you.' He sighed. 'And what makes me mad is, even if we catch our bloody murderer, the bastards who filmed that stuff, who organized those kids, those men – they'll get away with it.'

'No, they won't. They've created a Hell and they're already living in it.'

'Wishful thinking, Agnes. Unless Hell is driving fast cars, living like kings, drinking champagne in countries where people are dying of thirst. Think about it, Sister. The world's a shitty place.' Lowry's voice was bitter, and he stared out unseeingly through the windscreen. He shook his head, started the engine and they headed back to Chidding Ford. Agnes leaned back in her seat, her arms folded tightly across her chest, her eyes shut. She would think about all this later. But tomorrow – she had her plan. Tomorrow was going to be a busy day.

The next morning Lowry was at his desk early, unshaven and exhausted. A young constable, PC Meredith, brought him coffee. 'Where's Agnes?' Lowry barked. 'It's time we got Mellersh, before he moves on.'

'I don't know, sir, no one's seen her.'

'Have you tried phoning her where she's staying?'

'No, sir.'

'There's the phone, Constable.'

Agnes spoke softly to Carlo as she gently let down the ramp of the horsebox. She heard him snickering nervously, but when he saw the daylight and Agnes standing there, he stood calmly. She went in, murmuring to him, and gave him a carrot.

'You enjoy it, *mon vieux*. It might be your last decent snack for some time.'

She gazed around her at the Forest. The trees were still dripping from the overnight rainfall, but now their leaves were flecked with light as the morning sun broke through the branches. Everything seemed fresh and new and green, and Agnes felt a surge of energy which was echoed by her horse, who whinnied and nuzzled her.

'Let's get you tacked up, then,' she said to him.

'Riding?' Lowry shouted.

'That's what her friend at the house said.'

'What did she say?'

'She said that Agnes left early this morning to go over to her friend Arnie's, and she was probably going riding. And did I know that polite people didn't make phone calls before ten o'clock, except to tradesmen?'

'And where's this Arnie, then?'

'Er – I'll find out, shall I, sir?'

The horsebox was tucked away on a verge by the side of the road. Agnes checked that it was locked, before mounting Carlo and heading off at a steady trot along a bridleway. She took the reins into her left hand and felt with the right in her inside jacket pocket, where Julius's pistol nestled. The feeling this gave her was interpreted by Carlo as a call to arms, and he broke into a fast canter.

'A cavalry of one, eh, my boy?' Agnes murmured to him, restraining him gently, steadying his pace. 'But the best warriors go into battle at a trot.'

'There you are, Driscoll. What the hell's going on? It's nearly ten, Agnes has gone horse riding, and I've got some fool of a cadet constable trying to track her down.'

'But she said she'd tell you, sir.'

Lowry scowled at him. 'Tell me what?'

'About going to the Forest. I don't understand, I thought you'd asked her—'

'Take a seat, Driscoll. Let's start at the beginning, shall we?'

Agnes paused at the top of a gentle hill, and looked down into the next valley. Carlo nibbled idly at a ferocious-looking tree. She'd already passed the abandoned Vauxhall on the way up, and Carlo had picked his way carefully along the track beyond it. Now she could see the patchy slate roof and tumbledown walls of a tiny cottage, with its broken windows and leaning chimney. There was no smoke coming from it, but Driscoll's directions had been very clear. This was Mellersh's lair. Poor Driscoll, she thought, with a brief flicker of remorse. She gathered up the reins, and Carlo, still munching on a mouthful of branches, set off quietly down the hill.

'Were you born with no brain, or was it removed by surgery, Driscoll? So she tells you this claptrap about needing directions to Mellersh. Didn't it strike you as odd, Driscoll, that I wasn't asking you myself?'

'Not at the time, sir.'

'And now Meredith tells me that this Littlejohn fellow has

quite coolly let her go off in his horsebox, worth ten grand, apparently, with one of his horses, to confront a murderer in the Forest of Dean. Do you know, these upper classes only have one brain cell each? It's passed on from generation to generation with the family silver.'

'Hadn't we better go after her, sir?'

'What a brilliant idea, Driscoll. I hadn't thought of that.' Lowry stood up and reached for his coat. 'I am surrounded by madmen and fools, Driscoll. And that bloody nun is the maddest of all.'

'Yea, though I walk through the valley of the shadow of death . . .' The rhythm of the psalm echoed in Agnes's ears, the ancient words hanging in the air like the mist which clung damply to her face as she approached the cottage. She tethered Carlo outside and knocked at the crooked, peeling door. When at last it was opened, Agnes was surprised at Mellersh's appearance. He leaned unsteadily against the rotten doorpost, unwashed, his clothes crumpled, his eyes ringed with dark shadows. He seemed thinner. He peered at her from behind his glasses for a long time. She waited, and at last he said, 'Sister Agnes, isn't it? I must say it wasn't you I was expecting. Have you got anything to eat?'

Agnes released Carlo into the small field behind the cottage, and unpacked the saddle bags. Once inside the cottage she found some old tin plates and set out bread, cheese and tomatoes and a carton of milk. There were three old armchairs in the tiny front room of the cottage, and Mellersh settled down in one, eating hungrily. Agnes sat opposite him, and drank a little milk. She looked around her. A single cracked window pane let a dingy light into the room. Peeling wallpaper covered the walls; there was a slate floor, a fireplace filled with soot and ashes, and no electric light. Agnes noticed melted candle ends precariously balanced along the heavy slate mantelpiece.

'So, David, why are you here?' she began, conversationally.

He smiled craftily. 'You won't catch me that easily.'

'Did you return the thing they were after?'

Mellersh shifted uneasily in his chair and looked away. When he looked back at Agnes his eyes seemed hollow. 'That stupid boy, he wouldn't tell me.' Agnes thought he was about to cry, but then suddenly he grinned at her and took a large bite of bread.

'Wait till I've finished my breakfast,' he said, through the crumbs.

'How did you find this place?'

'Pip knew about it. One of her – clients – brought her here once, apparently.'

'Do you know why? Or when?'

'No.' He shrugged. 'But I worked out where it was, and here I am. No one's found me yet.'

'Sue's very worried about you.'

'Poor girl. You'll tell her I'm all right, won't you?'

'Yes, of course.'

'Except, now you won't get the chance.'

Lowry strode across the car park, his raincoat flapping behind him. 'Barlow, is it?' he barked to the officer who was running to keep up with him. 'Ten minutes I waited for you lot. Ten minutes too long. You've done this negotiation stuff before, have you? Good. And your men know how to fire those things, do they? Here, you sit in the front – Driscoll knows the way, don't you, Sergeant?'

Mellersh finished eating, took a long swig of milk and then wiped his mouth carefully on a filthy handkerchief. 'So,' he said, 'why have you come?'

'You know why,' Agnes replied. 'Why did you hide away up here?'

'I'm not hiding. I've done nothing wrong.'

'Then come back to town with me.'

'You've got the cops outside.'

'No I haven't. You saw I rode here. They've probably not even missed me yet.'

Mellersh smiled icily. 'More fool you then.'

Agnes leaned back in her chair. 'This is your only chance, Mellersh.'

In answer, he laughed. Agnes took a sip of milk. 'How did you meet Pip?' she asked.

'Dear Pip. It was at some do, for local businessmen. Local radio consortium for a new licence. It never got off the ground, but they were all there, her crowd. I noticed her at once. I'd already set up on my own, but it was going badly. I needed new blood.'

'Were you a blackmailer then too?'

Mellersh smiled. 'I was running a recruitment consultancy, mostly finding salesmen. Head hunting. But I realized there was a lot of potential in it. Personal data, you might call it. Information. People tell you things when they think you might find them a job. I'd put all their details on file, on my computer. And after a few months I began to wonder. I thought about what they weren't telling me. You see, that sort of information has a value; the more they want it hidden, the more valuable it becomes.'

'And Pip understood this?'

'She was a natural. With her previous experience—'

'Ah yes. In France.'

'Precisely. Though in those days, her services were more – direct, I think. The technology came later.'

'When you say technology—'

'We offered a range of services. The dressing up was the beginning – but also people could subscribe, through computer, to Fantasy Land.'

'Which was—'

'Oh, just stories really. But tailor-made to the individual client. Pip would write them. Computers really are wonderful things. We'd started doing pictures too, but I have to say the quality was very poor. We were working on improving it.'

'Was Pip good at the technological side?'

'She loved it. She'd spend ages on my machine.'

'Doing what?'

'Talking to people, she said. She said she was on to something that would help our business enormously.'

'And you never found out what?'

Mellersh sighed. 'I have no doubt that she stumbled upon something, or someone, connected to the menaces I received, and which led, ultimately, to her death. Some information is just too hot to touch. I wish she'd told me.'

The old, haunted look had returned to his face. Agnes was aware of a broken spring in her chair digging into her back. She shifted position, and said, 'Why did you kill Jez, then?'

David got up suddenly and began to gather the dud candle ends from the mantelpiece, his long fingers scuttering nervously amongst the dirty wax.

'Was it easy?' asked Agnes.

With a sudden movement he threw the candle ends into the fireplace. 'If some stupid kid overdoes the glue, it's hardly my fault, is it?' he said, harshly. He knelt down by the fireplace and picked up an old hearth brush. Its handle was broken off leaving a rough, splintery edge, and its bristles were worn and uneven. He began to sweep the cinders into a heap.

'I bet he took ages to die,' Agnes went on. The sweeping continued, rhythmically. 'I expect you had to hold him down. In fact, it was surprising, wasn't it, how strong he was, even at the end? Those compulsive kicking movements. Even with a plastic bag over his head.'

Mellersh's voice echoed strangely from the fireplace. 'If I were you I'd stop now,' he said.

Agnes shifted in her seat again. 'And it's very ugly, isn't it,' she went on, 'a suffocated corpse. Swollen tongue, bloodshot eyes – especially when you've never killed before, eh, David?'

Mellersh stood up from the hearth and turned slowly to face her. In his hand he held a pistol, which he now raised and pointed at Agnes. 'No,' he said. 'No, I'd never killed before. But now I have. So once more isn't going to make much difference.'

'Driscoll, you're not driving your granny to the dentist. Sergeant Barlow here is a seasoned police officer – I'm sure he can cope if we go over sixty.'
    'There's laws against dangerous driving, sir.'
    'And who enforces those laws, Driscoll?'
    'Er – we do, sir.'
    'Exactly, Driscoll.'

Mellersh sat down in the chair opposite Agnes, the gun still aimed levelly at her. The spring in Agnes's chair dug sharply into her. She sat absolutely still.
    'Jez didn't know anything,' she said, trying to keep her voice level. 'Why did you kill him?'
    'He wouldn't tell me. I meant to scare him into saying where it was. I meant him to be scared, scared like I was. So that he'd say. But he didn't.'
    Agnes moved an inch to her left, and watched as the gun barrel followed her. 'You might as well give yourself up, you know,' she said.
    Mellersh laughed, and his laugh became a fit of coughing. While he coughed the aim of the gun wavered, and Agnes's hand went to her inside pocket.
    Mellersh stopped coughing and with his free hand fiddled in his pockets for the filthy handkerchief. 'When your friends arrive, they'll find you dead and me gone. I've got my passport and everything.'
    Agnes made to stand up. 'Let's go, David,' she said, but then sat down abruptly as a bullet whistled past her head and cracked through the ancient window. The glass shattered into a web-like pattern around the bullet hole, but stayed poised and intact in the frame. Mellersh sat still, the gun in his hand, his eyes cold with resolve. Agnes took a deep

breath, and wondered why all sensation seemed to have vanished from her legs.

'Let me show you something,' she said, slowly reaching into her pocket and pulling out the antique pistol. 'Don't worry, it's not loaded. It's much too complicated. If you were going to load it, first you'd have to put the powder into the barrel of the gun, like this.' She glanced at David, who was sitting absolutely still, watching with an expression of great interest, smiling like steel.

'Then you put the bullet in here,' she continued. David seemed to be lifting his pistol as if to fire it. 'And then you prime the pan with more powder, like this. It's really terribly fiddly compared to modern guns—' Mellersh stood up suddenly, smiling oddly. His aim was steady, his hand unwavering. Agnes carefully cocked her pistol, and then laid it down deliberately in her lap. Mellersh laughed, and leaned against the fireplace, still aiming straight at her.

'Nice try, Sister. But your position is flawed.'

'Oh, the gun, I know. It's only for decoration really.'

'No, not the gun. I'm sure it could kill in the right hands. Are you really a nun?'

'Oh yes. Through and through.'

'And so you observe the Ten Commandments? Religiously, one might say?'

'Oh yes. Absolutely.' Agnes smiled up at him.

'How about, "Thou shalt not kill"?' He grinned at her.

Agnes watched his finger on the trigger. The broken spring in her chair felt as if it might draw blood at any minute. She leaned hard against it in an attempt to focus her mind and steady her voice.

'Theologically that's a very interesting point, David,' she said, stroking the carved butt of Julius's pistol. 'On religious grounds alone, of course I have no intention of killing you with this. To do so would be to condemn myself to Hell.' She looked up and smiled. 'More to the point, I should have no objection to your killing me. My faith tells me that life is simply a short step on the way to ultimate glory, when we shall be in the presence of the Lord for Eternity. As a nun, I should be eager for that moment; so if you were to help me on the way, in theory I shouldn't mind at all.'

She saw Mellersh's finger tighten on the trigger. 'On the other hand,' she went on, 'murder is wrong. So, as a religious person, I should prevent it taking place. Even if it is my own.'

Agnes heard the explosion before she was aware of having fired her gun. She saw flames from the muzzle, and was then thrown back in her chair by a violent jolt through her shoulder. In the cloud of smoke from the gun she could see nothing, although Mellersh seemed to be no longer in his place.

It was suddenly quiet. In the silence, the window pane trembled, and then shed its delicate web of glass. One by one the fragments shattered against the slate floor with a crystalline tinkle.

Lowry and his team were almost at the cottage when he heard two gunshots. They all stopped still and then dropped suddenly to the ground. Barlow and his two constables drew their Smith and Wessons. Lowry could hear glass breaking, then silence. Some moments later, the cottage door opened and Agnes emerged. Her face was blackened and she walked unsteadily. Lowry stood up, ignoring Barlow's hissed warning, and went towards her. Her eyes were glassy, and she came up to him and grasped his hand with a strange urgency. It was only then that he noticed the large dark stain spreading across her shoulder.

'Mellersh is wounded in there. Would've killed me. Phone Arnie, he can pick up the horsebox, on the Coleford Road. Carlo's behind the cottage.' Agnes spoke slowly, her stare unblinking, her gaze fixed on some point beyond Lowry's shoulder. 'Here's the tape,' she added, handing him a small cassette recorder, and then she fell forwards. Lowry caught her as she lost consciousness altogether.

'Driscoll,' he shouted, 'radio for an ambulance. Two

wounded, gunshots. And keep an eye on her.' He laid Agnes gently on the ground and covered her with his coat, then gestured to Barlow. 'Come on, let's go inside.'

# Chapter Seventeen

Agnes opened her eyes reluctantly. The first thing she saw was a ripe Camembert. Beyond that there seemed to be a starched, grey-haired nurse, making her feelings plainly known in a sharp voice.

'—bringing a mouldy old thing like that in here. Apart from the fact it's terribly unhygienic, there's the other patients to consider, Mrs – er—'

'Paneotou,' came the crisp reply. Agnes smiled and slowly turned her head.

'With all due respect, nurse, I don't think you should underestimate the healing qualities of mouldy old French cheese. I promise to wrap it in sterile polythene and keep it in my locker.'

In answer the nurse studied her watch for a long moment, then looked hard at Athena. 'Visiting time ends in twenty minutes,' she said, over her crisp white shoulder.

'My God, Agnes,' gasped Athena when she'd gone, settling herself down on the bed, 'you'd be better off in our village hospital in Greece. I mean, there it's a fifty-fifty chance whether you live or die, but at least while you're waiting to find out you can eat the half-sheep that your family brings in for you. Have a grape. You know, they wouldn't even let me in to start with? I came straight down as soon as I heard, but they said you'd been operated on and were asleep.'

'So was that about three days ago?'

'That was yesterday, poppet. Today's Thursday. I'll have to spring you from here if you're to keep your wits about you. So, tell me the whole story.'

The nurse reappeared with a large bunch of chrysanthemums in a vase. 'These just arrived. Ten minutes, ladies.' She strode away.

'Julius,' said Agnes, reading the card.

'I bet he's not too pleased with you.'

'Oh, I'm surrounded by men being cross with me. I'm surprised Lowry hasn't got me under police guard.' She mimicked his voice. 'I'd be acting within the law to arrest you for unlawful possession of a firearm and wounding with intent, Sister.' She laughed, and then lay back on her pillows. Athena noticed the blue rings round her eyes, the tension around her mouth.

'And anyway,' Agnes went on, smiling briefly, 'I should be cross with Julius, sending chrysanthemums when he should know that we French only send them to funerals.'

Athena nibbled at another bunch of grapes. 'Why did you do it, Agnes? The police were about to arrest him anyway.'

'It seemed quicker, that's all.' She sighed. 'You're right though. In retrospect it just seems clumsy. I should have left it to Lowry.'

Athena helped herself to more grapes. 'But you felt responsible. For Jez, I mean.'

Agnes looked up and met her gaze. 'Yes. Yes I did. An eye for an eye, or something.' She sighed wearily. 'And anyway, the police would have arrived with great pomp and circumstance and Mellersh would have run off, probably. So at least this way, with me and Carlo creeping up on him, we got him. And I taped my conversation with him, so it's all sewn up.'

'So why did he kill Pip, then?'

'Pip? Oh, no, he didn't kill her. Only Jez. He was being threatened by the same people who were after Pip, I think, because she'd got this – this thing they wanted. After her death they still hadn't got it, so they thought he had it. But he had no idea what they were after. All he knew was that she'd mentioned it to Jez. Jez's death came about out of Mellersh's despair. Great, isn't it. We're no further on at all.'

'But he must know the murderer, then?'

'Not necessarily. Pip's – clients – were often quite safe from Mellersh, while they paid up, anyway.'

'What will you do now?' asked Athena. 'I mean, from your hospital bed, there's not a lot you can do, is there?'

'Thanks for volunteering, Athena.'

She slept again, and was woken by a cool hand against her cheek. She opened her eyes.

'Julius.'

His hand was quickly withdrawn.

'Thanks for the funeral flowers.'

Julius smiled. 'I only remembered later. All those village burials at Savigny. Sorry. How's the shoulder?'

'Oh, not so bad. A clean wound, the surgeon said.'

'That's more than can be said for Mellersh, apparently. I assume you intended to hit him in the leg?'

'You should be pleased I managed it at all. Your pistol's hardly accurate, even if it is a work of art.'

'Another centimetre and you'd have killed him.'

'I don't understand—'

'The upper thigh is hardly a safe area, Agnes. I'd have gone for the shin, myself. You just missed an artery. The poor fellow might have bled to death.'

A tiny red spot appeared on each of Agnes's pale cheeks. 'Bloody hell, Julius, you're lucky I'm alive. If I hadn't managed to put him off balance by my shot, he'd have killed me. As it was I just got a glancing blow. Hasn't it occurred to you I might not have been here at all? Next time you can bloody well find me a more practical weapon.'

Julius sat still. His hand went to the crucifix at his neck. When he next looked at Agnes his face was grave. 'Do you think I don't – when I heard – can you imagine how I felt—?'

They looked at each other. Agnes stretched out her hand

and laid it over his for a moment. When she withdrew it, Julius stood up. 'Anyway,' he said, 'there won't be a next time. Your friend Lowry's already threatened to arrest me for having given you the damn thing in the first place. If he catches me dealing in any more weaponry I'll be for it. I'm going now. I'm staying with the Brothers out by Chalford, so I can pop back in the morning.'

'Did you find out anything suspicious from the Catholic charities?'

Julius turned, taking in the weary face, the drawn expression. He sighed. 'Well, yes, actually, but it can wait.'

'Wait? Don't be ridiculous, Julius. There's a killer at large.'

Julius sat on the bed and helped himself to some of Athena's grapes. 'I went through the lists of members of all the Catholic bodies I could find, all the charitable organizations and committees and things. There's a few possibles. I looked at the amount they'd donated – I assume we're looking for wealth? – and their business, nationality, where they live. Here are the photocopies – the strongest candidate is this one, from the Ignatius Mission, who has an address in Gloucestershire, one in London and one in Paris. Serge Roche. He's a Swiss-French businessman and he's in import-export, it says. He has connections in Brazil – Rio. They're listed too.' He placed some sheets of paper on her locker. Agnes immediately picked them up and began to scan them.

'Julius,' she said, the colour returning to her face, 'you're a hero.'

'Athena, is that you?'

'Agnes, where are you?'

'Where do you think? I had to wave your Camembert at the ward sister before she'd let me have this phone. I've got a task for you. A man called Serge Roche. He lives just outside Cirencester. Can you track him down? Invisibly, mind you, he might be dangerous. I'll give you his address.'

'But how – what—?'

222

'Use your initiative. I need to know as much about him as possible.'

'How do I get to find that out, then?'

'I'm sure you have your ways, Athena.'

The next morning Lowry appeared. 'How's it going, Agnes?'

'Well, it's good practice for prison, if you ever do arrest me. Woken at dawn with luke-warm tea that's so thick you have to chip it out of the cup, given a tiny so-called breakfast, and then left to wallow in boredom for hours. How's Mellersh?'

'Still in hospital, we're keeping watch.' Lowry shook his head. 'Why you couldn't have left it to us – my Superintendent's had words with me, you know. "I need some explanation about the decisions you've taken, Jim," he said. Oh, don't you worry, Super, I took no decisions, it's all being handled by a crazy nun—'

'We've been through all this, Jim. It seemed easier at the time. At least you've got him, and the tape. Have you charged him?'

'Yes, with the boy's murder and the attempt on you. Though he can plead self-defence to that, which complicates things. He'll be remanded in custody when he's well enough. If it wasn't for you being trigger-happy—'

'If it wasn't for me being trigger-happy I'd be dead. How's Carlo?'

'Who?'

'My horse?'

'Oh, him. Your friend picked him up as you asked. I expect he'll be suing you for damages, frightening his horse, risking his vehicle . . .'

'The horse enjoyed it.'

'Oh, that's all right then. No doubt he's selling his story to *Horse and Hound* even as we speak.'

'Is this man bothering you, Agnes?' Agnes smiled at the voice and eased her head round to greet Julius.

'Inspector Lowry, this is Father Julius. Though, of course,

you've already met. Jim's just been telling me what a headstrong fool I am.'

'You'll never change her, Inspector. God knows I've been trying to for years.'

'You haven't tried at all, Julius. You love me just as I am, and so does Jim really, underneath his bluff Yorkshire ways.'

'The wife sent you this.'

Lowry unwrapped a large chunk of rich fruit cake. 'In the part of bluff Yorkshire I come from, we eat it with cheese.'

'*C'est merveilleux.* I just happen to have a ripe Camembert in my locker.'

'When I said cheese, I meant cheese, Sister.'

On Saturday morning a huge bunch of expensive orchids arrived. The card said, 'You'll never keep away from danger. Hugo.'

Agnes stopped a hurrying nurse. 'Excuse me. Is there a ward which could do with some flowers? I – er, don't want these, thank you.' The nurse took them gratefully and hurried on.

Agnes lay back on her pillows, aware of the constant dull ache of her shoulder. Two more days. Two more days of repetitive routine, of ghastly English food, of bright lights and muted voices. Of shaky legs from too long in bed. The nurse reappeared.

'There's a phone call for you from the police. Can you walk over to the desk? I'll help you.'

It was Lowry. 'There was an attempted raid on Jeff's company last night. Foiled by his security people – he'd employed more of them, thank God. Two hooded men, armed, tried to break in, alarms went off, they ran off, pursued but started shooting, got away. No one was hurt. We traced the car, it was stolen. Just thought you ought to know.'

Back in bed, Agnes thought about the person she was hunting. Whoever he was, he was still out there. A shadowy figure with evil on his mind. She wondered whether he would ever become real to her – and if so, how? She closed her eyes wearily, and once again saw Mellersh standing over her, his face hard as iron, his eyes narrowed with fear. She wondered what Mellersh saw when he closed his eyes.

The weekend passed in sleeping, and waiting. Often when she dozed she dreamed of a man's face which appeared to her mistily, hidden behind a web of glass, or was it a cloud of smoke? There would be loud explosions, and in the chaos she'd be trying to recognize him. Just as she woke up, she would see him clearly. It was always Hugo.

After tea on Sunday, Athena arrived, wafting in on a cloud of perfume. To Agnes she seemed to be a bright splash of colour in the pale and sterile world, a blast of musical notes against the dull hum of boredom. She sat up on her pillows and grinned.

'I'm so glad to see you.'

'You'll be even gladder when you hear my news. I visited the Roche house this morning. I waited till now, because of my plan. I was a Jehovah's Witness, you see – what's so funny? You'd have been quite taken in. I'd have made a Protestant even of you.'

'God forbid,' giggled Agnes.

'It's a lovely house, one of those Georgian stone ones up on the hill.'

'And did you see him?'

Athena looked crestfallen. 'Ah, well, that's the bad news. I spoke to his housekeeper, who said Monsieur Roche had gone to Paris yesterday.'

'Was he still there on Friday night?'

'Yes. He left Saturday afternoon, she said.'

'When is he due back?'

'Not for several weeks, she said. He's visiting family in Geneva, and then doing business in Rio and Paris.' Athena deposited a few coins on Agnes's locker.

'What's that?'

'My profit. She bought my copy of the *Watchtower*. I'm

thinking of taking it up for a living.'

'I said, are you glad to be leaving Gloucestershire?' Julius shouted above the noise of the engine.

'Does this thing ever go above fifty?'

'It's perfectly serviceable. Well, are you?'

Agnes gazed out of the window. 'You want me to say yes, don't you.'

The engine roared suddenly, and Agnes noticed the speedometer creeping up.

'I want you to say whatever you think.'

Agnes turned to look at him. 'I like London, yes.'

There was a little pause. Julius's old Morris Traveller settled back to its comfortable fifty. Julius said, 'But?'

Agnes sighed. 'Oh, I don't know. Where do I belong? I seem to have cut myself loose – from the Order, from you. I owe you both more than that.' She opened the glove compartment, then shut it again. 'I wish – I mean – I always disappoint you.'

Julius shook his head. 'No, not me.' He smiled. 'I can't think why you need to make me your conscience when you've got such an active one of your own.' He changed gear. 'Anyway, you're glad to be going back to London to work on this murder of yours, aren't you.'

She looked at his profile which remained calm, his eyes firmly on the road. 'Yes.'

'Well, that's something then, isn't it.'

She turned away. Julius stole a glance at her before accelerating to sixty-five to overtake a large tractor.

'You've been cleaning in here, haven't you.'

Agnes surveyed her room, which seemed bright and welcoming in the afternoon sun.

'You're too good for me, Julius,' she said, and squeezed his hand. 'Now what I really need is—'

'A cup of tea?'

'No – all the London volumes of the Yellow Pages.'

She spent the afternoon with the phone by her bed, propped up on pillows, phoning every London number under the heading 'Screen Printers', asking for Angie. By teatime she had worked through all the names in the London South and East directory, and the London Central, and was just starting on London North. So far she had spoken to two Angies, one of whom was the Managing Director of Noisy Prints Ltd, with a manner to match; the other, a marketing manager, who, in her beautiful voice, was enthusiastically unable to help.

Agnes closed the book and began to think that there must be a better way of doing this. She picked up the phone and dialled the Department of Employment.

'I wonder if you could help me. Do you publish lists of all the people accepted on to the Enterprise Allowance scheme? Yes, I'll hold. Thank you.'

At length, after talking to two different departments, she spoke to the Press Office, who promised to send her a list in the post.

The next morning, to her amazement, she received a copy of an out-of-date press release which included a comprehensive list of new small businesses in London funded by the scheme. And there, amongst the fashion designers, photographers and independent video workshops, she found 'Smokescreen: silk-screen printing, badges and T-shirts; grant applied for by Angie Morton'.

Julius passed her on the stairs. 'Where do you think you're going?'

'Hackney. A silk-screen co-op. I'll be back this afternoon.'

'Agnes, you can hardly walk.'

'I'll take a cab then.'

Furnival House was a Victorian warehouse that had been completely renovated. Spaces that had once been occupied by carved wooden banisters were now filled with shiny chrome tubing. Where there had been heavy brass door handles, there were now plastic chunks of red, yellow and blue like children's bricks.

'Smokescreen' was on the second floor, its door ajar. The front office was filled with stacks of cardboard boxes and piles of T-shirts in plastic bags. The walls were covered with posters advertising rock bands. Two young women sat smoking on a foam rubber sofa, deep in conversation.

'Steve never, right. He never did it.'

'Gail says he did. Dunno who to believe.'

Agnes coughed. 'Er – is Angie here?'

The two women looked up. 'Out the back,' they said, in unison, and carried on talking.

'Out the back' was a large workshop area in which stood two presses. The concrete floor was splashed with layered, multi-coloured ink spills. A tall young woman was bent over one machine, talking to a spiky youth. She was thin, in black leggings and black suede platform ankle boots, with a bleached cropped bob.

'Angie?' said Agnes.

The woman looked up. 'Yeah?'

'I'm from Chidding Ford. From the kids there. Jez and everyone?'

The girl looked blank, then slowly her face lit up. 'Wow. Amazing. Who are you? Is it true that Fip got done in by her old man? Come and talk.'

Finding the two girls in the front office, Angie loaded them up with bags of T-shirts to distribute and shooed them out of the door. Then she busied herself making instant coffee while chatting happily to Agnes.

'Yeah, it's going really well. Had some problems at the beginning, trusted the wrong sorts of people. Lost a lot of stuff that way. God, I was ready to kill someone.' She grinned, handing Agnes a mug and then sitting down cross-legged on the floor. 'What happened to your shoulder?'

'Oh, it's a long story. So, when did you leave the Bunker?'

'Must have been just after Christmas. Late January, I think.'

'And did Sinead come with you?'

'Sinead? No, why?'

'Lisa and Latoya said she did.'

'Nah. She was going to, but she changed her mind. Said she'd stay with Fip, they had some plan. Shame, but there you are.'

'Do you know where she is now?'

'Thought she was still there. Though, her, she could be anywhere. Dope-head.'

'Was she religious?'

'Yeah, sort of. So was I, then. I know she took Fip to some group. But Sinead, even if she did find Jesus, she'd bloody lose Him again the next day.' Angie laughed. 'I miss her really. We had good times.'

'Did she have a family?'

'Her mum lived in Bath, I think. But she hated her. She had a sister in France. She kept going on about how she'd go there one day, the weather was better.'

'Do you know where in France?'

'No.' Angie gulped her coffee. 'Why do you need to know?'

'You see, Fip wasn't killed by her husband. Someone else did it. I'm trying to find out who.'

'Oh. But Sinead—'

'What was Sinead's other name?'

'Goodwin. But I don't see what she's got to do with—'

'It's just that I think she knows something that no one else knows. She may not know how important it is either. That's why I've got to find her. She might even be in danger.'

Angie grinned. 'She always bloody was. Mostly from herself.'

Agnes stood up. 'I'd better let you get on. Thanks for your help.' Angie got to her feet too and smoothed her leggings over her knees. Agnes took a deep breath. 'There's one more thing, I'm afraid. About Jez.'

'Jez?'

'Yes. He's – he died too.'

Agnes explained, briefly, the whole tale. She put her hand on Angie's arm, and they walked together in silence to the landing.

'I'm sorry I had to bring you bad news.'

Angie stood, her eyes fixed on her beige carpet tiles. 'Them bastards,' she said. 'Hope you bleedin' find whoever bloody did it.'

By the bus stop, Agnes bought a copy of the evening paper. She sat on the bus and idly turned to the Missing Persons List. Four faces stared out at her from the page, four fuzzy black and white prints of people who'd ceased to be where they were expected to be. A man in his forties with learning difficulties; a teenage boy; a young mum who walked out one morning to the shops and never came back, leaving her husband and two small children; and a teenage girl called Lucy, from Hastings. 'Your mum and brothers miss you,' it said underneath Lucy's picture. 'Please get in touch. Lucy has long red hair and was last seen wearing a black woollen jacket and jeans, and carrying a red duffle bag.'

Agnes stared at the photo, the bright eyes and youthful smile, taken in happier times before whatever caused Lucy to leave had happened, no doubt. Or perhaps this face had just become adept at hiding the pain. It was a sweet, pretty face, framed by dark waves of hair. Agnes stared at it again. She remembered Latoya's message from Jez. 'He wanted you to know what Sinead looked like.' Of course, she thought. Of course.

That evening she stood outside a shiny green front door in a Georgian terrace in Belgravia. The bell she pressed had the name Roche underneath. She waited. Eventually the door was opened by a Filipino maid. She shook her head. No, there was no one by the name of Roche there. The people she worked for had only just moved in. Last week, April 5th. No, there was no forwarding address.

The next morning she phoned Lowry.

'It's Agnes here. It's urgent.'

'How's the war wound?'

'Never mind the war wound. I need your help. How do I get permission to look through Foreign Office records?'

Lowry sighed heavily. 'So the track leads to spying activities in Iraq, does it? Or the debris of the Cold War? Do you need to ask MI6 who's still active in the Soviet bloc, is that it?'

'I need to know who bought a temporary passport for France early this year.'

'Oh, easy-peasy. That's Home Office. I'll get back to you.'

'Hurry, please. It's Easter this weekend.'

'I thought your sort liked Easter. Spiritual renewal and all that.'

'And God knows I'm in need of it too. It's just, I'm getting fed up with the trail going cold whenever I start to follow it.'

Two minutes later:

'Agnes, you're supposed to be convalescing. I promised your nurse—'

'Does she phone to check up on you?'

'No, but—'

'I'm so nearly there, Julius. I'll be at the Passport Office all day.'

'Don't forget the Maundy Thursday service is at seven tonight.'

'As if I would.'

She was shown into a dingy little room with grudging ill will by a large female clerical officer. The woman gestured with her head to an assortment of dusty box files piled on a table. There was one chair.

'There,' she said.

'Thank you,' said Agnes.

Lowry had arranged for her to look through all applications for temporary passports from January to March of that year. She opened the first file, and saw lists of names, dates, place names, all carefully inscribed in black biro. Agnes took a deep breath and began to scan the lists. One name was all she needed. One name, to confirm what she already knew.

She looked up with a start as the door opened and the officer reappeared. Names swam before her eyes in scratchy black biro. She had been there three hours and was still only on January 21st.

'Lunch,' said the woman in a surly manner.

'No, really, I'm fine—'

'We stop for lunch. You can't be here unsupervised. One hour.'

At ten to four she opened the first file for February. At twenty to five, and dreading the jangling keys of her warder again, she noticed the name Goodwin.

Sinead Goodwin. 7 February. Purchased a temporary passport at Chidding Ford Central Post Office.

Four days before Pip's murder.

That night, Agnes lay on her bed leafing through Philippa's diaries. Of course, she thought. Of course. She took a pencil and circled the words, 'I'm frightened of him. I think he wants to kill me,' then closed the diary. She held it in her hand, thinking how strange it was that she'd had the evidence here in her possession all this time; all this time spent dealing with blackmail and computer discs and attempted murders. And real murders.

She opened the drawer of her shabby junk-shop desk and put the diaries into it, then took out a small envelope which contained the lock of Philippa's hair she'd cut on impulse at the mortuary. She scribbled a note to Athena, put both note and hair into an envelope which she addressed to Sparkbrook Terrace, and then went to bed.

The Tuesday after Easter was bright and sunny, and the air was filled with birdsong and with the grumbles of people on their way to work after the cold and drizzly Easter weekend. Julius unlocked the side door of the church, anticipating the backlog of paperwork awaiting him. As he opened the door he heard the phone start to ring. He hurried to answer it.

'Hello, Father Julius speaking – ah, Inspector Lowry, what a pleasant surprise. You're lucky to find me at my desk.'

'Is she there?' came the gruff voice.

'Might you be meaning Agnes, Inspector?'

'Who else?'

'I'm afraid Sister Agnes has gone to Paris.'

'Paris?'

'Yes. She left Saturday morning.'

'I suppose she thinks she'll find our murderer there, then?'

'Oh, I rather assumed she was making an Easter pilgrimage to Notre Dame. It was certainly a miracle that she found a flight.'

'It was nice of her to tell me. While I'm here, can I just check the whereabouts of your pistol, Father?'

'In my safe, Inspector. Where it belongs. With its powder and bullets separate, of course.'

'Well, that's something anyway. No doubt I'll read all about her daring capture of a multi-national porn-dealer and killer in the newspapers in due course.'

'I'm sure she'll contact you soon.'

'Oh, don't worry about me, Father. It makes a nice change to get back to parking offences and mislaid canaries.'

# Chapter Eighteen

Hugo was bewildered. It was surprising that Agnes should phone him – even more surprising that it should be from Paris. It was odd that she sounded so friendly. It was even odder that she should ask him to host a party for her. In his house. Inviting people, some of whom he'd never even heard of. Who were these girls, Lisa and Latoya, for God's sake? But he'd said yes. Life was dull, he had to admit it. Anything to liven it up a bit.

He sat at his big heavy oak desk. His face was reflected, tiny and distorted, in the polished brass desk lamp. He made a face at it and wondered what had changed. Where had all the women gone? There had been a time when he'd had no shortage at all, all beautiful in their different ways, all so willing to be his lover that he'd had to resort to devious means to keep them all secret from each other.

He thought about that girl – last week, wasn't it? – at that cocktail do over at the lockkeeper's cottage. A lovely thing, she'd been, wearing a sheer black mini dress and nothing else, that was clear – and she seemed keen, that was clear too, it wasn't that he'd lost the knack – but halfway through chatting her up he felt bored, a universal, cosmic boredom which ate right through him; and some moments later, when she was in the middle of telling him about the time she went backstage and met Mick Hucknall, he made his excuses and went for another drink.

He smiled grimly at his gargoyle reflection. He couldn't even find one woman now; and yet he felt he'd come to a point in his life where one would be enough. The irony was not lost on the ugly little face in front of him, which jeered from the shiny yellow metal.

And now here was Agnes insisting he host a party. He wondered why on earth he'd agreed. Next Saturday, she'd said. That gave him six days to order the food, send Colin out to find some cheap booze. He was damned if he was opening up his cellar for Agnes's motley collection of friends and acquaintances.

Six days later, at ten in the morning, his doorbell rang. He answered it himself.

'Isn't this fun, darling.' Athena stood on Hugo's doorstep clutching a large bunch of white roses. 'You know, she's not even due back from France until lunchtime today, it's all so cloak and dagger, isn't it? Don't look so alarmed, sweetie, they're not for you. She's instructed me to come and help, and I thought these would look nice on the table. I suppose you are doing food for us all this evening?'

'Aye, well, I don't know. She said party. And to me party means wives. Or husbands, where appropriate.'

'Don't worry, dear. Not that I've ever met her, but I'm sure she's got it all worked out.'

'All the same, I'd rather have you on my arm this evening than Driscoll.'

'I'm sure Sergeant Driscoll will look very decorative, James. Anyway, I'd already promised to go bowling with the girls. That tie's not quite right with that shirt, dear.'

Julius took one hand carefully from the steering wheel and checked his watch. Six o'clock for drinks, she'd said in her postcard. Sometimes, he thought, Agnes really overstepped the mark. To have to accept a drink from that man, in that house. The very place where he'd – really, she was asking a lot of him. Julius sighed. But then, Agnes always did. And each time he delivered it. Something about this thought irritated him, but he pushed it to the back of his mind.

The last rays of the spring day shone into the lounge, glancing off shiny folds of brocade. Hugo closed the french windows and drew the curtains.

'Sweetie, surely it would be nicer to leave them open?'

Hugo opened his mouth to speak, and at that moment the doorbell rang.

'I'll go,' beamed Athena, and swirled out of the door in her new cream chiffon number. A tiresome woman, thought Hugo, opening the curtains again. 'I just have a feeling about this evening, that's all,' she'd said, making a great performance of getting changed in the bathroom. 'A sense of occasion. I love dressing up, don't you?'

She answered the door to Lowry and Driscoll.

'Mrs Paneotou,' nodded Lowry.

'I think you can call me Athena, now, don't you? And the charming Sergeant Driscoll. Do come in gentlemen. Agnes isn't here yet.'

'Typical,' muttered Lowry under his breath, handing his coat rather awkwardly to Colin who had appeared from the kitchen.

'Do go through, Hugo'll fix you a drink. Oh, look, here comes Arnie, with – er—'

'Hello Athena. This is Lisa, this is Latoya. I gave them a lift. Agnes's instructions.'

'Don't tell me, a phone call from Paris. She is a bossy old ratbag at times, isn't she, darling,' beamed Athena, and the two girls exchanged glances and giggled.

Half an hour later, Colin showed Julius into the lounge. The first thing that struck Julius was the sense that everyone was in suspense, arranged somewhat artificially, their drinks in their hands, as if waiting for their photo to be taken. Julius managed to take a glass of whisky from Hugo without even looking at him, and then joined Lowry who sat alone on the smaller of the two sofas in the room. Opposite them

Driscoll sat with Lisa and Latoya either side of him. Arnie was leaning against the mantelpiece talking to Athena. Hugo lurked awkwardly by the drinks trolley.

'I was hoping to arrive after her,' Julius said to Lowry.

'You'd have thwarted her sense of drama,' said Lowry.

'That was the idea.'

Lowry looked at Julius, and smiled with one side of his face. 'Yes. I know the feeling. Does she treat all of life like a parlour game?'

'Well, that's just it—' Julius began, but was interrupted by Agnes herself, breezing in through the door, looking fresh and cheerful in a crisp white cotton blouse and black silk jacket and trousers. Hugo, looking at her, briefly recalled the girl in the sheer mini dress, and the thought occurred to him that young women were oddly insubstantial these days, unsexy even. He tried to catch Agnes's eye, but she seemed not to notice him.

'How nice of you all to come,' she said, beaming around the room. 'Julius, dear,' she said, bending to kiss his cheek. He blushed and she turned to Lowry. 'Jim, I've missed you, really I have. Athena—'

'The food's all set up, darling,' Athena said. 'Shall we serve it now? It's a cold buffet, we can eat off our knees in here.'

When they returned, with plates piled high with ham, smoked trout, salad and warm bread rolls, Colin had set up a large colour television and video machine, and Agnes had arranged the chairs around it.

'I went to Paris, you see,' Agnes was saying as they all found a place, 'and I made a home movie of my holidays. I thought perhaps you'd like to see it.'

'Bloody parlour games,' murmured Lowry, and Julius grinned at him.

Agnes pressed the Play button and the film began.

The video was of a rather amateur quality and showed a room with two chairs, and behind them a balcony. Into this room walked Sister Agnes, and behind her a thin young woman with short brown hair. They both sat down. The sound was scratchy but audible, and everyone heard the young woman laugh and say, as if in the middle of a conversation, 'Well, at least we have Hugo in common, you and me.'

'Oh, I think we're more alike than that,' Agnes on the screen replied. The brown-haired young woman looked quizzically at Agnes. 'How about a taste for running away?' Agnes went on. 'And dressing up. We're both rather good at hiding inside our clothes when we want to.'

Julius glanced across at Hugo, and saw he was ashen white. His hands were gripped against the arms of his chair. Julius saw Lowry flick a glance at Hugo too.

On the screen, Agnes was asking, 'So did you mean Hugo to get put away for your murder?'

The girl looked at the floor and fiddled with her sandals, then looked up again.

'That's how it started, yes. I set up the silly plot with Athena and the money so that I could provoke a row. And it worked. You know what he's like. He hits me for any old excuse. I just made sure he went further than usual. And then I made sure that the old busybody from the village saw the bruises on my neck, asked her the time or something.'

'And then you went to meet Sinead. And nicked a car?'

'Yes.'

'Not for the first time?'

Philippa shrugged.

'And Sinead hid in the back?'

'Yes.'

'And that's when you combed out her hair, in the car? To make it look like yours?'

'Yeah. It was a laugh. She dressed in my clothes, I dressed as a bloke. When we got to the house I dressed as Hugo.'

'And she dressed as—'

The young woman looked brazenly, mockingly, at Agnes.
'She looked a treat, didn't she. When I saw her, I thought,
she could earn a fortune looking like that.'

Agnes said quietly, 'And the fingerprints?'

'Well, when me and Sinead nicked the car, I was wearing gloves at first. Then I realized that they'd get my prints
from the house so it didn't matter. When we got to the
house, I made her touch everything to mix her prints with
mine.'

'Even your diaries?'

Philippa grinned at the memory. 'Even my diaries. I
pretended it was a game. Running through the house.
Like make-believe. We pretended that she could turn into
me, so everything she touched she could have. We were like
children.'

'So that's what she thought it was – a game?'

The girl on the screen laughed, a harsh, brutal laugh. 'It
was. A game.'

'Ending in murder.' Agnes's voice was cold. Philippa
shrugged. 'I wanted out.' There was a pause.

In the silence, everyone in the room looked across at Hugo
who was staring at the screen with glassy eyes. He suddenly
pulled himself out of his chair and strode from the room, the
door banging noisily behind him. Everyone turned their
attention back to the television. On the screen Agnes was
saying, 'Do you know that Mellersh killed Jez?'

The girl's mouth dropped open. 'M – Jez? David killed – I
don't understand. They didn't even know each other.'

'That disc you stole. Mellersh was being threatened to give
it back – as you were, I imagine.'

'Typical of David to panic. He was always an amateur.'

'So, what were you running from?'

'That disc was gold dust. That and the others. Gold dust,
all of them.'

'I don't see—'

'I contacted – someone – through the Network. We were

talking pictures, moving pictures – and big money. He said, come to France, they're living in the future there already. He said, leave no traces. Vanish. So I did.'

On the screen, Agnes blinked. And frowned. 'So – Sinead – all that—?'

'Watertight, I thought. The bondage gear was a brainwave. I found it in Hugo's things, stuffed in the bottom of his wardrobe. I was puzzled, he hated anything like that, so then I wondered why. Why he should have it. He'd threatened to kill me a few times by then – and that's when I realized he meant it. Use the gear, make it look like an accident – I dunno, something like that. And when I thought about – vanishing – faking my death, and I knew that I couldn't let Hugo get too close to the body – I thought, that's it. Disgust would overpower him, he'd just nod when asked to identify me, and by the time he saw me naked – I mean her – if the police asked him to, he'd just believe it was me – and I was right, wasn't I?'

Agnes nodded, distaste clear on her face. 'But it was a bit stupid to leave the disc behind.'

'I was sure I had them all. In the lining, you said? I can't believe it.' She shifted impatiently in her seat. 'So did they think David had stolen it? He's an idiot bastard, isn't he. And killing Jez—' She shook her head.

'Who threatened David?'

Philippa smiled. 'Now, that would be telling.'

'We'll find out,' said Agnes.

'I doubt it,' said Philippa, icily. 'You see, even I don't know. The great thing about the Network is that it's anonymous. As long as you pay up. If you don't, that's when you might meet one of them. Better not to.'

Agnes looked out of the window, and then back at Philippa. 'When you married Hugo, was that a vanishing act too?'

'You are nosy, aren't you. I met him through friends. I was running a business, doing rather well. Rather too well, it was time to go. He was in debt, a shambles. I quite fancied him too. I thought, bail him out, on condition he marries me, come back to England as Mrs Bourdillon. Easy. New life, new person.'

'This business you were running—'

'My business has always been what I'm good at. Selling people's fantasies back to them. In various forms. I learned long ago that I have a huge talent for it.'

'And it gets you into trouble?'

'Oh well, you see – fantasies can be subversive things. Dangerous too.' She smiled again, but this time with an effort. She seemed suddenly very young.

On the screen, Agnes got up and paced across the room. 'So, you two really looked alike, then, you and Sinead?'

'People said so. But they didn't realize how alike. I only saw it one day when she showed me a photo from her school. She had long hair, like mine, when she was younger. And then when I needed to – disappear – I suppose it just occurred to me. She had dreadlocks, so I got her to change those. Put in extensions instead. And then a day or two before, we did a red rinse, just a wash-in one, 'cos her hair was almost as red as mine. This is dyed,' she said, with a self-deprecating laugh, pulling at her short fringe.

'Poor Sinead,' said Agnes.

'Poor nothing. She wouldn't have lasted long. They never do.'

'She trusted you.'

'No one should trust anyone in this life.'

'She was your friend.'

Philippa looked at the floor and shrugged again, and pouted like a child.

'Just because she looked like you—' Agnes went on.

Philippa suddenly jumped up, her fists clenched at her sides, her eyes tearful. 'She looks nothing like me. Nothing at all. Not now, anyway. I should know. I saw her yesterday. She ran after me along the rue des Ecoles . . . It's not the first time—' She flopped down into her chair and stared in front of her for a long time. Then the screen went blank.

The silence hung heavily in the room. No one took their eyes from the screen. Lisa and Latoya were gripping arms. Agnes stood up.

'There's more, wait a minute.' She forwarded the tape until the screen showed the same two figures, then pressed Play again. On the screen, they heard her voice.

'But didn't you think you'd get caught?'

Philippa laughed. 'What have I done? I've done nothing illegal. That's the wonderful thing about the Network; you can never find us.'

'How about murder?'

Philippa fiddled with her sandals again. 'Oh. That.' She looked up at Agnes with suddenly flashing eyes. 'So, have you got a squad of Riot Police waiting outside?'

Agnes shook her head.

'Are you about to arrest me?'

Again, Agnes shook her head. Philippa smiled. 'Well, no doubt you've put all the procedure in motion for my arrest. But you see, this has happened before. By the time they come for me, I'll be somewhere else. Gone.' She snapped her fingers. 'Like that.' Her smile was vacant, her eyes glittered. The screen went blank again. Agnes got up and switched off the set.

Everyone assembled in the room eyed the television in silence. The door opened, and they all looked up to see Colin, who went over to Agnes and whispered something to her. She got up and left the room with him. Outside, the light had faded. The windows were dark. The curtains swayed slightly in a sudden draught. Athena got up and drew the curtains, and switched on a table lamp. A moment later, Agnes reappeared with coffee. Athena helped her serve, and the silence was broken with murmured thank yous. Lowry cleared his throat.

'This hair dye—' he said. 'How did you—'

'I sent it to Athena. She's a hairdresser – she knows about these things.'

'I tested a lock of Sinead's hair for dye,' broke in Athena. 'I found a semi-permanent colour on it. And I knew it couldn't have been Pip's because I always did her hair.'

'How did you get to video her?' asked Lowry.

'Secretly, of course,' Agnes replied. 'I bought an old junkyard wardrobe, drilled a hole in the back, set the camera up and left it running – same old techniques that she used on all those poor men.'

'But what made you think—' Lowry said again. 'I mean, why should it have been someone else, the dead girl, I mean?'

'I think,' Agnes began, 'I think I began to get a very clear picture of Philippa. And the most obvious thing about her was the one most familiar to me. She was someone who had to get away. Desperately. The clues fell into place after that. The diaries were very helpful. You see, Pip only talked about herself in the first person when she could reward herself for losing weight. She allowed herself to be "I" then. Everything else is as "she", and half the time she's describing the girl in Hugo's painting, with whom she identifies. But once she's worked out her plan, she fakes some diary entries. There's some made-up dates written into her engagement diary, and there's the last entry in the personal journal, all written in the same blue biro; and she says, "He wants to kill me" so that whoever read them would think she meant Hugo. It rang untrue when I first read them, but I couldn't work out why at first. It was the "me" instead of the "she". And you see, I know what it's like to be like that. Fragmented, not knowing who you are. On the run, really. She was just as desperate as I was; only she was much cleverer.'

There was a pause. Lowry scratched his head. 'And you tracked down her victim, then, Sinead?' he asked.

'I knew they were friends. And Jez had obviously thought about it too when he sent me a message about what Sinead looked like. But it was only when I glanced at a photo of some missing girl in the paper, and I thought about how her family saw her as an ordinary schoolgirl, and how her appearance in reality, now she had run away, was probably very different; and I looked at this pretty schoolgirl and thought that Sinead, if she looked more ordinary, would have looked like that – and I suddenly saw Philippa. And I realized. Then I just had to check out the passports, as I guessed that Pip would have taken on Sinead's identity to get away.'

Everyone in the room shifted and breathed, but then looked up with a start as the door opened noisily. Hugo stood in the doorway, a half-empty bottle of whisky in one hand. He lurched towards Agnes.

'Enjoy your charade, did you? You knew all along.'

'Hugo—' began Agnes, but her voice was weak. Hugo took another, unsteady step, the bottle raised. Suddenly Julius was there, walking into Hugo's advancing path, saying to him calmly, 'Put that down, now.'

Hugo's mocking gaze fell on Julius. 'You? Of all people? My whore of a first wife organizes this little performance, and I'm foolish enough to allow her to. I'm humiliated in front of all of you, because that fucking bitch who became my second wife thought she could stitch me up—' His voice reached shouting pitch, and he threw the bottle. At least, that was what it looked like, except that somehow Julius's arm went across Hugo's, and the bottle landed heavily in Julius's other hand. He replaced it calmly on a table. The next moment, Hugo aimed a punch at Julius, which missed, and was then grabbed by Lowry and Driscoll, one on each side. Driscoll led him, stumbling and shouting, from the room. In the calm that followed, everyone sat down again.

'I suppose that's the end of the party, then,' Lowry said.

Lisa murmured to Latoya, and they both stood up. 'We'll go now, if that's all right.'

Arnie stood up to drive them back. In the doorway, Latoya turned. 'You know, it's always people like us who get it in the end, innit. No one would've missed Sinead, would they? Just another runaway, another missin' bleedin' person, eh? And

Jez? Just another drugs death. Just like normal.' She stood there, biting her lip, suffused with anger; then she turned and left, with a dignity beyond her years.

Athena, Agnes, Lowry and Julius sat in the lounge, which now seemed empty and dishevelled. Lowry looked at Agnes.

'How did you know where to find her?'

'She used to live in Paris, that's where she met Hugo, and it turned out we had acquaintances in common. I just looked up some old friends, asked some questions . . .'

'What will you do now?' asked Arnie.

Lowry spoke. 'Extradition, I suppose. Though she'll have moved on by then.'

Agnes stood up. 'I doubt it. There's a police guard on her house. I had a word with the Gendarmerie before I made myself known to her. It's a matter of a phone call, I should think, Jim. As long as your continental colleagues are as efficient as you are.' She went across to the video, took out the tape and handed it to Lowry. 'And here's your evidence.'

Athena poured more coffee. 'So, what happened to our Mr Big, the porn merchant?'

'Serge Roche? I met him in Paris. A charming man. I'm afraid it wasn't him. Yes, he has a house in Gloucestershire, and yes, he's in import and export. He deals in glass and china. You'd like him, Athena, he has a fine collection of eighteenth-century Leeds ware. But he's nothing to do with Pip's little network.'

They drank their coffee in silence. Some minutes later Hugo came into the room, poured himself some coffee from the jug, took two large spoonfuls of sugar and sat down, the rattle of his spoon against the cup the only sound in the room. Agnes looked at the floor, Julius looked at Agnes. Athena sighed.

'Well, Hugo – what does it feel like to have a wife return from the dead?'

Hugo looked across at her wearily. 'Pretty bad. But no

worse than when she was alive.' He darted a glance across at Agnes, who looked away.

'Did you know?' Athena went on.

'That I'd married a criminal?' Hugo laughed harshly. 'Not the details, no. At the time I couldn't afford to ask. But she was bad all right. I stopped being surprised at just how bad a long time ago.'

Athena drained her cup. Julius self-consciously patted Agnes's hand. 'We should go,' he murmured to her. There was a clinking of coffee cups being put down, and then they all stood up and wandered awkwardly into the darkened hall. Hugo switched on a light.

'Well, everyone,' he said in a jaunty voice, 'thanks so much for coming to my party. We all so enjoyed it, didn't we?'

'Hugo—' said Athena, her arm on his sleeve. He brushed it off angrily. 'So nice to see you again, Inspector,' he continued. 'I do hope we meet again soon.'

'As long as you remain bound over to keep the peace, Mr Bourdillon, I doubt there's any danger of that,' said Lowry. On the drive he turned to Agnes. 'Pop into the station tomorrow before you go back to London, won't you?'

Julius was walking away down the drive. 'I parked in the road,' he said. 'Come on, Agnes, I assume you arrived by taxi.'

'I'll join you in a minute,' Agnes called to him from Hugo's porch. Julius hesitated. The light from the door threw long shadows on to the gravel, into the shadows beyond. He could see Agnes silhouetted next to Hugo. Athena joined him in the darkness.

'They'll always have to have a last word to each other, those two,' she said. 'Wherever they meet, whenever it is.'

Julius's feet crunched noisily on the gravel. 'As far as I'm concerned they had their last word a long time ago,' he said sharply.

'Things are never that simple,' Athena replied.

Julius turned. He could see the two tiny figures in the

lighted porch. They seemed to be standing very close, but it was difficult to tell from so far away. 'Don't torture yourself,' Athena said quietly.

'As you say, things are never that simple,' Julius replied. A few moments later they heard Agnes's steps on the drive, and she joined them at the gates.

'Fond goodbyes?' teased Athena.

'Hardly,' said Agnes shortly. But Athena saw how her eyes shone bright in the darkness.

'How were the Brothers at Chalford?' asked Agnes the next morning as they set off back to London in Julius's car.

'Devout. How was Athena?'

'Whatever the opposite of devout is,' laughed Agnes. 'We had a great evening, you should have joined us. Ate loads, drank wine, talked until the small hours.'

'About Hugo?' said Julius tersely.

Agnes looked at him as he stared fixedly at the road. 'Partly, yes.'

'And what did you conclude?'

'I don't think there are conclusions about Hugo,' said Agnes.

'That's what I thought you'd say.' Julius was quiet for the rest of the journey.

Some weeks later, Julius arrived in the office one morning. Agnes was on the phone.

'Yes, we'll have a bed for her this evening. What's the child's name . . . Right . . . Same old story . . . Uh huh. That's fine. Just let them know.' She put down the phone.

'Coffee.' Julius said. 'Why have you got your coat on?'

'I'm going to Heathrow, and then to Gloucestershire.'

'It's astonishing the places one can fly to these days.'

Agnes grinned. 'I'm meeting Inspector Lowry and his Superintendent at Heathrow. Philippa's been extradited, they've flown to Paris to pick her up. Jim said I could join them at the airport if I liked. Sweet of him, wasn't it.'

'I'm surprised you want to see her again. Nasty bit of work.'

Agnes sighed. 'No worse than . . . No, you're right. Nasty bit of work.'

'And why Gloucestershire?'

'I'm going in Jim's car.'

'I asked why, not how.'

'I'll be away overnight.'

Julius's expression flickered. 'Hugo.'

'Why can't I?'

He got up and looked out of the window. 'No reason. No reason at all. You know what's best for you.'

Agnes looked at him with troubled eyes. 'But that's just it.'

Julius went over to her. He placed his hands gently on her shoulders and looked into her face. She stared at the floor. After a moment he said, 'Pray.'

She looked up at him. 'I do.'

'Well, then.' He smiled at her and took his hands from her shoulders. 'You'd better be going.'

She touched his cheek. 'I wish I had your faith, Julius.'

'Oh no,' he laughed. 'You must have your own. Mine would be no use to you at all. Off you go, now.'

At the doorway she paused. 'It's only dinner. I'll be back tomorrow.'

'Dinner. Yes.'

She hesitated, as if to say something else, then turned quietly and left. Julius stood by the window and watched her as she went out into the street, into the muggy, drizzly day, striding away from him, her coat flapping against her knees. Later, he supposed, she'd tell him about it. About how Philippa had seemed – jaunty and relaxed? – cowed and humiliated? About the drive to Gloucestershire – would the prisoner be handcuffed, flanked by police officers? Would Agnes have travelled with her? And maybe even about dinner with Hugo. At least, he thought, watching the tiny figure merge with the hurrying crowds, she would tell him about the restaurant décor, the steak *au poivre*, the vintage of the wine. In other words, nothing at all.

Standing by the window, Julius felt a curious contentment. He remained there, watching the drizzle, long after Agnes had vanished altogether into the rumbling traffic and grimy London air.

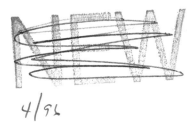

7/2